The COVER STORY

Kim M. Lowrey

PublishAmerica
Baltimore

© 2008 by Kim M. Lowrey.
All rights reserved. No part of this book may be reproduced, stored in a retrieval system or transmitted in any form or by any means without the prior written permission of the publishers, except by a reviewer who may quote brief passages in a review to be printed in a newspaper, magazine or journal.

First printing

PublishAmerica has allowed this work to remain exactly as the author intended, verbatim, without editorial input.

All characters in this book are fictitious, and any resemblance to real persons, living or dead, is coincidental.

ISBN: 1-60563-631-2
PUBLISHED BY PUBLISHAMERICA, LLLP
www.publishamerica.com
Baltimore

Printed in the United States of America

Marge,

There's nothing like good friends. Thanks for your support and I hope you enjoyed the book.

With warmest regards,

Ken M. Savory

Dedication

I would like to dedicate this book to my parents, Floyd and Esther Lowrey. Without them I wouldn't be here to have written this book. It was through their nourishing love and encouragement that I developed an attitude that nothing would be out of my reach, it was just a matter of extending my arm far enough to grasp whatever it was that I wanted. One of my goals in life was to share that theory with my children, which I believe has been achieved.

I also include my children in this dedication. Through hard times as well as happy times, my children have grown into young adults that continue to make me a very proud mother. Through the struggles of everyday life, I found that I needed them as much as they needed me. Thank you for making me become the role model I needed to be and for loving me in spite of my short comings. I love you all! My children: Tifini Mills Haddad, my favorite daughter, and Edward Mills Jr., my favorite son. An honorable mention also goes to the adopted child, my nephew, Christopher Brand.

And last, but not least, I want to include a remembrance to my best furry friend, MacKenzie. Her unconditional love warmed my heart endlessly and I miss her terribly.

I would like to extend a gratifying 'Thank you' to Roberta Chilson, my aunt, and Teresa Guilliams Murphy, my good friend, both critics and wonderful cheerleaders!

And my good friend, Stacy Carpenter Decker, my thesaurus and dictionary, as well as a critic and cheerleader. Thank you all for supporting and helping me to believe that I could do this.

ONE

Stretching long, slender arms high above her head as a large yawn escaped deep from within, Nicole tried to pull herself from a pleasant slumber. Eyes, still half glazed from sleep, lazily searched in the direction of the clock. Finally landing on the target, the green numbers glowing in the darkened room weren't the numbers that she had wanted to see. Bolting to an upright position to get a better look, she realized the alarm hadn't gone off again!

"Oh shit, I'm going to be late if I don't get my ass in gear," she cursed to herself.

Throwing the covers back, she flew out of bed. There was one thing Nicole Bentley really hated, and that was being late. Running to the bathroom, she washed her face, raked the comb through her hair and brushed her teeth. Moving at an ultra-high speed, she flipped through the clothes hanging in her closet and tossed an outfit onto the bed. A rainbow of pantyhose and underwear flew out of a dresser drawer just missing the bed. Balancing on one leg to pull on the pantyhose, she reached for the deodorant and nearly tipped herself onto the floor, face first. Taking a deep breath, she steadied herself and continued the tussle with the pantyhose. Nothing ever goes smoothly when one is in a hurry. Quickly dressing, making sure everything was facing the right way, she glanced at her reflection in the mirror, said 'to hell' with the makeup, grabbed her things and headed down the stairs.

Ready for the everyday battles of New York City, she hit the street in record time. Here, you didn't merely stroll to work; you took your place on the sidewalk, and allowed yourself to be shuttled to wherever you needed to go. The pace was always fast, the crowded streets were relentless. The atmosphere was charged with such a high energy level. The city was a place that could just swallow you up and then spit you out, if you weren't careful. You almost had to be equipped with an invisible body armor to reside in the metropolis. Nicole seemed to have it, and she wouldn't dream of living any place else. Entering the building, her pace didn't slow until the elevator doors closed behind her. It was still hard to believe that she had really made it to 'The Big Apple'. As the doors opened to her floor, she grabbed the briefcase and adjusted the stack of newspapers in her arms and headed for her desk.

"Mornin' Glorie, mornin' Rose, is the coffee ready?" she smiled to herself, and mumbled to no one in particular, "If you didn't know better, it would sound like I was greeting a garden."

"You're pretty chipper this morning. Coffee's ready, I'll get you a cup," Rose replied as she came around from the receptionist desk and headed toward the coffee pot.

Everybody knew that Nicole didn't function effectively until she had that first cup of black energy steaming in front of her.

"Have you had a chance to go over any of the papers from the weekend? I checked the Variety, and the Sun. I didn't find anything inspiring in either one of them. Same old stuff," Gloria rattled on, as her fingers toyed with the corners of the newspapers that were deposited on the desk.

Most of the working class people hated Mondays, but they were just like any other day to Gloria. Bouncing into the office, she was always raring to get the day started. There was never any weekend lag to her spirit. Nicole admired the spark that Gloria ignited in everything and everyone that came in contact with her. Not only was she Nicole's assistant, she was also one of her dearest friends.

"Nope, I had a pretty quiet weekend. I took the phone off the hook, curled up in front of the fireplace with a good book, and just totally unwound for the whole weekend. I did manage to drag myself out on Saturday to pick up a few papers from upstate. I thought maybe I'd snag a lead on something exciting in the outskirts. Sometimes big things come in small packages." Nicole picked up her cup and took a smooth sip of coffee as she opened one of the small town papers and said, "That's what I've been told anyway."

The magazine she worked for, *Who Are the People*, often wrote about citizens who contributed to effective causes. Not just the people who donate great sums of money to charities, but the ones who give their time and effort to help others. Nicole made it a habit to scan the local papers for articles of that nature; they had gotten some of their best leads that way. There were so many wonderful human interest stories out there just waiting for someone to uncover. Who could ask for a better job? Writing was her passion. To be working for the top magazine in New York City was *the* job. Writing articles and interviewing a person who had made life a little better for someone else, that was the topping on the cake.

Nicole came up the ranks just like everybody else. Starting at the bottom of the food chain, she learned to cover a little bit of everything while writing for a local newspaper. Moving on to the larger papers where there was a lot more action, a much bigger challenge, she learned to investigate everything, from whose cat was up a tree, to who was sleeping with whose neighbor. Young and eager and bound to make her name a household fixture, she was relentless. Not even the corrupt politicians, the homeless victims, the poor, the rich, or the insane had escaped her byline. All the hard work paid off in the end when she landed her dream job.

A second cup of coffee finally shooed the Monday morning blues away and Nicole got down to work. Papers scattered across her desk and with elbows buried in black ink and wrinkled paper; she finally came across an article that sparked her interest. The paper was an issue from a small town in northern Pennsylvania. Having no idea where Jasper was, she grabbed a nearby atlas and flipped to the Pennsylvania page. Apparently the town was too small to be found in the atlas, so she got a state map out of the filing cabinet and searched again. Low and behold, there in the very northern corner was a little speck with Jasper for a name. The story was about a rather large donation given to a shelter for battered women and abused children. What had caught Nicole's attention was not the actual donation, although it was a sizable contribution, but the recipient and the donor. It seemed odd that a wealthy owner of a production company and well renowned investor living on the west coast would donate a million dollars to a women and children's shelter on the east coast.

After finding the town on the map, it seemed even more odd that anyone would donate so much money to a place so small and so remote; a place that wouldn't seem to be significant to anyone. The thought of that gave a rise to her curiosity. It had to be significant to him, somehow. Not many people would make a donation of that size, unless there was a specific reason.

"O.K., Time to do a little research..," the adrenalin was starting to pump as she spoke to herself. Think... what do I know about this guy? J. Collins Savage, that name sounds so familiar. Rubbing at her temples as if it would bring something to mind, she dug into her memory banks. Let me see, self-made millionaire. Umm... born in Texas, hit oil on his ranch and moved to California. It was all coming back to her, purchased a production company after striking it rich in the investment field.

If memory served her correctly, there was a time a colleague on the paper tried to get an interview with him and was rudely denied. The scuttle-butt was that J. Collins Savage was a cold, calloused and viciously, mean person. If he didn't grant interviews then, there was probably a pretty good chance that there hadn't been a change of heart after all these years. Why would a man with a reputation like his, give a donation to a shelter of that nature? Why that particular town? The dots just weren't connecting.

Turning to the computer, she logged on to the internet in search of information about the Savage Production Industry. There was a listing for the company, its share holders and other details concerning the business, but not much about the founder. The facts did state that he was from Texas, but that she already knew. The internet couldn't produce anything else worth reading, so she decided that a trip to the library would benefit more.

The library was such a wonderful source of knowledge. Finding an article on 'Who's who in America' gave her a little more information on Mr. Savage. Born in 1960 in a little town just outside of Beaumont, Texas, to parents, Austin and Jessica Collins, both deceased. There were no siblings, and the article didn't state any other living relatives. After his father's death, he inherited the family ranch. Although that region of Texas wasn't known for oil wells, J. Collins decided to purchase a rig and try his luck anyway. After three years of relentless drilling, he finally hit a small well. It produced enough oil to get him out of Texas, and to set up a financing company. The financing company did well enough to help purchase the production company, which was when the name J. Collins Savage emerged. J. Collins was his given name, he added the Savage after acquiring the production company. The name seemed to fit the reputation he had also acquired.

The information she had uncovered gave her more insight to the man than she had before; but it still wasn't enough to explain why he had made such a generous contribution. There were questions she wanted answers for. Like…what did the J stand for in J. Collins, not that it made any difference, did his parents die from natural causes? There was a picture of J. Collins just above the article she was engrossed in. The photograph revealed an extremely handsome man. The blonde hair had bleached highlights that apparently came from a lot of exposure to the sun. The most beautiful blue eyes seemed to glare back at her, but there was something haunting about them. Even the stunning color of blue couldn't hide the cold, empty look they held. Although she couldn't tell his height from the head shot, it was easy to imagine that he was tall, lanky and muscular. The lean face with high cheek bones and a chiseled jaw line probably looked very striking when he smiled. Something told her that he wasn't the type of person who indulged in that pleasure too often. Staring deeper into the picture, she couldn't help but wonder what the real story was behind this man. What could have happened in his life to make his features appear so defiant? Clearly, a man with his looks and stature should have led a fairly comfortable life.

Nicole immediately scolded herself for that thought. Of all people, she should know you can't judge a person by their looks. Something had cast that haunting look of despair he bore. As she stared at the photo, she didn't realize her thoughts were slipping back into her own childhood.

Being an only child had been a lonely existence for Nicole. Oh how she longed for a sister to share her time with. Someone to laugh and to cry with and to whisper her deepest secrets to. She remembered plaguing her mother, day in and day out, to have another baby. The fact that there would be nine years difference between the two of them didn't seem to bother her.

"Mama, please, can't we have another baby? I'll help you take care of her. I'll be the best big sister there ever was. I need someone to play with," Nicole pleaded again.

She just knew if she asked enough times, her mother would finally give in. Even though she had tons of little girl dolls, they just weren't the same as having a real, live baby.

"I'll be good forever. *Please*, can't you ask Daddy?" As she spoke she dramatically dropped to her knees and folded her hands together in prayer fashion.

"Nicole," her mother sighed, as she pulled her daughter back on her feet. "We've been over this a hundred times. We don't need another baby. We've got you, and Daddy and I think that's enough. Now stop your whining and go play."

Explaining to the child why there would be no more babies had grown very tiring.

"But, Mama, if we had another baby, I would have nothing to whine about! I would have someone to play with, and I'd be quiet as a mouse! Please ask Daddy. If he knows how badly I want one, he'll say yes. I know he will!" The urgency in her voice matched the look in her eyes.

Looking sadly, down at the pleading little face, how could she possibly tell her the truth? Maybe she should just discuss it with her husband, one more time, and get it over with. The worst he could say would be 'no'. Then, at least, she could say she had tried.

When there was no response from her mother, Nicole just knew she would talk to her father and she would get the baby she so longed for. Finally she would have someone of her very own to pour all her attention onto.

Nicole could hardly contain her excitement for the rest of the day. When her father came home in an extremely good mood, she knew the timing would be right for her mother to approach him about her request. Dinner that night dragged on and on, lasting longer than forever. Nicole was getting a terrible case of ants in the pants. It seemed as though time was standing still as she watched the hands on the clock tick at their own sweet pace, until they finally reached her bedtime. Without the usual struggle to get her upstairs, she pecked her mother and father on the cheek and rushed off to bed. Laying on the bed waiting with anticipation, she finally heard her parent's heavy footsteps climbing the stairs to their own room. Butterflies danced in her little belly, and the roar of excitement rushed in her head. When enough time had passed for her parent's to settle in, she crept quietly out of bed. Crouching as close to the carpet on the hallway floor as she could get, she slithered to her parent's doorway. Quiet as a mouse, trying ever so hard not to breathe, she put her ear to the crack in the doorway and listened. So many times since that night, she wished she had stayed in her own room.

"She wants what?" her father's voice had risen considerably. "I can't believe we're even having this conversation again!"

The harsh words ripped through the quiet night. Normally he didn't speak to his wife in that tone of voice and it frightened Nicole a bit. It was hard to remember her father's voice being anything but gentle.

"If you remember correctly, we agreed before we ever got married, there would be NO children. I realize that your pregnancy for Nicole was an accident, and I have had to accept that fact. But, I will be damned if there will ever be any more children brought into this household. I can't believe you would even consider discussing the subject!"

"It's just that I feel so sorry for her," her mother's voice was just a whisper. "She's such a lonely child. She caught me in a weak moment, and I didn't think it would hurt to ask, for her sake. I know how you feel, but we have Nicole now, what harm would another baby do?"

Kneeling down beside the bed, her father gathered her mother in his arms.

"I know she's lonely, Babe, but she'll just have to learn to cope with it. I just don't want anymore children. I don't want to share your attention with anyone else. Nicole will just have to get over this foolishness and she should learn to be grateful that she's even here. I know that sounds cruel, but those are the facts. It would be less painful for you, and for her, if we don't discuss this subject again. In nine more years, she'll be grown up and gone, then it will be just you and me again, the way it was suppose to be. The way it always should have been. You know I love Nicole, but she gets in the way. We can't just drop everything and take off to the places we have always dreamed of going. We would have to wait that much longer if we had another child. I'm not willing to do that! Now let's just forget this silly baby business and show me how much you love me."

Nicole couldn't bear to hear any more. Her father had just broken her heart into tiny little pieces. The words 'getting pregnant for Nicole had been an accident' played over and over in her mind. Clamping her tiny hands over her ears still wouldn't stop the words from singing in her head. Creeping back to her room on rubber legs and climbing into bed, she cried herself to sleep. Never again would she utter the word 'baby' around her parents.

Life for Nicole was never the same after that dreadful night. Finding out that your total existence was an accident would be hard to accept at any age. But at nine years old, it turns your life up-side-down, with no clue when things will ever right themselves again. Sometimes, they never do.

Nicole withdrew from her father completely. The thought never left her mind that if she messed up or made him angry, somehow he might make her disappear. That fear was very real to her. Making sure she kept herself in the background made her feel like nothing more than a shadow on the wall. What hurt even more, was the fact that neither of her parents seemed to notice the change in her. Spending so much time alone ultimately made Nicole a very independent person.

Somehow, through all the turmoil, she grew into a rare beauty. Not only was she delightful to look at, she had developed a wonderful personality, as well. It never occurred to her to use her looks or appeal as a tool to get ahead in life. The easy going manner she had acquired was the direct result of trying to gain the acceptance that was clearly missing at home.

With time, she learned to bury all the old memories, the hurt and the anger. Life really began with the job at *Who Are the People* and she loved all of the staff at the magazine. They showered her with loving affection in return. Gloria and Rose were like the sisters she never had. Sister's that not even her father could take away from her. Sam Bailey, her editor, was also her mentor. Keeping her on the right track at all times, he also served as a father figure whenever she needed a shoulder. Knowing it was well within the realm of her capabilities, he wanted to help her reach her ultimate goal at the magazine. That goal was to finally achieve the highest award a journalist could seek. She wanted a cover story.

At one time, she had nearly achieved that. Nicole had pulled out all the stops on a piece she was doing on a wealthy heiress, Nora Stockwood. After the death of her husband, Stockwood seemed to have vanished into thin air, along with her staggering inheritance. Long after the trail had grown cold and other reporters went onto bigger and better stories, Nicole stuck with it. For some reason, the story had really intrigued her. Lead after lead came to a dead end, but she still persisted. How did a person that wealthy and that renown just vanish? The big break finally came with an anonymous phone call. The tip was that Nora was alive, but not doing well. The address she had written down led to the Bowels of Hell in Harlem. Fighting the elements of an extremely cold winter with filth and debris surrounding the area, she found Nora Stockwood, living homeless and shattered in a cardboard box. Just standing there in raw garbage, littered with human feces and the stench filling her nostrils was almost more than Nicole could bear. Not even the disgusting background had prepared her for the sight of the woman she had once known as Nora Stockwood. Gone was the elegance and beauty that once gave Nora her elite standing with the upper echelon. Apparently, gone too was all her wealth. Nicole could hardly believe that this pitiful, distorted figure before her was really Nora Stockwood. It took her two days to get her cleaned up enough, and sober enough, to interview her.

They sat in a little run-down coffee shop. Even in the dimly lit, hole-in-the-wall establishment, Nora looked out-of-place. The long, dark hair was matted to her head and appeared to be lice-infested. The skin on her face was puffy, red, and totally distorted from the alcohol. The clean outfit Nicole had given her to wear had gotten shoved in the back of her box for future need and the grubby, filthy clothes she wore reeked of body odor and stale booze.

"Nora, what has happened to you?"

Nicole tried to hide the pity she knew was pouring from her eyes. How could a person, once so beautiful and so proud, end up like this?

"How could a person of your wealth and stature end up living in a cardboard box?"

Nicole still found it hard to believe that this was really her. A picture of Nora standing on the deck of her yacht flashed through Nicole's mind. It was obvious that she was born and bred to be aboard that yacht, she carried herself so regally. Who would ever think to look for her in some cardboard box in the midst of Hell's fury?

"What do you care?" she protested, her words slurring from the alcohol that reeked from her body. "Why are you bothering me anyway? Go away and leave me be. All I want to do is die," her voice was gruff as she spoke with no feeling or energy.

"Nora, why do you want to die when you should have so much to live for?"

Why would someone like her wish for death? Especially the way Nora intended to die. With no dignity or grace. Just a cold and empty shell of a person. A person who once was so vibrant and alive.

"Is this what you call living? A cardboard box and a bottle of cheap wine?" she asked as she glared at Nicole as if she was the one who had lost her mind.

"What happened to all your money? Why are you living here, in this filth? Where are your family and friends? Don't they know how you are surviving, barely at that? No one should call this living!"

As she spoke, the anger poured from the tone in Nicole's voice. Someone had to feel the anguish; she didn't seem to care enough to be angry for herself.

It took some time but eventually, Nicole dragged the whole sordid story out of her. The one and only love in her life had been her husband, John. When he had died in the automobile accident, there had been another passenger in the car. A woman. The newscasters stated that the unidentified female was his secretary, but Nora knew better. The delusion drove her to hire a private detective to investigate the whole situation. The PI did his job very thoroughly, and turned up some pretty horrible details. It turned out the woman was a hooker. John had been seeing her for years. When her pimp found out she was carrying the HIV virus, it put a real damper on the business and he threw her out on the street. Sometime over the period of years, John had apparently fallen for the harlot so he set her up in an apartment to keep her for himself. Whether or not he was aware that she had AIDS, he must have contracted the disease from her. After his death, the family medical doctor contacted Nora with the results of John's recent tests. Not only was it the law, but she also had a right to know. It wasn't the fact that she may have contracted the disease from John that made her come completely unglued.

It felt as though she were sinking into a big, black, bottomless pit with no way to claw herself out. The poor-little-rich-girl had lost the only thing in life she had ever loved to a sleazy Jezebel. Even though she had enough money to buy and sell most people, that didn't matter to her. The money didn't matter to her, it never did. The only thing she wanted was her husband to come back to her. John was the air that she breathed, the light that showed her the way, the reason for her being. Without him, she didn't want her money, she didn't want her home and she didn't want to live.

Marrying John had enraged her father. It was probably the only thing she had ever done that had really gotten his attention. The fact that her father hated her new husband made her love him even more. There were never questions about his acts of infidelity, but the relationship with the hooker somehow managed to slip past her. The fact that he married her for the sake of the money didn't faze her in the least. The reason it didn't matter was because she truly loved him. Even if the truth caused pain or heartache, he never tried to hide anything from her. Right from the start, he was up-front with her, told her how things were going to be. Just like any other luxury she possessed, he had been bought and paid for. As simple as that. As long as she took care of him, he would stay, but he never promised to be faithful to her. In fact, he boldly told her he didn't think it was a possibility, but it never became an issue. The fact that John was so honest with her from the beginning of their relationship was probably what made her care so deeply for him. It was something she had never had, something that money couldn't buy. There was nothing she could do to tame him; but in return, he wouldn't expect her to make changes on his behalf either. Yet, no matter what or even who might be taking up his time, he was fully aware of the moment when Nora needed him. And when she needed him, he was right by her side for as long as it took...until he died. Hate for his for dying and leaving her alone consumed her. The hate was compounded for the hooker that took her spot in the accident. Why couldn't it have been her? If she could have bargained with her soul to be in the car the night John died, she would have. But she couldn't, so now, she not only hated John and the hooker, she hated the whole world, including herself.

    One day out of the clear blue sky, she contacted her lawyer. Much against his wishes, she donated all her money to various charities and sold her house with all of her belongings and just disappeared. The cardboard box didn't start out as her home. Drifting from one bar to another until closing time, she went home with whoever would take her. When the cash finally ran out, she traded sex for alcohol and drugs. After a while the effects from all the booze and drugs started to take a toll; her sex-appeal was lost to any decent men. The free rides came less often, right along with the free meals and the use of a clean towel with soap and water. Nora still didn't care; all she wanted was to die. Finally, she ended up in the cardboard box, in a place worse than any slum imaginable; hoping every night would be her last. When the sunshine would wake her for another day in hell, it would make her physically ill.

It must have never occurred to her to overdose on some prescription medication. Such a quick and painless death would have been too cowardly on Nora Stockwood's part. It was as though she sought the worst possible way to land on death's front door. Living from one extreme to another, she took advantage of every luxury known to man when she had money, and groveled in the filth of the impoverished when she chose to die. In a perverted sort of way, it made the aristocrat in Nora really standout.

As the interview came to a close, Nicole could see Nora's hands were shaking. Looking paled and exhausted, she had been too long without a drink. Nicole could not will herself to buy a bottle of wine. There was no point in assisting the woman down the path of self-destruction. All she wanted to do was get her back on her feet. Walking back to the box, Nicole made a silent promise that she would return the next day with someone that would help Nora. Living in a filthy box was no way for any human being to exist.

Unfortunately, when she did return with help in tow, it was too late. Nora had gotten her wish and died in her sleep from over-exposure. At least there would be no more torment for her to go through. Nicole decided to write her story anyway. Even though the end seemed to justify the means, her heart ached for Nora. Hoping that when the story was published someone would come forth and give Nora a proper burial, it surprised her that no one ever did. It was like her life hadn't mattered to anyone and neither did her death.

Sam thought the story was a ringer and it was sure to make the cover, until the Intern Scandal hit the street. Everything else became second rate to that, even Nicole's work.

Taking the news in stride, she knew there would be other cover stories. At least poor Nora's distorted face wouldn't be plastered on a cover for the whole world to see.

Nicole pulled herself back to the present and quickly glanced around to see if anyone was staring at her. Time had escaped and she didn't know how long she had been sitting there in oblivion. Whatever made her sink into the past like that was beyond her. Usually it was easy to keep her mind closed to the unpleasant chapters in her life. It was her motto that things didn't change by dwelling on them, so why put yourself through the unpleasantness again. Usually, it worked. Realizing she had lost all train of thought, it was time to call it quits. Closing out the information she was researching, she packed up her belongings. It wasn't the only project she was working on so she could come back to it later.

TWO

As Nicole walked to her car, she couldn't get the picture of J. Collins out of her head. There was just something about his appearance that bothered her. In the photo he seemed to look sad, or maybe a better word would be empty. When she got back to the office, she decided to call the paper or even the shelter and see if they could offer her any information. Intuition was screaming that there was a deep story here and she wanted to get to it first.

"Rose, would you find the number for the *Tribune* paper in Jasper, Pennsylvania? I would like to talk to the editor, please," Nicole requested as she handed over the paper that she found the article in. "Just send them over to my desk when you get the call through. Thanks."

Nicole sank down into her chair just as the phone started to blink.

"Good morning, Nicole Bentley, how may I help you?"

"Good morning Miss Bentley, this is Janet Ryan from the *Tribune*, you wished to speak with me?" a very cheery voice spoke over the line.

"Oh yes, Janet. Thank you for taking the time to talk to me this afternoon. I was reading through your paper this morning and I came across a very interesting article. It was about the rather large donation given to the Sunshine Shelter for Battered Women and Abused Children. I do human interest stories for our magazine. This one sounds like it could be a good one and I'd like to follow up on it. Do you have any further information that would help me out?"

There was an uncomfortable moment of silence before the voice came back on the line.

"I'm terribly sorry, that was a huge misunderstanding. I don't have any information on that subject," her voice was trembling as she finished her sentence.

THE COVER STORY

Nicole heard a soft click, and the line went dead.

Holding the phone away from her ear, she stared at the receiver with a puzzled look on her face.

Gently putting the phone down, Nicole tried to figure out what the heck had just happened. What was the huge misunderstanding? Was it the amount of the donation that was mistaken? Was the donation itself in question? Was it the placement of the donation that may have been the error? What started out to be a simple and gracious deed certainly was in question now, but who had the answers? Deciding to call the shelter next, she thought it would be better to take some precautions, just in case she was stonewalled again.

"Gloria, look in the directory for the Sunshine Shelter in Jasper, Pennsylvania. Find out who the director of services is and who it is that handles donations. When you get that information, get me some phone numbers to go with those names and bring the information to me right away."

In the mean time, Nicole retrieved the paper and reread the information to make sure it wasn't she that made a crucial error. As she read, absentmindedly she ran her hand through her curly, auburn mop, a habit she had when she was thoroughly engrossed in her work. The article read the same way it had that morning so the mistake wasn't hers.

"Ilene Ross, director of services and Darla Gates, head of donations. The phone numbers are right there. Anything else I can get for you?" Gloria asked as she dropped the information in front of Nicole.

"Wow, these are some tough names, which one do you think I should call?"

Nicole glanced at Gloria with that gleam in her eye and she knew immediately the game that she was playing. Get the younger one, she'll talk a lot easier, a lot longer and give a lot more information.

"I think I'd go with Darla. It's a toss up though. Good luck!" she laughed at Nicole's little predicament and headed back to her desk.

Nicole dialed the number for Darla. Crossing her fingers as the phone started ringing, she didn't want to wind up at another dead end.

"Hello, Sunshine Shelter, this is Darla speaking," a whiny, overworked sounding voice came over the telephone line.

Hearing a voice like that could sometimes mean trouble. If the person was overworked, they might want to get off the line quickly if they thought the particular call will cause them any kind of extra work. Nicole rushed in with her sweetest sounding voice.

"Hello, Darla, this is Nicole Bentley from *Who Are the People* magazine. I was wondering if you could help me with some information. I'm doing a human interest story on J. Collins Savage. I understand that he made a sizable donation to your shelter."

"Human interest story, on that guy?" she interrupted before Nicole could finish her spiel.

"Have you ever talked to that S.O.B., he has got to be the rudest man alive. The temporary help made the mistake, his temp, mind you, not ours. Apparently there was a request that the donation was to be made anonymously. The person working from his office sent us the details with his name posted right on the paper work. We, of course, were so happy to get such a generous donation; we wanted the recognition to go where it was due. When we called the local paper, they were more than happy to make an announcement on his behalf. Some McCormick guy telephones with the big news, they might decide to sue us. Can you believe it? Thank goodness he had made the donation in care of his mother, or he probably would have taken it back. We were warned, seriously, not to give out any information, whatsoever. They warned the newspaper staff too." Pausing long enough to catch her breath, she asked, "Who did you say this was anyway?"

The way she had carried on, somebody must have made a great deal of noise over the mix up. Nicole was glad Darla wasn't her employee. It was obvious that she couldn't withhold personal information, even though that's what she had been hoping for. Having gotten more details than she was obviously supposed to, she decided it would be better not to push her luck. Gently placing the phone back in its cradle, Nicole smiled at Gloria and mouthed the word 'Bingo!'

It was at that moment she decided to call Mr. J. Collins Savage to see if she could get an exclusive interview. Before putting the cart ahead of the horse, she decided to check it out with Sam, the editor. After all the final say had to come from him so she had better get a good line ready.

"Sam, ya got a minute?" she asked hanging half in and half out of his doorway as she spoke.

"Yeah, come on in Red."

THE COVER STORY

That was the nickname he always called her by. Sam was an easy going guy if everything was on the right track. It was well known that he could bellow like a bulldog if things weren't going his way. On a real bad day, he could be caught baring his teeth like one. Apparently, things were going pretty well today, he seemed to be in a pleasant mood.

"Sam, I found an article in a Pennsylvania paper this morning. It was about a large donation given to a shelter. There is something about the whole ordeal that doesn't seem quite right. The donation was supposed to be given anonymously, but something got messed up in the transaction. The gentleman who donated the money is a big player on the west coast. I called the paper it originated from; they're pretty scared to give any information out. I called the shelter, and as luck would have it, I got a talker. There's an issue about a pending lawsuit resulting from the announcement that was given to the paper. Something really fishy is going on and I'd really like to do some more investigating, if it's all right with you. I'd like to get an interview with this guy. Even though he hasn't granted interviews in the past, but I'd like to give it a shot. Lying underneath the turmoil caused by this donation, I think there's a hell of a story."

"What makes you think you can get an interview if he's never done one before, Red?" he asked as one of his famous smirks emerged from his lips.

"I don't know that I can, but you know I can be pretty persuasive at times!"

It was easy to tell she had him hooked by the look on his face.

"If you can pull it off, you got five days and no more. I want you back in two if the story's not there. We've got Fourth of July coming up in nine days; there will be stories you need to cover from here. Five days from the time you leave, so you had better get your ass in gear and get somebody to agree to an interview. Now if that's all, get out of my office."

That was Sam's normal procedure for dismissal.

"Yes, Sir!" she exclaimed as she closed the door and practically ran to her desk.

Picking up the phone, she dialed Savage Production Industry in Los Angles, California. Closing her eyes tightly, she shoved her arm behind her back and crossed her fingers, an old habit she couldn't seem to break.

THREE

"Who the hell did you say was on the line," J. Collins Savage bellowed in a voice so loud that it produced an echo that bounced off the walls. "And what the hell do they want?"

It was very evident to Tami, his personal secretary, how angry he was because the protruding veins made his neck look like a road map. According to Collins Rule #4—talking on the phone was comparable to eating cow pie, neither of which he enjoyed. In theory, his theory anyway, companies of any magnitude hired secretaries to take care of that shit. That's what they got paid to do. If they couldn't take care of a simple little phone call, why were they still on the payroll?

That wasn't really how J.C. felt about Tami; he was just blowing off steam. A rare commodity, that's what she was, and he knew it. There seemed to be some type of telepathy that existed between the two of them. Before her next assignment could even leave his lips, she was right on top of it. Ninety percent of the time, she would finish the sentence he started and be right on the money. A diamond in the rough, that was Tami. Yes, he was tough on her, but by God, she could take it. If he even remotely came close to crossing the line, she wasn't afraid to put him in his place, but she didn't push that issue too often. J.C. was lucky to have her so he compensated her well for her services. Even though the money was abundant, it wasn't the key to what kept her there; it was the loyalty. That was why she stayed. J.C. could be compared to a pit-bull when it came to her and Garret. If anyone tried to mess with either of them, there wouldn't be a doubt that he'd sink his teeth so deeply, that he would draw blood. That was the kind of security Tami needed. Even having three brothers of her own, whom she loved dearly, still didn't compare to the bond she felt for J.C. and Garret. No matter how strong that bond was, one of J.C.'s black moods could still manage to intimidate her. At that particular moment, she was wrapped in intimidation that fit her like an old fashioned corset!

"It's a reporter from New York City; a Nicole Bentley," as Tami spoke, she stood just inside the doorway, not wanting to enter the room. "She said she writes for a magazine and wants to interview you on a human interest story."

J.C. looked up from the paper work he had been studying on his desk with sparks flying from his eyes and said, "I don't give a shit what her name is, where she's from, or what she wants! I don't do interviews, remember?" In an even more pious tone he barked, "Human interest my ass. Where do these people come up with these angles? They just want to find a way to get your picture spread across the page and then try to make you look like a jackass."

The more he spoke, the angrier he became. Glaring at Tami, making her feel as though she had two heads, he finally waved his hand toward the door in an obvious dismissal.

When J.C. looked up from his desk and saw Tami still standing in the doorway, he gruffly said, "I thought I told you to go away!"

"Um, J.C.," Tami stammered, as she shifted her weight from one leg to another in a nervous quirk. "The call is about the donation for the shelter."

Knowing that the subject of the donation was taboo around the office, she really didn't want to be the one to bring it up again. Especially after the way he ranted and raved when he first found out about it. She could still hear him shouting 'heads were going to roll, someone was going to pay dearly, an investigation was going to be conducted'. After all the commotion that was stirred up, he still hadn't found out who was responsible for the screw up. Tami knew the tirade wouldn't be over until he knew and he would find out, no matter how long it took.

"Son-of-a-bitch," he sighed in a bewildered tone. As he leaned back in his chair, locking his hands together, he placed them behind his head and asked, "How the hell does she know about that?"

In an instant, he was angry again.

Bolting straight up in his chair he shouted, "Where the hell is Garret?"

Just as Garret came around the corner, he hit him with both barrels loaded.

"I thought I told you to make that go away, damn you!" J.C. screamed at him.

Garret entered the office and stood calmly waiting for J.C. to get a grip. The tyrant attitude didn't have much of an effect on him; it was just J.C.'s way of expressing himself. It would be nice if he found a different way to vent his frustration, but Garret didn't think that was going to happen any time in the near future.

"I'm sorry J.C. I thought I made it perfectly clear what the consequences would be if there was any more information leaked. Apparently nobody took me seriously, but I will take care of that, too. As for the reporter, I'll get rid of her."

Possessing the patience of a saint, Garret was always the one who had to smooth things over. Lord knows, he needed all the patience he could muster to handle J.C. when his temper was in an uproar.

Turning his head in Tami's direction, he said, "Why don't you just transfer her over to my line? I'll take care of it."

Satisfied that the situation was finally under control, J.C. put his head back down and started going over the papers in front of him. Taking that as a sign that they were no longer needed, Garret headed toward the door and Tami stepped back into her office.

"Close the damn door on your way out," J.C. barked, making sure he got the last word in.

"Human interest story. What a crock of shit!" J.C. sighed, in defeat.

It was supposed to be an anonymous donation, a simple, quiet deed. How the information had leaked out was beyond him. With a staff he knew so well and trusted, how the details escaped his domain really baffled him. He would get to the bottom of that enigma if it was the last thing he ever did.

Presenting the donation to the shelter had felt like the only good thing he'd done in so long. Not that he wasn't a giving man; he just gave in ways that kept him out of the limelight. That was the specific reason for donating to a shelter that was in such a remote region. Anonymity. Privacy was a very important issue to him, and he resented anyone who tried to invade his space.

The memory of his mother was the whole idea behind the donation. It was the only thing he was ever able to do for her. So vibrant and full of life, she was such a beautiful woman. Picturing her long, blonde hair flowing in the wind as they ran together by the river, he could still hear her laughter filling the air as she chased after him. It seemed like such a long time ago, he was so young back then, and so was she.

The memories of the time he spent with his mother were good; there just weren't enough of them. For that, he felt cheated. Life for her had been cut too short and because of that, he wouldn't allow himself the luxury of remembering much at all. As he sat in his chair with his head tipped back, he couldn't seem to stop some of those memories from drifting in. His mother's big, blue eyes, as pretty as the sky on a clear day, came into view.

"We'll get out of here someday, my little prince. You wait and see."

Over and over again, she would tell him that with so much conviction in her voice. So much so that he truly wanted to believe her. They would be sitting by the river, eating a picnic lunch packed with all his favorite foods.

"I'll find a good job, and we'll buy a nice little house. Just for you and me. And we'll get a dog! We'll be so happy."

She'd wrap her arms around him and rock him back and forth. A faraway look would creep into her eyes. J.C. always wondered what she was picturing that he couldn't see. Whatever it was, it always brought a tiny, little smile across her beautiful face. She spoke with such assurance; it was hard for the young boy not to believe her.

But, that someday never came for his mother. Well, it did, but not the way she had wanted it to. J.C. quickly blocked what would naturally follow. Instead, he pictured another beauty with honey-colored hair. His beautiful Elizabeth. They were strolling hand in hand down by the river. When they found the perfect spot, they spread a blanket on the soft, grassy knoll. J.C. stretched out on the blanket, and Elizabeth cuddled next to him. After a while, she leaned toward him and propped her head upon his shoulder.

"I love you Justin," she whispered softly in his ear. "I want to be with you forever. Please tell me that nothing will ever keep us apart."

"I promise you with all my heart that nothing can keep us apart," he spoke in a voice sounding soft and tender, as he leaned over and kissed her deeply, claiming her as his, forever. "Because I love you, too."

Holding each other for what seemed like hours; they lay there, touching, exploring, and feeling the heat of their bodies rapidly climbing. Eventually that just didn't seem like enough. Although they had made a vow they'd wait until marriage; an insatiable hunger devoured them and they ended up making love under the soft light of the full moon right there by the river. It was the sweetest thing he had ever experienced. Just touching her skin was like enveloping himself in the softness of velvet. When she kissed him it felt like little sparks riveting through his veins, making his blood rush and his heart beat faster. When he couldn't stand it any longer, he placed himself inside of her and gave way to his longing. Every inch of his body trembled as wave after wave of sensual desire pulsated through his very being. It sounded like a choir of angels singing when she called out his name as she started to peak. Finally, in what felt like a thunderous explosion, he climaxed. Totally spent, he collapsed on top of her, feeling more complete than he ever had in his life. It was the greatest pleasure he had ever experienced.

Holding her in the glowing aftermath, he had no way of knowing that the first time would be the only time, or the best time would also be the last. It never occurred to him as he laid there next to the woman that he loved that she would rip his heart right out of his chest. At that specific moment in time, he didn't know he was never going to love like that again. But worst of all, he had no way of knowing how much he was going to miss her. So many years ago, so much time gone by.

Feeling the pain as if it were fresh, he shook his head to clear the ghosts. It seemed like only yesterday when he thought about her like that. He had loved her so much. Still did, as a matter of fact, he just wouldn't allow himself to admit it. Going back never did much good, but sometimes he couldn't help himself. Just then a knock came at the door totally pulling him from his nostalgic state.

"Yeah, what is it?" he asked, in a raspy tone.

"It's Garret, J.C.," he poked his head around the door as he spoke. "Can we talk for a minute?"

J.C. nodded his approval so he entered the room and quietly closed the door. A quick glance was all it took to see that J.C. had been traveling down memory lane because his cold, hard eyes were just a tad misty. That didn't happen very often, and God help the poor soul who might dare to make a comment on it. Garret waited until J.C. composed himself before he spoke again.

"Boss, it might not be a bad idea to do this human interest story. This reporter, Nicole, has some pretty good credentials and she writes for one of the top magazines."

Garret was studying J.C.'s facial expressions while he spoke to see what kind of reaction he was going to get.

When he didn't seem to be getting too excited, he continued. "I spoke with her for a bit and she says that if you will consent to the interview, she'll print only the material that you agree to. I think you need to give the public an idea of what you're all about. We both know that you haven't got the kindest reputation there is going for you. It's time that we squash this 'recluse' image and besides, it will be better for business." With a little smirk playing around the corners of his mouth, Garret added, "I know you're meaner than a grizzly standing on an anthill, but you don't have to let everybody in on that."

You can take the man out of Texas, J.C. thought, but you can't take Texas out of the man.

"Garret, I don't want to do the damn interview. If I do one, then they'll be camping all over the place, wanting more," he said stubbornly as he stood up and came around the front of his desk. Leaning casually against it, he crossed his arms over his chest and continued, "I don't want people knowing my business. I don't want people trying to get close to me. It's bad enough I got stuck with you!"

The truth was J.C. didn't know what he would do without Garret. There was no one left in the family, and he was the only true friend he had. Hell, he didn't need anyone else; Garret was enough friend, enough family, and even sometimes, enough foe. But, no matter what Garret was, he was enough. Garret had been through some pretty rough times with him. He stood by him, was right there, every step of the way, when Elizabeth disappeared. No matter what J.C. unloaded on him, Garret took in stride. It would have been impossible to make it through without him.

"Look, Garret," he said in a softer tone. "I'll sleep on it." After a slight hesitation, he added, "Don't expect much, but I'll sleep on it."

"Boss," Garret goaded him on, "She's got a real sexy, little voice. Got that Yankee accent too," he added, as he ducked out the door half expecting something to come flying at him.

FOUR

With long legs sprinting toward the boarding gates, and just minutes left to spare, she was bound and determined she wasn't going to miss this flight. For some reason, she was more excited about this interview than she had been about anything else she had worked on in a while. There was no tangible evidence that there was going to be something earth-shattering to uncover. Call it a 'woman's intuition', because she had a strange feeling deep in the pit of her stomach. Hardly containing her excitement, she checked her ticket with the stewardess and boarded the plane headed for Chicago. Nicole's mind, and not to mention her heart beat, was racing as she slid into her seat. As she briefly nodded to the passenger occupying the adjoining seat, he leered at her for several, uncomfortable seconds, before nodding back. Something about that exchange gave her quite an odd feeling, but she couldn't quite put a finger on it. Ah, its just nerves, she thought, as she settled back for the ride.

It was no accident that Jason Deveroe was sitting next to her on the plane. Every ounce of persuasion he could muster went into getting that seat. No one jilted him and got away with it. Mr. Charles Donovan III didn't know that yet: but he would find out soon enough, right along with a million other people. When he got done spilling his guts to this reporter, the whole world would know. With that comforting thought, he settled back in his seat too.

Jason had been ridiculed and teased all of his life. Even as a young child, he knew that he was different from the other boys. It seemed as though he had spent an eternity trying to hide his feelings, especially from the other guys. It didn't come to him for a long time exactly what he was trying to hide, or why he had to hide it, he just knew he was different. The light finally dawned on why he was different, but the thought of getting the same reaction he had gotten from his mother when she found out about his secret kept him from making any friends. The memory of that horrible day still haunted him.

Not having any interest in girls, Jason was probably what some would call a late bloomer. Even he didn't realize what direction his sexual interest had taken until he happened to notice his mother's *Playgirl Magazine*. After Jason had gone to bed one night, she was flipping through it and left it lying on the coffee table. In comparison to other twelve year old males, he seemed to have matured rather quickly and was reasonably well endowed. Trying to mimic the other boys in school he had nicknamed his penis, 'Big Red'. It was the latest rage and he quickly joined in so as not to feel left out. There wasn't much he had in common with the other kids, so this little adventure kind of made him fit in with the crowd.

That particular evening had been unbearably hot and the air in the apartment was stifling. Jason wandered downstairs to get a drink and as he walked by the coffee table, he glanced down at the magazine his mother had left behind. Knowing he shouldn't be looking at it enticed him even more to pick it up. Flipping slowly through the pages and admiring the strong, bare chests, the muscular arms and the steel hard abs, when he finally reached the centerfold, the sight of the picture before him sent his blood rushing and he could feel 'Big Red' stirring and rapidly coming to life. As he stared longingly at the most beautiful, nude body he had ever seen 'Big Red' had grown into a full, blown woody. Totally surprised by the sight as he looked down at the hard mound in his tight, white briefs, he grabbed the magazine and raced off toward the bathroom. With 'Big Red' in one hand and his eyes glued to the magazine in the other, Jason was about ready to have his first sexual experience. Full of mounting excitement and finding it hard to catch his breath, he was pretty close to a release when his mother came barging into the bathroom. When she saw what he was holding in his hand, her mouth dropped open and she almost lost her false teeth. To make matters worse, when she finally took the focus off from his private parts, her eyes averted to the magazine he was holding in the other hand. Gasping for air as she tore the magazine out of his hand and turned it around, there was Mr. July, in all his glory, smiling back at her. All the excitement of getting caught with his pants down, so to speak, caused 'Big Red' to erupt and an unwieldy mass of the thick, milky substance dropped, heavily, onto his mother's slipper.

Slowly and painfully she lowered her gaze to her feet and with a dreadful look of disgust, raised her brow to her son. A heinous noise ripped from her throat as she slammed the magazine to the ground.

"Damn you, you little pervert!" she screamed at him. "I have one child, one son, and he has turned out to be a freak! You're nothing but a pervert. You're a freak!"

Pushing her face damn near against his, she kept yelling it over and over; you're a freak…a freak…a freak…until he began to believe it. When she got over the initial shock of what she had just witnessed, she balled her hands into fists and started to beat the hell right out of him. No one would ever tell Jason his mother couldn't throw a punch as well as any prize fighter. It wasn't until he collapsed to the floor, still holding his arms over his face and ears that she finally stopped. Lying on the floor sobbing as quietly as he could, Jason thought that the fierce beating would be the end of it. It was quite obvious that his mother was going to be angry with him for a long time, but surely he had been punished enough. How sadly mistaken that thought turned out to be.

When he returned home from school the next day, tired and badly bruised, he went directly to his room. Trying to avoid all contact with his mother, he was surprised to see that she was sitting on the edge of the bed. Giving him a look of disgust, she shoved the bag she was holding into his severely, sore chest. Slowly pulling the bag open and peering inside, the sight of the contents nearly made him regurgitate.

"You want to act like a pervert, it is only fitting that you will dress like one," was all she said.

Turning on her heel, she stomped out of his room.

Jason quickly ran to the dresser and pulled open his underwear drawer. The fear of what his mother might have done became very evident when every single pair of his Fruit of the Looms was missing. At least a dozen pair of lacy, pink, woman's underwear identical to the pair he was holding in his hand filled the drawer. Sinking to his knees and sobbing quietly, he tried to reassure himself that he wasn't really a freak, he was just different. It didn't matter what words he tried to use, his mother made him feel like one.

Jason and his mother's relationship became rather strained from that day on. Once he graduated from high school, she helped him pack his few belongings and practically pushed him out on the street. Walking away from home that day, he never looked back. As far as he was concerned, his mother could go to Hell, he never planned on seeing her again. Every now and again, he'd wake up in a cold sweat hearing his mother's voice yelling... freak...freak...freak.

Finally, for once in his life, there was a way to get back at someone who had hurt him and Charles had hurt him deeply. Knowing there wasn't a possibility that he could make Charles wear woman's underwear, he had planned a way to humiliate him just the same. After what Charles had done to him, he was going to enjoy this revenge immensely! Hoping he had picked the right person for the job, unconsciously he glanced in Nicole's direction.

It had taken her nearly three days to convince J. Collins Savage to give her an exclusive interview. In order to get the interview, she had to promise Mr. Savage that she wouldn't mention his donation to the shelter. That was easier than convincing her editor, Sam that it was going to be a great story even without the information about the donation. What the hell, no one had ever interviewed with him before. A gut feeling said that he had a least one good story to tell and she wanted to be the one to get the man with the cold, haunting eyes to talk.

When the plane arrived in Chicago there was an hour layover for the connecting flight. Giddy with anxiety, Nicole wandered to the lounge to kill some time. Thinking that maybe it was a good time to jot a few notes, she soon realized it was a fruitless effort and put the stuff away. The excitement was mounting and she could feel the restlessness raging through her.

After purchasing a soda, not knowing what to do with herself, Nicole wandered over to a window seat in the lounge. Tossing thoughts around in her head, she tried to figure out what the best approach would be to begin the interview. Should she be direct or quietly feel him out before she tried to invade his innermost, private space? Gazing out the massive window, weird feelings began to envelope her and send shivers down her spine. It was a prickly feeling that made her skin crawl, like someone was staring intensely at her. Slowly, she glanced around the lounge. There were only a few other people in the small place. Two pilots appeared to be deep in conversation at the counter and a woman sat at a near by table reading a book. The only other occupant was a man who was sitting at a table in the corner with a newspaper propped in front of his face. Just as she turned her head back toward the window, he lowered his paper to take another peek at her. Sucking in a quick breath, it took her by surprised when she saw that it was the man that sat next to her on the plane. Remembering the eerie feeling she got from the first time she saw him, Nicole quickly picked up her things and decided to wait by the boarding gate.

I don't know what it is about that guy, she thought, but he gives me the creeps. There's such a hostile look about him, like a wolf ready to jump its prey. I certainly hope he's not sitting by me on the next flight. Shaking her shoulders to drive away a chill, she continued to wait for the plane.

Damn it, he thought, when he was sure that Nicole had spotted him. Knowing that he was being too obvious, he would have to try to be more careful. It was way too soon to make a move. The excitement of exposing Donovan was beginning to build up; but the timing meant everything. Having the precise entrance was vital to his plan. If he was discovered prematurely, it would ruin what had taken him months to put together. Quickly he yanked the newspaper up to hide his face again. Good, he thought, she's leaving; it would give him some time to think.

A mental picture of Charles Donovan filtered through his mind. They had been truly happy together, until that arrogant father-in-law of Charles' ruined everything. If Bartholamuel Bordoe, better known as Buck, said jump, Charles would ask, how high? Jason would love to see the look on old Buck's face when he found out his prominent son-in-law was nothing but a faggot! Yes, it was a poor choice of words; but after everything he had done to him the name seemed to fit Charles. Jason had rolled into Dalton, Texas about five years ago but he had no intentions of staying.

After a heart wrenching break-up with a long time lover, he wasn't really looking for anything, he was just wandering. Texas was the last place he expected to find a new partner.

When Charles stopped in for a cocktail, he was already sitting at the bar of the Long Horn Steak House. Scanning the room for an empty stool as he entered the bar, the search ended when his gaze fell upon Jason. In an effort to draw his attention, Charles loudly cleared his throat. When Jason turned his head in that direction and their eyes finally met, there was an instant connection. Pulling himself up to full height, Charles puffed up his chest and sauntered over to the stool next to him. There was never a question of the man's sexual preference; he was practically drooling at the sight of Jason. Charles was starving for male attention and Jason was at a very vulnerable stage. The rest was history; they had spent five wonderful years together. Without a clue that the relationship was going to be over with so soon, Jason was totally crushed. The end came the day Buck decided Charles should run for Mayor. Charles broke the news to Jason after a hot, steamy session of passionate sex. Acting as if it were no big deal, he explained that he couldn't take the chance of anyone finding out about the two of them. With his father-in-law's connections, Charles was already a shoe-in for the mayor's position. If they broke off the affair right then, there would be less chance of anyone digging up any dirt about him by the November election.

While he was getting dressed, Charles explained to Jason how much he cared for him. It had been a wonderful experience that he would never forget. Adding a 'thanks, take care of yourself' to the exit speech, that was it…boom, he was gone. It would have been more appropriate if Charles had left a fifty dollar bill on the dresser; the way he walked out left Jason feeling like a mere prostitute.

Unable to comprehend what had just happened, Jason laid there unable to function in a state of bewilderment. After five gratifying years he got dumped. Just like that, with absolutely no warning. For five years he had been at Charles' beck and call. All he had to do was say where and when and Jason would drop whatever he was doing and go to him. Spending time with Charles had always been worth the time and energy. The plans they had made together were long term plans. Jason hadn't found 'just' a partner; he had fallen deeply in love. It was unspoken knowledge that Charles would never divorce his wife; her family carried too much clout in the small town they lived in. It wasn't a secret that Charles had never had any sexual contact with her; that was something he bragged about at the beginning of the relationship. Thinking of that made Jason wonder whether Elizabeth knew her husband was gay. It was very unlikely that she did because it appeared to him the she was too wrapped up in her own little world. Frankly to him, her actions implied that she was one cold-hearted woman. Well, he had information that would definitely thaw her out. It wouldn't be long now, before her husband's little world would come tumbling down around him.

In the five years he had spent as Charles' lover, Jason had learned almost everything there was to know about the Bordoe and Donovan families and the scorned lover's theory had never changed. There was a lot of dirty laundry that needed to be aired and Jason planned on doing just that; but all in good time. When he was finished, Buck Bordoe and Charles Donovan III would be railroaded out of town. Charles obviously hadn't considered who he was dealing with. Oh, but he would soon find out! If luck was with him, Charles wasn't going to be able to show his face for the November election. It was imperative that he didn't lose sight of Nicole Bentley. This particular reporter was the key to his whole plan. Although she had no idea what she was getting into, she was going to be responsible for the unraveling of the tightly knit families that had crushed Jason's future and destroyed his wonderful past. All he had to do was make sure the timing was right. There were so many secrets and he didn't want to leave any stones unturned. It was going to be his pleasure to watch Charles and his father-in-law bleed, so to speak. Patience was never one of his virtues.

So for the hundredth time, he said under his breath, "Timing is everything. Make sure the timing is right."

FIVE

When he spotted her coming out of the gateway; he knew it was her in an instant. The most natural smile spread quickly across her face displaying perfect, glistening teeth. A soft glow seemed to radiate around her angelic face. The color of the Caribbean Sea matched her glistening, green eyes perfectly while her curly, auburn hair whisked around her face. Anyone could have mistaken her for a model instead of a reporter. Garret wanted to stand back and just study her for awhile; but he could see that wasn't going to happen when she was headed right in his direction.

"Miss Bentley," he yelled to her as he waved his arm in the air for her to notice.

When she finally reached him, he took his huge cowboy hat off and offered her a very large hand to shake.

"Howdy Miss Bentley, I'm the one that you're looking for. Name's Garret, Garret McCormick."

If she hadn't already known that he was from Texas, his drawl would have definitely given him away.

"I believe I could have spotted you from a mile away Garret, Garret McCormick," she laughed, poking fun at the way he had said his name.

When she shook his hand, she gave him another terrific smile that made Garret's heart leap in his chest.

"Please, call me Nicole."

"What gave me away, this ole hat?" he asked as he raised the hat in question and gave her a little wink.

"Well it was that, plus the fact that you're the only guy dressed like a cowpoke in the whole airport! Not that it's a bad thing," she kidded with him as they headed toward the luggage return.

"How was your flight?"

Instantly Garret felt completely at ease with her.

"It was pleasant. I had forgotten how long the flight was because I haven't been out here in quite some time. A little time in the sun will do me some good. On the way here I was thinking that I might just stay for a few days after we complete the interview. I haven't had a vacation in quite a while. Speaking of the interview, when will I get to meet with J.Collins Savage?"

Garret's mannerism had put her at ease right away. Talking to him was like chatting with an old friend.

"You sure do get right to the point. Is that the New Yorker in you, or the reporter in you?" his laugh was deep and had a pleasant ring to it. "You can call him J.C., everybody does."

After they retrieved her luggage, Garret took her elbow and steered her toward the exit.

"We've got a car out front. I'll take you to your hotel so you can get some rest. They have an excellent dining room there, or you can order room service if you like. I'm really sorry that I can't accompany you to dinner. Because this was done on such short planning, I already had a previous engagement; but I'll send a car for you in the morning. We'll tour the production company and have lunch. You should be able to meet with J.C. in the afternoon. I hope that's O.K. with you, it's the best that I could manage," he handed her luggage to the driver as he finished speaking. "Your chariot awaits, my lady."

Bowing from the waist he opened the door to the limo. As she entered the car, Garret slid into the seat beside her and gave the driver the address for the hotel. Just as the car sped out of sight, Jason Deveroe stepped out of the shadows.

"Taxi," he shouted as he waved his arms frantically. When the Yellow and White pulled along the side of the curb he flung the door open and jumped in and yelled, "Follow that limo. Don't lose them!"

Having come this far already, he had no intention of losing her at that point.

The ride in the limousine was very pleasant. The scenery in California had always impressed Nicole. There were skater's rollerblading down the sidewalks; most of them were dressed for the beach. People were just strolling along the street in no real hurry, as though they were all on one big vacation. A few of the drifters on the street looked as though they belonged on a different planet, but you found that in New York too. The coolness of the air-conditioning camouflaged the heat wave going on outside. It was typical California weather for the end of June.

"How long have you known J.C., Garret?" Nicole asked as she broke the silence between them.

Having taken in enough of the scenery, she was ready for a little conversation.

"I've known him for a long time. After his daddy died, he needed some help on the ranch so he hired me, I've been with him every since. J.C.'s been a real good friend to me, and he's the closest thing I've got to family, and vise-versa. I don't want to appear out of line and I certainly don't mean any disrespect Nicole, but I don't want you to write anything in your article that will harm J.C. I'm the one who talked him into doing this interview, and I really don't want you to make me sorry that I did that," he said that with real conviction in his voice.

In that moment, Nicole knew that Garret would give his right arm to J.C. if it ever came to the point where he would need it.

"Garret, I have no intention of printing anything harmful about Mr. Savage. I'm just looking for the story, so to speak."

The loyalty he openly displayed made her smile. Friendships like that don't come along everyday and she found that she was a little bit envious of theirs.

"Oh, there's a story, all right, I just don't know if your going to get it out of him." he mumbled just loud enough for her to hear.

But if anyone can, my money's on you little filly, he thought. As they rode along they fell into a comfortable silence, giving Nicole a chance to study him a bit.

It never occurred to her how large he was until she was seated next to him. Even in the expanse of the limo, his legs didn't look entirely relaxed. Upon further investigation, she noticed that he was quite a handsome man. Of course, that god-awful hat he sported at the airport had hidden most of his appealing features. Thank goodness he had taken it off to fit into the car. The tone of his skin had a bit of a weathered touch; but it didn't give his face a rough looking appearance. The long, broad nose had a couple of small, flat spots that indicated it may have been broken once or twice. Coupled with the well groomed mustache, they added a certain amount of character to his appearance. Short, unruly curls covered his head and matched the color of his soft, brown eyes. She wondered how this cowboy from Texas fit into the California chaos. As she was pondering that thought, they pulled up in front of the hotel.

"Well, here we are. I hope the accommodations will suit you, Miss Bentley, uh Nicole," Garret said, as he was exiting the limo. "I hope you have a pleasant evening, and if you need anything, here's my card. Don't hesitate to call," he was handing her luggage to the porter as he spoke. "Reservations are taken care of; all you have to do is just check in at the desk. I'll see you tomorrow," he added as he got back into the car.

The place was indeed suitable. Garret insisted on J.C. picking up the tab for Nicole's stay. He had given the girl such a hard time about the interview, Garret thought it would help his image if they put her up in the most impressive place in town. She glanced around the grand foyer as she headed for the front desk. No expense spared here with the Italian marbled floors, teak woodwork, and a massive front desk. Nice, very nice indeed, she thought, as she proceeded to the desk to check in.

"Hi, I'm Nicole Bentley, I believe there is a roomed reserved for me."

As she waited patiently for the clerk to look up her reservation, she noticed how well the young man was dressed. He was clean cut and conducted himself in a very professional manner.

"Oh, yes, Miss Bentley, we have a suite reserved for you on the seventh floor," he was summoning the bellhop as he spoke. "Carl will take you to your suite; I hope you have a pleasant stay." Handing Carl her key, he gave her a genuine smile and added, "If you need anything, anything at all, just call the front desk."

The young man stared at Nicole a little longer than he wanted to, but he couldn't help himself. As she stepped onto the elevator with Carl, she caught a sudden movement out of the corner of her eye. Recognizing the face, she realized it was the strange man from the plane again. Was it a coincidence that he was at the same hotel, or was he following her? Somehow she was going to have to find out who he was. If he was staying at the same hotel, that shouldn't be too difficult. She was going to have to put some feelers out on that one. The whole thing was beginning to spook her.

THE COVER STORY

As Garret eased himself down into the seat for the ride back to the studio, he thought of his friendship with J.C. There was a strong and loyal tie between them. Garret had always hated the regular ritual of ranching. When J.C. had approached him about drilling for oil, he jumped at the chance. It was a given that he had always been the black sheep of the family, so breaking away to work with J.C. hadn't brought about any big surprise to them. There wasn't an awful lot of pay those first couple of years. J.C. shared his home with Garret, and the promise of a percentage of the profits should they ever hit oil and he had been true to his word.

There had been a lot of rough spots they had to endure, but together, they managed to pull things through. Now, they were sitting quite comfortable, and things weren't as hectic as they used to be. Garret sort of missed the staggering pace. There was a lot more time on his hands to fill and nobody in particular to fill them with. That was something that was going to have to change.

SIX

The porter opened the door to an exquisite suite and paced the bags inside the room. It was obviously designed to pamper its occupants in luxurious comfort for the length of their stay. The elaborate décor didn't escape her attention, but she was starving and her thoughts weren't really on where she was going to sleep. All she wanted was to hang the clothes that would wrinkle and wash some of the traveling grime from her face. After the unpacking was done, Nicole went down to the dining room and had a delicious dinner that totally satisfied the hunger pains.

Feeling rather bored, the thought of taking a walk sort of appealed to her, but it looked as though it was still pretty hot outside. The waiting was killing her. For some reason, she had it in her head that the meeting with J.C., as Garret called him, would occur right after she had gotten off the plane. When she realized that wasn't going to happen, she hoped that Garret hadn't detected her disappointment; he seemed like such a nice person. It wasn't going to do any good to drag a bunch of writing material out tonight, as wound tight as she was, there would be no way to focus on anything. Looking at the time and calculating the difference, if she were at home she would be in bed fast asleep, so she decided to just call it a night.

Finally giving in to the need for sleep, Nicole crawled into bed but all she could do was toss and turn. No matter what position she laid in, no matter what kind of pleasant thoughts she tried to drum up, she just couldn't get to sleep. Part of the insomnia was due to the difference in the time zones. The other part was pure, raw excitement. A premonition kept taunting her that something big was about to unfold. A little voice inside kept nagging at her. Who was the guy on the plane? Was he really following her, or was it just a coincidence they kept ending up at the same places? How did the newspaper from Pennsylvania end up on the desk? It wasn't one that she brought in; but the thought never occurred to ask Rose or Gloria where it had come from; she had been too excited about finding the article in the first place. Why was the donation made in J.C.'s mother's name? Was she originally from Jasper? Could she have been a victim of abuse? All these questions kept swimming around in her head.

I guess the answer is to work on one question at a time, she thought. I'll start with the mystery of the newspaper first thing in the morning. Before leaving with Garret I'll call the office and see if either of the girls might know where it came from. But right now, if I don't get some sleep, I'm going to look like death warmed over. Turning out the light she hoped sleep would come as quickly as the darkness had enveloped the room.

In the distance, a faint, irritating noise kept repeating itself. It got louder and louder, until the wailing echo became very disturbing.

"What is that awful racket?" Nicole wondered out loud.

It felt like sand had filled her eyes and she was having a difficult time trying to pry them open. Lying there in somewhat of a fog, it finally it dawned on her that the blaring sound was coming from the alarm clock. How could the alarm possibly be going off when it didn't feel as though she had slept a wink? Trying to find some sort of motivation she rolled, lazily across the huge bed and stretched her slender frame. Out of the corner of her eye she spied a coffee maker on the wet bar that sparked a tiny little bit of ambition. Coffee was probably the only thing that was going to put some life back into the empty shell. Dragging the limp body over to the bar, she summoned enough strength to get the pot started. As the aroma wafted into the air it worked like a small jolt of energy and she finally managed to crawl into a steaming, hot shower. As the pellets of sizzling water pelted against her head and back, the feeling in her body started to come alive.

There is nothing like a good, hot shower, she thought, while rinsing the shampoo from her hair. Grabbing the soft, complimentary robe from the hook, she waltzed into the other room feeling invigorated. The only thing missing to complete the moment was a steaming cup of coffee. The heavenly scent of ground coffee beans drifted to her nose as she poured the dark liquid into a cup. Perched on a stool in front of the bar, she toweled her hair with one hand and sipped at her beverage with the other. When most of the moisture was gone from her hair, she set the towel on the counter and grabbed for the phone. There wasn't much time before Garret would be there and there was still a lot to do. Absentmindedly she started punching numbers.

"Gloria, good morning, this is Nicole." she said, as she took a sip of the strong, hot liquid.

"Hi, Nicole, how is everything going? Have you met J. Collins Savage yet? Where are you staying and what's the number?" Gloria just kept firing questions at her left and right.

"Go easy on me, Gloria; I can only answer one question at a time," Nicole laughed. "First of all, Garret is picking me up in a little while. I'm going to guess that he's J.C.'s assistant. I'm staying at the Bayside Plaza Hotel, very nice if I might add. I'll fax you the numbers that you need a little later. I think I may be starting the interview today. The reason I'm calling is because I'm not sure where the *Tribune* newspaper came from the morning I found it on my desk. I didn't bring it in with me. Did you?"

"No, I'll check with Rose, but I know I didn't bring it in. That is kind of odd that we had a paper from Pennsylvania available on Monday morning. They don't usually come until the middle of the day. I'll get right on that. O.K., so come on, tell me, have you met him yet? What's he like?"

"No, Gloria, I haven't," she chuckled at her enthusiasm. "I hope he will be as pleasant and as easy to look at as Garret. I'm probably wishing for way more than I'll get! Gotta go, Garret's here and I'm not ready. Call me as soon as you get this phone number with that information."

While she was talking on the phone, she heard a knock at the door and assumed it was Garret. Putting the phone down, she scrambled to get dressed. There wasn't any point in making a bad impression by being late the first morning. Just as she was finishing the last button on the sundress, she heard a second knock. Taking quick strides to cross the room, when she opened the door, there was no one there. Looking up and down the hallway, there was not a soul was in sight. Just as she was about to close the door something caught her attention. There was a white envelope lying on the floor just outside of the room, so she bent down and picked it up and stepped back inside.

THE COVER STORY

There was nothing written on the front side of the envelope so she turned it over to check the back side. That too was blank so she really couldn't be sure that it was meant for her. Curiosity was testing her as she tapped the envelope against her hand trying to decide whether or not to open it. Anticipation finally got the best of her and she ripped the envelope open. There was a regular sized piece of notebook paper with the words '*WHEN YOU ARE READY FOR THE REAL STORY, I'LL BE IN TOUCH*' written in bold letters.

That's it? she thought. Reading the few words over one more time, she opened the door and looked down the hallway again. Still, there was no one there. Where had the envelope come from she wondered. It didn't just fall out of the ceiling tile. 'When you are ready for the real story, I'll be in touch', she repeated in her mind. Taking the envelope and its contents and jamming them into her purse, she decided it was something that would have to be dealt with later.

Quickly running a brush through her hair and checking to see if there was any need for makeup, she grabbed the coffee cup and drained the last drop of liquid. While she was applying a bit of sunscreen the phone began to ring. The shrill noise broke the silence in the room startling the hell out of Nicole.

"Hello," she stammered into the receiver as though the call had frightened her.

The envelope with the note in it must have had a bit more of an effect on her than she realized.

"Miss Bentley, this is Oliver, your driver. I have the car downstairs. I'm supposed to drive you to join Mr. McCormick for breakfast. I'll be waiting for you out front."

"Thank you Oliver, I'll be right down," she said, recovering quickly.

Finishing with the sunscreen and grabbing the purse, she almost forgot the room key and had to run back to the nightstand and grab it before heading out the door. By this time, the adrenaline was pumping into overdrive.

Oliver pulled the car up in front of an outdoor cafe. The view of Garret's huge hat loomed from the window. Oliver opened the door and helped Nicole out of the car. With that hat, you could never lose him in a crowd, she laughed to herself as she crossed the floor over to the table. Standing as she approached, he tipped the beastly hat.

It was a lovely morning. A soft, cool breeze was churning up a delightful aroma from the nearby blossoms. The cafe was a great choice for breakfast and she was pleased with the decision to wear the sundress.

"Morning, Nicole. You look lovely, as usual, I'm sure," he exclaimed as he gave her a radiant smile. "This is a great little place to eat and their coffee is wonderful. I know I said we'd have lunch, but noon is too far away. My morning appointment cancelled and I'm starving right now!"

Nicole took a seat and picked up the menu. When the waitress brought her coffee, they ordered food. Garret ate like a bear. Nicole figured it was his hearty appetite that produced enough energy to carry that large frame around, plus a little extra to carry the hat. They chit-chatted about nothing in particular, just getting to know one another. When they finished with breakfast and got into the car, Nicole couldn't stand to wait any longer and decided to ask a few questions about J.C.

"Garret, what were J.C.'s parents like?"

Not knowing whether Garret would talk to her or not, curiosity was getting the best of her and she didn't want to wait to get the answers.

When Garret appeared to grow a little rigid, she thought she had ruined the moment. The muscles in his jaw started twitching as though she had hit a raw nerve. Hoping she hadn't said anything to offend him, she waited quietly for some sort of response. It would be awful if he was angry with her because he was so enjoyable to be with and she didn't want to spoil the mood.

"I don't know if I should be the one talking to you about J.C.'s parents, Nicole. Maybe you should be asking J.C.," he concluded rather shortly as he looked out the window.

"I'm just curious about his background, Garret," she smiled sweetly at him as she spoke, not wanting him to be angry at her for prying.

There must be some reason that Garret wouldn't want to talk about his parents and she wanted to know what it was. The hesitant manner to speak on the subject peaked her intrigue.

"Besides, nothing that you say to me will go any farther than the two of us. I won't use any of the information you give me as a tool to get to J.C. I just thought it might help to give me some insight to what kind of person J.C.

was. If it's a difficult subject for you to talk about, then never mind. I don't want to upset you."

She gave him a look that said she was sincerely sorry, but her eyes were pleading with him to give her any kind of enlightenment.

"I don't know what it is about you, girl, but I'd bet you could draw blood from a stone," he said as he was shaking his head. "What is it that you want to know?" he finally answered, in a defeated tone.

"What was his mother like?" she questioned Garret, giving him her undivided attention.

Maybe he could shed some light as to why the donation was made to the shelter in her name.

A long sigh escaped from him, and then he spoke, "I guess she was a beautiful woman. She had long, blonde hair, and pretty, blue eyes. From what I could tell, she was very petite, and it looked as though she kept herself in pretty good shape. I never actually met her. I did see a few pictures of her at the ranch house, but she had already passed on before I met J.C. I guess they were really close and he took it pretty hard when she died."

"How did she die?" Nicole asked, curiously. "Was it from natural causes?"

"Oh no, far from that," he paused for a moment and then slowly said, "I don't know if I should be telling you this stuff."

Nicole looked at him with those turquoise eyes surrounded by those long lashes and Garret knew that he had lost the battle, but hopefully not the war.

"Oh hell, you're just going to pry it out of me anyway."

Garret thought for a moment, before continuing. It felt like he was betraying J.C. in some way by talking about his parents like that. But sitting there next to Nicole, her subtle beauty smothering his common sense, it was hard not to give her anything in the world that she wanted. And all she really wanted was a little bit of information. What could that possibly hurt? So, he put his conscience aside and continued with the story he had started.

"J.C.'s daddy was a very brutal man. After spending a whole evening drinking in a bar, he'd go home and beat the hell out of his wife. J.C. would do everything he could to try and stop him, but he was no match for the old man. He'd end up lying in a heap somewhere then his daddy would go finish the job he started. It was under the assumption that he beat her because he thought she was cheating on him. That, of course, wasn't true. Finally, the day came that she just couldn't take anymore. One day when they were out working the fields, she drew a bath, slit her wrist, and bled to death right there in the tub. J.C. was the one who found her. He went crazy. He ran out looking for his old man screaming that he was going to kill him. When he couldn't find him and returned home, there was his old man holding his mamma in his arms. Just rocking back and forth, howling like a wounded animal. J.C. figured that his old man died that day too."

Garret paused and looked out the window for a minute, remembering the pain on J.C.'s face the night he told him the story.

"The old man never spoke a word after that. He'd just go get liquored up and then just sit there and have himself a good cry. Finally, he killed himself on the way home from the gin mill one night. Drove his old truck right into a tree. After his daddy died, J.C. finally found a little peace of mind. I believe he hated that man until the day he did die. Rightly so, I guess. It was his fault his mamma killed herself. For J.C. to find her that way, it must have been awful," he finished and then grew quiet for a moment. As he gave Nicole a guilty look, he said, "And I talk too much."

No one spoke as Nicole digested the information that was shared and Garret continued to berate himself for having shared it.

"Garret did J.C.'s mother come from Pennsylvania?" she asked, thinking the answer might be a little piece to the puzzle.

"Yes, she grew up in Jasper. That's why he made that donation there; plus it's a small town and he didn't think there'd be a big hoopla made out of it. It was her birthday and that was his way of dealing with it. I don't know how that information got out, about the donation. I thought J.C. was going to kill me."

He spoke softly and she had to strain to hear. There was no mistake that she could hear the compassion that he felt for J.C. in his tone of voice.

"Look, we're almost to the studio. Let's not talk about this anymore. If J.C. finds out,"

"Garret," she said, cutting off his words. "I promise, J.C. will never know what you told me. Thank you for sticking your neck out and helping me. I think I will be able to understand him a little better."

As the car pulled up to the guard shack, Nicole's mind was reeling from the story she just heard. Knowing full well that she had just told Garret a tall tale; the information he had given her wasn't going to help her to understand J.C. any better. The only thing that information did was to get her curiosity level spiked even more. It may have explained some of the reason for the cold and empty look in his eyes.

Nicole and Garret took their tour of the production company. Although it was a fascinating place, Nicole's thoughts were a million miles away. She was really getting anxious to meet with J.C. Just as they were about to finish their tour, Garret's cell phone started ringing.

"Hello, oh, hi Boss. Yeah, we're just about done here. Fifteen minutes, O.K., we'll be there."

Garret flipped the end of the phone back into position, indicating the call was finished.

"J.C.'s ready to meet with you. We need to give him about fifteen minutes. He wants to speak with me first, so we'll go over to the office."

As he spoke, he was steering her in a different direction.

"Is there a fax machine somewhere I could use, Garret? I need to send some phone numbers to the office. They'll be frantic if they can't get a hold of me."

"Yeah, you can use the one in Tami's office while I talk to J.C. By the time you get finished, he should be ready to see you. Before we get any closer," he paused for a second and looked deeply into her eyes. "I want to wish you luck."

The tone in his voice had become very serious and he had a look of concern on his face. A worried look broke out across Nicole's brow. What am I getting myself into she asked herself. Garret saw what he was looking for, the expression of fear, and burst into laughter.

"I was only kidding, Nicole. He's not really an ogre; he just wants people to think he is."

Garret was smiling at her mischievously.

"Very funny, Mr. McCormick!" was the only come-back she could muster.

The sudden approach to humor caught her completely by surprise. For her own sake, she certainly hoped that was what it was.

"Here we are." Stepping back, he let Nicole enter first and said, "Tami, this is Nicole Bentley." Turning to Nicole, he finished the introduction, "And this is J.C.'s right hand—no she's the left, I'm the right hand-oh, I can't ever keep them straight! Anyway, this is Tami. Nicole needs to use the fax machine, Tam. I'm headed in to see J.C."

With that, he crossed the room and rapped on the door. Nicole heard a faint 'it's open' and Garret disappeared inside.

"This is a very nice office," Nicole replied as she glanced around, taking everything in.

It was small, but comfortable. Tami had a few plants scattered here and there. Some personal photos occupied a portion of her desk. Everything was neatly organized and in it's place.

"J.C.'s pretty much a neat freak," she laughed as she got up from her desk. "I'm pleased to meet you, Nicole," she said as she extended her hand for a shake. "It must be exciting, your job, that is. You must get to meet a lot of famous people."

Tami was headed toward the fax machine while she spoke. When she reached the machine, she turned around and leaned against the counter looking very relaxed and waited for her response.

"It does have its moments," Nicole replied. "Not all of them are good ones though. I can't decide if the next moment is going to be a good one, or the alternative."

She laughed as she spoke, but she was really hoping to get a reaction from Tami.

"Oh, don't worry about J. C.; his bark is bigger than his bite," she gave Nicole a warm smile. "Here's the fax machine, there's paper right next to it, take what you need. If you need any help, just holler. If you'll excuse me, I'm working on something pretty important and I don't want to hear the Boss's bark, or feel his bite, if you know what I mean," she said, and grinned as she headed back for her desk.

"Thanks, Tami."

Nicole grabbed a sheet of the paper and started to write down the number to the hotel and then got out the card Garret had given her yesterday. His cell phone number and the number to the studio were both on it so she jotted them down, too. Beneath the phone numbers she added a little note '*heading into the lion's den shortly, wish me luck!*' and signed it, *Nicole*. After she punched the phone number in and fed the paper into the machine, she smiled to herself. Having written those words in jest, she could only hope they didn't back-fire on her.

SEVEN

J. C. spent a lot of time in his office, so he wanted plenty of space to spend that time in. When entering the room, a massive oak desk sat to the left of the door and in front of a huge wall of built-in shelves. Lined with books, magazines, and film cartridges, the shelves held all the tools of the trade. There were two over-stuffed, leather chairs positioned in front of the desk for clients. When Garret entered the room, he chose to by-pass the chairs and opted for the sofa in the further room. That room was used, more or less, as a sitting room. There was a large window directly above the sofa and the natural light gave the room a relaxing ambience.

Garret plopped down on the sofa and jacked his boots up onto the table in front of it. J.C. came around his desk and followed Garret into the adjoining room. Leaning against the wall in the doorway, his hands were behind his back and one leg was bent and a foot rested on the wall.

"Garret," he hesitated for a moment, "I don't know if I really want to do this." Fidgeting with an imaginary piece of lint on his pants, he looked up again and said, "I think it was a stupid idea."

It was plain to see how uncomfortably nervous he was as he squirmed around against the wall. Garret watched in amusement. Standing in front of him was one of the most powerful men he knew; yet here he was, reduced to a nervous wreck by one little female!

It was quiet for a moment, and finally, he asked, "What's she like?"

Garret grinned at J.C., he'd never seen him so out-of-control. This is what it must feel like to get cold feet on your wedding day, he laughed to himself. Without hesitation he gave his description of Nicole.

"She's intelligent and definitely beautiful, she's got compassion, and she's a real sweet person, J.C. If you give her half a chance, you might really like her, Boss."

THE COVER STORY

"You gathered all that from the little time you've had to spend with her?" J.C. asked, looking at him in disbelief.

"She's like, oh…how would you say it?" he hesitated, trying to find the right words to describe how easy it was to form an instant bond with Nicole. "Like the girl next-door or your kid sister. She has a way of getting right under your skin; but it feels so comfortable, you don't mind when she burrows right in like she's gonna stay awhile. She's got a personality that you just can't help but get attached to." Rising abruptly from the sofa, he strolled over to the door. Turning to face J.C., he added, "Guess you won't know that until you meet her for yourself."

There were things he needed to get done and holding J.C.'s hand while he met with the reporter wasn't one of them. Turning back toward the door, he moseyed across the office floor and sauntered out.

J.C. bounced off the wall with a start. Lost in thought while trying to digest what he had heard, it finally hit him that Garret was going out to get her.

"Oh, Jesus, why did I let him talk me into this shit?" he mumbled.

There was no way, no shape or form, that he was ready for this. As Nicole entered the room, J.C. was standing with his back toward her, hands on hips, looking every bit as intimidating from the backside as he did from the front. As a rule, the person being interviewed would normally be facing her, usually giving some sort of spoken greeting. It looked as though someone stuffed a steel rod up his back; he stood there so stiffly with his shoulders squared off. Making no moves to turn around and face her, she could feel the tension mounting in the room causing her to go a little weak in the knees. Don't let him get to you, she warned herself. Quickly taking the focus away from him to gather her bearings, she glanced around the mammoth office and was pleasantly surprised at the warmth it generated. He certainly was a neat-freak, she noticed, as her eyes fluttered around the room. The office decor was very pleasant, but definitely masculine in taste. Allowing herself another glance, her eyes fell back on J.C. Ignoring the ram-rod stance this time, she gave herself plenty of time to evaluate the tall, lean, muscular build. Well, he gave her plenty of time because he still hadn't moved a muscle.

Finally, when J. C. slowly turned around, his cold, hard eyes were sizing her up. Looking every bit like the picture she had seen of him at the library, she really wished Garret had come in with her to ease the uncomfortable tension that was now stifling the room. There were two chairs on either side of the sofa. J.C. sat in one and pointed to the other for Nicole to use.

Garret had been right about her being a beautiful woman, J.C. thought as he gave her the once over. The soft, green eyes coupled with the auburn hair, complimented the porcelain complexion of her skin. If she was as intelligent as Garret said she was, she wouldn't try using her looks to win him over. It wouldn't get her anywhere because he'd stopped caring a long time ago about how a woman looked.

"J.C.," Nicole spoke softly, trying to break the ice between them. If she had waited for him to speak, they would be sitting there, silently, all day.

The writing was on the wall, nothing about this interview was going to be easy. Sensing that he wasn't going to voluntarily give her anything to work with, she was going to have to drag every word out of him. Taking a deep breath, she tried to settle the fluttering sensation that was causing the uneasiness in her stomach. How could one man make an experienced journalist feel as though this were the first time out? When she realized that she was the one allowing a man that she hardly knew to diminish her level of confidence, she finally got pissed off. Getting things back into perspective, she decided not to hesitate with the start of the interview. If she just charged in and got started, maybe the intimidation he was projecting would disappear.

"I'd like to use a tape recorder while I'm doing this interview," she spoke gently, trying to reassure him. "Is that O.K. with you?"

There was a very uncomfortable silence and when he finally spoke, his voice was deep and the words were spoken in monotone.

"Why do you need the tape-recorder?"

As if the situation wasn't already bad enough, he glared at her like she was some kind of thief that was trying to steel his words by using a tape recorder.

"It's pretty much a standard procedure during an interview. If I were to take notes, sometimes it will delay the conversation and we may lose our train of thought. On the other hand, if we use the tape-recorder, our conversation can remain steady and unrestricted. Sort of the out-of-sight, out-of-mind concept."

Even mustering up her most winning smile didn't appear to have any effect on its intended receiver.

J.C. just sat there, staring at Nicole. He didn't like the idea of the tape-recorder one bit. And he sure didn't like the idea of someone else having control of the situation either. It was beyond reason how a person could sit across from you, flash a smile, and expect you to unload your whole life in their lap. This interview shit just wasn't going to work.

Suddenly, a tiny smirk came over his face as he had a revelation. If she wanted him to talk about his past, his childhood, his parents, then damn it, she would have to talk about hers first. Let her see for herself how humiliating it would feel to tell a total stranger things about your life that you could barely tell a friend. Of course, a woman like her probably didn't have any dark or illusive stories hidden deep within her past, but he really didn't care. She was going to tell her story first, or this interview wasn't going to happen. Let her sit on pins and needles while he watched her squirm. J.C. wasn't about to be the only uncomfortable person in the room.

"Go ahead and use it if you have to," he grumbled.

Wouldn't she be shocked when she realized that she was going to use that damn little thing to get her own words on tape!

Nicole took the small recorder out of her briefcase and placed it on the table in front of the sofa. Pushing the record button, she sat back, ready to begin. As she closed her eyes for just a moment in an effort to select just the right words to begin the interview, J.C. spoke and interrupted her thoughts.

"What made you decide to become a reporter, Nicole?" he asked, taking the lead as he leaned back and got comfortable in the chair.

The sudden change in his tone startled her so that her eyes popped open. As she looked in his direction, to her surprise, she couldn't help but notice how relaxed he looked as he sprawled out in the armchair. The tone of his voice was so calm and smooth, all the gruffness from before had miraculously evaporated. Gazing intently at him, she wondering what had caused the sudden change. Without skipping a beat, she eagerly took the bait he dangled in front of her.

"I knew that life was exciting out there. I figured if I couldn't be right in the middle of the action, the next best thing would be to write about it on the sidelines. So, I became the real, live, Brenda Starr."

It was kind of a corny answer, but knowing the beginning of an interview could be difficult, she just blurted out whatever had come to mind.

"And what about you, what made you decide to become the owner of a production company?"

The conversation was moving slowly, but at least it was moving.

"Well, I had images of what life should be about, too. Here at the studio, they can create any image they desire. I liked that concept and I decided I wanted to be a part of it."

O.K., this is good, she thought. Now we're going to go with some direction here. Having no inkling of the irony of her thoughts, she was pretty sure that she had him just about where she wanted him.

Feeling pretty confident, she asked, "What kind of childhood did you have J.C.?"

"It wasn't pleasant."

Instantly his voice had gone flat again. As he spoke he pulled his body straight up in the chair.

It couldn't have been more evident if the floor had opened up and swallowed her whole that she had picked the wrong subject. Even his body language screamed at her to choose a different path. Sheer stubbornness and a need to take charge prevented her from noticing the mistake she was making. Skating on thin ice, she shot forward with a different angle.

"What were your parents' like?"

No sooner did the words leave her lips when fire seemed to flare from his eyes. In the next instant his expression turned hard and cold and definitely unreadable.

From a voice that didn't even sound like it belonged to J.C. she heard, "I don't want to talk about them."

Goose bumps flared across her arms making the fine little hairs stand on end as the icy tone enveloped her. Finding herself at another dead end and possibly at the end of a rope, it was time to try a different approach.

"Did you grow up in Texas?"

The strain in her voice was becoming too audible. The tension in the room threatened to grow fingers and slide themselves around her throat.

"Yes." A single syllable response was all she got.

Being a man of such few words, she thought, no wonder he didn't interview. This wasn't going in a good direction. Knowing that she wasn't getting anywhere, Nicole released an exasperated sigh. Reaching over and turning off the tape-recorder, she leaned across to J.C.'s chair and gently placed her hand on top of his.

"J.C.," she said softly, looking deeply into his eyes. "I know this isn't easy and it's not something you're used to, but I'm not getting any information out of you. If you would just relax and open up, I could get a better picture of what you're all about. Please try and work with me. I'll try and make this as painless as possible."

Slowly pulling her hand back, she straightened herself back in her chair.

The empathy in her eyes almost made him feel badly, but it was going to take a little more than that. J.C. leaned forward and put his hand gently over Nicole's.

"Nicole," he said softly, but with a snarl on his lip. "Why should I bare my soul to a woman I hardly know?"

Sitting back in the chair, he enjoyed the look of confusion that appeared on her face before he continued.

"On the other hand, if you were to tell me your story maybe that would give me a better picture of what you're all about."

Throwing her words back in her face gave him such satisfaction it left a cool look of defiance glowing in his eyes. There was a silent struggle of wills battling on between the two of them. Nicole could feel the victory being sucked away from her by the instant. Seeing her slump in defeat, J.C. plucked the imaginary prize from the air, declared himself the winner and a devious smile broke out across his face.

"Let's start over, O.K.?" Leaning toward her with a sincere look on his face he asked, "Now then, what kind of childhood did you have, Nicole?"

Sarcasm dripped from each of the words he spoke. Nicole slowly got out of her chair and walked across the room to the window. Triumph sprung from every part of J.C.'s being. Now he had her where he wanted her, he was the one in control.

What the hell is he doing she wondered. What kind of interview is this going to be? J.C. watched as she nervously wrung her hands together behind her back. If I don't handle this right, she thought, I know I'm going to lose the story. After talking with Garret, she knew there was definitely one there.

Maybe he's looking for my trust. If I'm absolutely honest with him, tell him what he wants to know, maybe then he'll open up. This is so absurd, she screamed to herself. I'm the damn reporter. I'm supposed to be asking the questions. Yeah, and he's the one with the story, she argued to herself. He's going to make me play it his way or I'm going to be hitting the highway. The bitter truth of the situation had found its mark. If J.C. didn't get his way, there would be no interview. Period. End of story.

"O.K., J.C., we'll do it your way," she replied as she crossed the room and sat back in her chair. "Where do you want to start?"

Her tone sounded as defeated as she felt. This was such an unorthodox way to conduct an interview. Boy would Sam be chewing her butt if he could see the predicament she'd gotten herself into this time.

"Uh, tape-recorder on?" he asked, smugly.

"Is that really necessary?" she snapped back at him.

"Was it really necessary to record me?" he snapped back at her as he glared at her with those steel blue eyes.

Finally, she reached over and pushed the record button with a little more force than was needed. You may have won this battle, J.C., but you haven't won the war, she thought to herself.

"Now then Nicole, what was your childhood like?" he asked again, this time without the sarcasm.

Leaning back in the chair, she studied the swirls on the ceiling. How in the hell was she going to put her childhood into words? She didn't want to tell this total stranger the bitter facts about how she grew up. Isn't it ironic, she thought to herself, that's exactly what you barged in here expecting him to do. Thinking along those lines seemed to shed a little light on her precarious situation. J.C. was going to make her endure what she expected him to suffer through! How could she possibly refuse to give him precious information, and then expect him to pour out his heart and soul? She finally saw the logic to his request. It was still a rather odd situation, but at least she could see where he was coming from. Just do the best you can, she told herself. Slowly, she put her thoughts together and began the best way she knew how.

In a small, trembling voice she started at the beginning, "Well, my mother was a second grade teacher, and my dad was the only barber in town. They loved each other, oh…how would I describe it?" she hesitated, her eyes roaming in every direction, except in J.C.'s, searching for the right description. "They loved each other to the fullest extent, I guess you could say."

Still collecting her thoughts, she was quiet for a moment more. It was a lot harder than she thought to talk about her personal life.

"When I was a child, my parents were attentive enough. There was always a home cooked meal. They provided me with a roof over my head and participated in my education, but there was something missing."

In her mind she could picture her parents holding hands, always hugging and clinging to each other.

"They never did anything unless it was together. When they gazed at each other, it was like there was no one else in the universe, just the two of them," she continued, and with another pause while she searched for her next words, "It was like I was just there." she said softly.

The lonely feeling that had always accompanied her when she was at home crept inside and filled her as she spoke. The sad face of the lonely child popped into her head. Her father's words, 'an accident, an accident, an accident,' burnt into her mind, like the needle, stuck in the groove on a record. Even though she tried to camouflage them, her mixed emotions played nakedly across her face. Those feelings kept pulling at her, trying to bring her back to where she didn't want to go. It felt like her chest was being sliced open and her broken heart was lying there, bleeding for everyone to see. Nicole fought hard to keep her composure.

"It was as though they realized they had to love me. It was their responsibility, it was their job. But they didn't want to share what they had with anyone else; so I got what little extra love they could scrape together. Most of that extra was pretty lean."

The last part was barely audible. J.C. had to lean toward her to hear her at all. She cleared her throat so she could continue.

"When I got older, and could take care of myself, I felt like a third wheel in my own house. My parents hardly came out of their room. We ate some meals together, but they figured I was old enough to fend for myself. It was a pretty lonely existence at my house. It never felt warm and cozy there, like a real home. It made me pour myself into my school work. I was a pretty good student, and I had won some scholarships. My parents bought me a car for my eighteenth birthday; so, I went away to college." Looking directly at J.C., she boldly said, "I don't think they even missed me. That was my childhood."

Sarcasm had taken over her soft voice by the time she finished. There was no way she was going to humiliate herself any further by telling him about the conversation she had overheard as a child. She would never be able to share that with another person. If she had been an accident, so be it. There were only three people who needed to know that. And he wasn't one of them.

J.C. could see the naked pain in her eyes. He had watched the turmoil spread across her face as the untold portions of her story went through her mind. It was plain to see she was leaving the difficult parts out. It couldn't have been pleasant to discover that her parents had given her just enough love to get by, if indeed, it was enough. That had to be hard enough to share with a stranger. Love was the one thing his mother had showered him with. Too bad it was for such a short time. He didn't know if he was ready to tell his story. Oh, he wanted to. It was tiresome to carry all that pain and heartache around. He had read somewhere that if you could face your pain, you could make it disappear. If he shared his story with Nicole, maybe that would be facing it. Maybe, just maybe, all the hurt would go away.

Nicole sat there quietly waiting for J.C. to say something. Anything. She felt as though she had made a fool of herself and the silence was just making it worse. J.C. got out of his chair and went to the window. If he wasn't looking at her, avoiding any eye contact with her, maybe it would be easier to begin.

"My childhood wasn't pleasant either, Nicole."

She let out a soft sigh of relief. Not because of his unpleasant childhood, but because he finally broke the silence.

"My father was a bastard. He was a real hard working man; but he drank as hard as he worked. My mother was a beautiful woman. Much too good for the likes of him. My mother and I were very close. She didn't work, so every waking hour was spent with me. When I was a boy, she'd always tell me that one day, we'd run away. Get away from him."

There was venom in his voice as he talked about his father.

"He'd come home from drinking, couldn't hardly stand on his own two feet. Then he would start screaming at her. He'd get himself so worked up that he'd start hitting her. I think he felt guilty because he knew she could have done much better if she had married someone else. So he blamed her for her own misfortune. I'd try and stop him. It killed me to see him beating on my mother. He'd be in such a rage; he'd send me flying like a rag doll. He was a strong man."

J.C. had grown quiet. He felt like there was an old movie running through his mind. His father was yelling at his mother.

"Who was here, Jessica? Answer me, woman!"

As he screamed at her, his arm was raised above his head in striking position.

"No one, Austin, I swear!" she pleaded with him in a low voice as she cowered as close to the headboard of the bed as she could get.

"You got the winda' wide open for somebody to run away soons' ya heard me comin'," he slurred at her as he pointed toward the open window.

"Austin, its a hundred degrees outside. We don't have any air-conditioning. I was hoping for a little breeze. It's stifling in here."

She couldn't stop the tears from gathering and spilling down her face. To the old man, tears were a sign of guilt. To his mother, they were a sign of the beating she knew was going to come. If only she had remembered to shut the window.

"Ya lying slut!"

At that moment, the raised arm came crashing down and connected with Jessica's delicate face. There was barely a whimper heard at the force of the blow. She always tried to keep as quiet as she could when he beat her so she didn't alarm her son. Sometimes it was impossible to leash the screams. The pain was unbearable. Again, the fist came flying at her. This time it connected with her right eye. J.C. came running to his mother's defense, jumping on his father's back and swinging his little fists at the back of his father's head. Austin Collins just shook him off like a bull brushing away a pesky fly. J.C. landed in the corner of the room in a rumpled pile. The assault continued on his mother until his drunken body ran out of steam. Only then did he fall to the side of the bed, passed out cold.

Nicole watched J.C.'s face as the storm of a memory took over his expressions. It was like watching a ship at sea as the wave's crash into it and threaten to swallow it whole. She kept quiet and just watched, waiting for him to return. Finally, he cleared his throat and proceeded with his story.

"She took his shit for years. I think she stayed because of me. We didn't have enough money for both of us to go, so she stayed. Finally, one day she committed suicide. I was sixteen at the time. I really needed her, and she was gone. It was so hard to believe. I wish it had been him. Oh, how I wish it had been him."

He let out a deep sigh. The memory of finding his mother in the bathtub, a pool of red water swimming around her, clouded his mind. His heart still ached for the lifeless body she left behind. The feeling of hot moisture began collecting in his eyes, threatening to show up in the form of tears. He had shed all the tears he was ever going to in this lifetime so he willed them away before he could continue.

"He ended up killing himself, anyhow," his speech was slow, his voice exasperated. "Why couldn't he have done it before my mother died?"

He knew he hadn't told her the whole story either, but hell; it was hard enough getting that much out. Garret was the only other person he talked to about his mother. Even then, he hadn't told the whole truth. The rest just hurt too much. Walking back to the chair, he sunk heavily into the seat. That had been enough on that subject, she wasn't getting anymore. Things were pretty quiet for a moment.

"What's next, Brenda Starr?" he said with a little sneer.

"Were there any sweethearts?" she asked trying to lighten the somber mood they had both put themselves into.

They could have stopped right there and she could have just walked away, but he wasn't going to get the best of her, or so she thought.

"I don't know, Nicole, were there any sweethearts?"

Giving her a harsh look that could have split a hair, he was silently daring her to go first. Wincing from the knowledge that telling about her childhood was a breeze compared to what he was asking her to reveal next. That wound hadn't healed after all these years. She was beginning to wonder if the interview was really worth it.

"Let's get all of the skeletons out of the closet, shall we?" she threw at him.

Those were memories she had shut out a long time ago. Those were thoughts she would never allowed herself to think about. Very private, hurtful memories better left alone.

"Yes, lets," he threw right back at her, "But you go first, remember? It's your game."

He flashed her a wicked smile.

Nicole hadn't thought about Bobby Bailey for a long time. In fact, she had made a vow to herself to never think about it, mainly to preserve her sanity. If any little thought came creeping in, if anything triggered a memory, she'd immediately divert her thoughts to something else. Something more pleasant, something that didn't hurt. J.C. not only wanted her to break that vow, he wanted her to share the horrid details with him! His eyes were glued to her face as he was watching her go through this torment. Wondering if he was getting some sort of satisfaction out of witnessing her agony, she just sat there staring at him. He continued to stare, coldly, right back at her. The thought of getting up and walking out certainly passed through her mind for a second time. Coward, she said to herself. Just get it over with.

"Bobby," she said slowly, "Bobby Bailey."

Finally managing to get his name to come out of her mouth, she didn't realize it came in the form of a whisper though.

"I couldn't hear you Nicole. What did you say?"

She said something, he knew she did because he had seen her lips move, but there was no sound.

"His name, it was Bobby Bailey."

The unnatural tone in her voice sounded so hollow. It was quiet for a few moments as she looked up at the ceiling and then down at her hands, not knowing where to begin.

"Bobby and I met in High School when his parents had bought a big farm across town. I think it was our junior year. Yeah…that was it. He was the quarterback on the football team. The best looking guy in school. I couldn't believe it when he asked me to the Homecoming Dance. We had a great time; he was so easy to be with. We were pretty inseparable after that."

She had loosened up a little by then, talking a little easier.

"By Christmas, we were going steady. The whole family really liked me. We spent all our spare time at the farm. It was better than being at home. Bobby would pick me and Sara up for school every morning." At that point she looked at J.C. and added, "Sara was my best friend." There was a big emphasis on the 'was'.

"Anyway, we did a lot together. Sara never seemed to have a boyfriend of her own. So the three of us went just about everywhere together. Bobby and I got closer in our senior year."

Nicole was getting a far away look in her eyes. It seemed as though she was talking more to herself than she was to J.C.

"That Christmas, Bobby gave me an engagement ring. It was so beautiful. The ring...the way he gave it to me. I remember the whole family sitting around the tree. Bobby gave me this huge box. When I opened it, there was another wrapped box inside. I kept opening boxes until I finally got to the last one. In it was the most beautiful ring. It was the happiest moment in my life, when he slipped that ring on my finger. I felt like I was in a fairytale."

Feeling herself slipping back in time, she could smell the faint aroma of pine. The lights on the Christmas tree were twinkling on and off. The sound of happy voices chattering and laughter was filtering through the house. That was such a delightful sound to her. One she never heard at home. That was the way holidays were suppose to be, and she was so glad to be sharing it with people she loved. She continued talking softly as though she were relishing the memory.

"We set the wedding date that night. I would begin my first semester at school and Bobby would work with his Dad on the farm. We'd get married when I came home for winter break, on Christmas Eve. Everything was so wonderful. I felt like I finally had what my parents shared and I could almost forgive them for loving each other so much."

Suddenly she quit talking and stared off into space. A mental picture of Bobby's handsome face smiled down at her. His strong arms were around her, holding her close. She remembered all the happy times they had together, how she was so much in love with him, how she would melt when he kissed her. They had made so many plans for the future and went over all the details for a perfect wedding. J. C. was getting worried about her but he didn't know what to do. She was acting like she was in some kind of trance.

"What happened then, Nicole?"

Maybe if he could keep her talking, he thought, she might come out of it.

"Hmm? Oh...um...yeah," she faltered, trying to remember where she left off. "I, uh, came home from school early. It was two weeks before the wedding." Her speech was slow, labored and her voice was shaky as she continued, "I was anxious to see Bobby. I had found the perfect wedding dress and I wanted to tell him all about it. It had snowed, just enough to cover the ground. Bobby's truck was there, so I ran in the house to find him. When I couldn't find him in the house, I went back out by my car. That's when I spotted the two sets of prints going to the barn. I followed them to the big barn doors. I never thought…," she broke off in the middle of the sentence, picturing the hideous scene that followed. "I stepped inside, the doors were open wide enough for me to slide through. The top of the barn is where they kept the hay and straw. I heard voices, but I couldn't see anyone. So, I followed the sound of the noises. They must not have heard my footsteps because of the loose straw on the floor. When I found them…," she hesitated again, a painful look crossing her face. "They were making love, in the corner, in the straw. Bobby and my best friend, Sara," she managed to say as she felt a riveting pain shoot through her.

It was just like the one she felt when she had found them together. It was as though someone had closed the curtains and everything went black. There was a rumbling in her stomach as it did flip-flops, threatening to toss all it's holdings up and out of her throat. The feel of her skin was clammy and she was nauseous and dizzy all at the same time. The barn floor could have opened up and swallowed her and she would have been happy to disappear, because she couldn't quit staring at the two of them. And the two of them just stared right back at her. Neither one of them attempted to cover their naked bodies. When she finally got a grip on her emotions she ran from the barn, only stopping long enough to get sick. She jumped into her car before the tears unleashed in huge drops, cascading down her cheeks. Once she was far enough from the farm, she had to pull over. The tears were falling so hard, she couldn't see anymore. The sobs had come from so deep within; she swore they were tugging at her toenails. Never, never again would she set herself up to be hurt so deeply. Not even real love was worth such excruciating pain.

Once she settled down and thought about the situation, things sort of came to light. That must have been the reason Sara never had a boyfriend of her own. It made her wonder how long their affair had been going on. The writing on the wall had probably always been there. Wanting to be a part of the family so badly, she never saw it coming. It was like they were waiting to get caught.

Bobby had never even apologized to her, neither had Sara. They had made her look like such a fool in front of the whole town. She had loved him so much, and trusted her to the farthest extent. It was as though they wiped her life right out of theirs, just like her parent's did, and continued on like she didn't even exist.

Taking a deep breath before she dared speak, she asked, "Do you have any water?"

J.C. jumped up and got a bottle of water out of the corner frig. When she opened it, he could see her hands were shaking. Taking a couple short swallows, she screwed the cap back on and set it in her lap.

"Bobby and Sara got married, on my wedding day. They didn't change any of the wedding plans. They just changed the bride. They have two little boys now. I don't go home much anymore. Every other year, for Christmas or Thanksgiving. Never both, sometimes neither. Oh gosh, now I'm rambling."

Nicole had never felt so completely out of control in her life and it made her feel absolutely helpless. She knew the pain had lain nakedly across her face for J.C. to see. As naked as Bobby and Sara had been in the barn. Embarrassment flamed in her cheeks. J.C. felt like a prick for making her go through that. Walking over to her chair, he gently took her hands in his.

"I'm sorry, Nicole. I shouldn't have made you do that."

There was sincere warmth in his eyes.

"No, no, it's O.K. J.C., really. It's the first time I have ever said the words out loud. I guess I let myself believe that if I didn't think about it, it couldn't have really happened. It's gone way past the time to face it. In a way, it felt good. It really did."

She was beginning to feel a sense of freedom. All that buried misery finally coming to the surface. The whole sordid thing was finally out in the open. It wasn't just her dirty little secret anymore.

"If you don't mind though, J.C., I'd like to call it quits for today. Even though that felt good to get it off my chest, it sure took a lot out of me."

Her nervous laugh justified her words. Pulling herself out of the chair, she stood still for a moment to get her bearings and then walked over to the window.

"I'll have Garret take you back to the hotel. Are you sure you're going to be O.K.?"

The genuine concern he was revealing touched her.

"Yeah, I'll be fine. A nice hot shower and a good night's sleep will do the trick. If you don't mind, I'll wait outside for Garret. I need some fresh air."

It was meant as a statement more than a question, and she wasn't really expecting an answer. Hastily grabbing her belongings, she headed as quickly as she could for the door. As soon as she stepped outside, it felt like she was going to keel over and quickly leaned up against the wall for support. Boy did I ever blow that one, she thought. I'm sure I've lost all credibility as a reporter with him. I feel so damn foolish. It wasn't going to do any good to keep scolding herself, but she couldn't seem to stop.

"Hey, you!" Garret hollered from his ragtop BMW, "This O.K., or do you want the limo?"

Nicole looked up and attempted a smile. Making a feeble attempt to compose herself, she walked across parking lot. When she finally reached the car, Garret jumped out to open her door.

"This is great, Garret. It's just what I need. The fresh air will do me some good."

She slid into the seat so he could shut the door.

"So, how'd it go? You appear to be all in one piece," he said, teasing her.

"He's a tough cookie, Garret. I'm not really sure what happened in there. I do know it wasn't pretty. I really need to get some rest so I'll be ready for round two tomorrow."

She gave him a smile, but it didn't quite reach her eyes. It looked like she was pretty beat. It made him wonder what the hell did happen in that room.

EIGHT

Garret found Nicole's silence almost unbearable as he drove her back to the hotel. Several times that day he had totally lost all concentration as his mind kept floating back to the morning he had spent with her. He could compare the conversation they had shared to a re-run of a television program; he had played it over in his mind so many times. In fact he could almost recite it, word for word. Filled with disappointment, the silence was deafening to his ears. There was no pleasant bantering back and forth, like there had been at breakfast. It was hard to believe that the person sitting beside him was the same bubbly spirit he had spent the morning with. What could J.C. have said or done to snuff out that wild fire that burned inside of her? All that seemed to remain was the smoldering ashes.

Any kind of conversation seemed fruitless at that moment; she looked so miserable and acted as though she were physically drained. Garret had to fight the urge to put his arm around her and comfort her. What was coming over him? He hardly knew her. Yet, there was something about her that drew him to her like a magnet. As he pulled up in front of the hotel, he shut the engine off.

"Nicole, would you have dinner with me tonight?" he asked gently, hoping to catch a glimpse of that familiar spark he had seen in her eyes earlier.

"I really appreciate the offer, Garret, but I don't think I'd be suitable company tonight."

Seeing the anxiety written all over his face made it really hard for her to turn him down, but she needed to be alone for awhile. After spending the horrendous morning with J.C., she really didn't think she had the strength for it anyhow.

"I'll tell you what, how about a rain check?"

"Rain check it is, then. See you tomorrow!"

THE COVER STORY

He shoved a lot more cheer in the tone of his voice than he was feeling. Trying to preserve her dignity, she waited outside the door until he drove away. Garret glanced back at her as he pulled out into traffic. A wave of disappointment had rushed over him when she declined his dinner invitation. For some reason Nicole made him feel giddy, like a school boy. A tingling sensation would flow through him whenever she was near him. In all of his thirty-nine years, Garret had never been in love. He had been in lust a lot of times, but never in love. Truthfully, he had to admit he was afraid of it. After witnessing the gut-wrenching torment, leaving wounds that would never heal, and the pure hell J.C. went through when Elizabeth Bordoe disappeared, he didn't want anything to do with it. Love seemed to do strange things to men.

To fill the void that Elizabeth's disappearance had left, J.C. threw himself into the drilling of his oil wells, driving himself from daylight until dusk. Garret was right there every step of the way and he felt his pain. It wasn't the same kind of pain J.C. was experiencing, but it was still pain, none the less. Every muscle and every bone in his body would be throbbing like a wicked toothache by the time they dragged themselves back to the ranch. J.C. was relentless, day in and day out. It was fortunate that all that hard work had paid off in the end. The whole situation made Garret a little leery about giving his heart away. But after meeting Nicole, he realized that the choice of who he falls in love with may not be totally in his hands.

You better slow down there big guy, he thought, as he realized he was starting to get attached to her. Hell, who wouldn't? She was very pleasing to look at and she had a very good head on her shoulders, too. It made him wonder if she had a boyfriend back east. When he had glanced over at her hands earlier to see if there were any rings, her left hand had been as bare as a baby's bottom. In his mind, that made her fair game.

Garret was entering a time in his life when he would enjoy the company of a steady female. Up until then, he hadn't given it much thought. Since meeting Nicole, he thought of nothing else. It was such a pleasure to spend time with her and their conversations came so easily. Things had slowed down a bit since J.C. had acquired the production company. More organized would be a better choice of words. Garret found a lot of his nights were empty. He could have his choice of women, but there were none that appealed to him. Well, not until Nicole came into the picture. He didn't know if there was a chance that he could spark her interest, but then, he'd never find out if he didn't try.

Nicole went to the front desk to check for messages before she retired to the room. As she placed the slip of paper the desk clerk had given her into a pocket she decided it could wait until she reached the suite to read it. Feeling absolutely drained, she leaned against the back wall of the elevator. When she reached the room, she kicked off her shoes, put her things on the wet-bar and flopped on the bed. It was definitely going to be an early night.

"Ah," she let out a deep sigh. "That feels so good."

Stretching her arms above her head, she closed her eyes for a few minutes. When she finally felt a little energy surge back into her tired body, she removed the paper from her pocket.

Nicole, it read, *paper was Fed-Exed from P.A. No return address. How are things going? Call me tomorrow—Gloria.* Going over it in her mind, she realized that the message just added another twist to the story. Obviously, someone deliberately wanted her to see that article. The message from Gloria made her think about the envelope she had shoved in her purse that morning. Could there be some kind of connection between the two incidents? When she tried to figure what the common link could be all she drew were blanks. The only alternative she had was to sleep on it; maybe something would come to her then. A long, hot shower helped to calm her nerves and she welcomed the comfort she found between the sheets.

Sleep didn't come easy for her though. Tossing and turning she relived the horrible day in her dreams. A vivid Christmas scene appeared in her nightmare. There was a big tree with broken boxes beneath its ugly branches. The large diamond rings that floated in the air would take off like bullets, flying toward her face, only to drop on the ground at her feet and turn to coal. Bobby Bailey's face drifted in and out of the scene as he maliciously bared his teeth as he laughed louder and louder each time his silhouette would leap forward at her. J. C.'s penetrating eyes kept glaring at her, staring right through her. Undistinguished noises kept popping into the background. The noises were getting louder and louder making a ringing sound in her ears. As she awoke with a jump, she realized that those were real noises she was hearing. The ringing sound was coming from the telephone. With sleep still clouding her eyes, she looked around trying to find a clock. The bright red numbers on the alarm clock read 4:00. Four o'clock in the morning! Who the hell would be calling her at such an ungodly hour?

"Hello," she said, grogginess still hanging in her voice.

"Did he tell you about the baby?" a raspy voice slowly whispered to her, taunting her.

"What baby?" she muttered, clueless as to what the person on the other end was saying.

"The baby, Rae Anne," the caller whispered. The raspy voice sent cold chills down her spine.

The sensation rattled all of her senses and totally woke her up. Who the hell was that maniac and why was he calling her about some baby?

"Who is this?" she asked in a frantic tone. Who else knew she was staying at this hotel? What did a baby have to do with anything? Whose baby was he talking about, anyhow? Just as she found enough courage to ask the questions, she heard a click. The other end of the line went dead.

Sleep was out of the question, she was too keyed up to even lie back down. Pacing the floor, she went over the questions she needed answers for. Who was Rae Anne? Who was the man that had called her? Who was the 'he' the man on the phone was referring to? First, there was the strange man on the plane who kept popping up in the same places as Nicole, and then the mysterious envelope appeared with the note that didn't make any sense. Then Gloria sent her a message saying that basically they don't know how the newspaper appeared on her desk. To top everything off, she receives a startling phone call in the middle of the night from some frightening stranger. After reviewing the list, she decided she couldn't keep this to herself any longer. First thing in the morning, she was going to go to J.C. and Garret. Maybe between the three of them, they could figure out what was going on.

NINE

"When did you get the envelope?" J. C. was asking Nicole. Garret had picked her up from the hotel bright and early that morning. It was J.C.'s idea because he wanted to take her to the beach to work on the interview. He thought it would be less confining than working in the office. Besides, his train of thought was better at the beach. Knowing that it was his turn in the barrel, he wanted to be on familiar ground when he gave Nicole the next bit of information he had for her. The beach was definitely where he needed to be. Nicole had wanted to go over something with them first, so they put the interview on hold.

"It came yesterday morning. Someone knocked on my door and I thought it was Garret. When I answered it, there was no one there, but I found this on the floor," while she spoke she was waving the envelope back and forth through the air. "It didn't make any sense to me; so after I read it, I shoved it in my purse and forgot about it. Then, I had a message from Gloria when I returned to the hotel. She said that the *Tribune*, which was the paper I found your article in, was Fed-Exed to the office with no return address. That's what made me think of the envelope. Then at four o'clock this morning, I got a phone call from some maniac, asking me if *he* told me about the baby? What does that mean? Who is the *he* that the caller is referring to?"

Nicole was looking at the two of them, waiting for some kind of answer.

"Is that all they said? Was it a male voice, or a female?" Garret asked, his brows were knitted together with worry.

"I'm pretty sure it was a male. His voice was real scratchy, like he was trying to disguise it.

That was all he said, did *he* tell you about the baby," hesitating for a moment, she added, "No, wait a minute!" She was beginning to get excited and added, "He said more. He said...oooh," she was trying hard to remember. "He said, Rae Anne, yeah that was it. He called the baby by a name, Rae Anne."

By then her eyes were dancing with excitement.

"What does that mean? Whose baby is Rae Anne?"

Looking from Garret to J.C., she expected one of them to come out with the answer. Both men looked at each other in bewilderment. Neither one of them knew any women that had babies, let alone one with the name Rae Anne.

"Have you seen any suspicious looking people around you, anybody doing anything weird, out of the ordinary? Think, was there anyone following you to work?"

J.C. was trying to cover every angle he could think of, partly to make up for the fact that they were no help with the baby named Rae Anne.

As she sat there staring off into space, Nicole was deep in thought. Several minutes had gone by when finally, her face lit up. The stranger who kept popping up everywhere had entered her thoughts.

"Ya know, when I got on the airplane to come out here, I sat next to this weird guy. I remember him because he stared at me in a real strange manner as I was sitting down. The look sent shivers up my spine. When the plane arrived in Chicago, we had to wait for the layover, so I went to the lounge to kill some time. That's when I noticed that same guy was leering at me from behind a newspaper. And when I checked into the hotel, I saw him again out of the corner of my eye as I got on the elevator. I'll bet he's the one, it's got to be him."

When she put all of the pieces together, she figured that it couldn't possibly be just a coincidence that the same man was staying at the same hotel. He had to be the one that was leaving the trail of puzzling information; but her question was for what purpose? What did he expect to accomplish? The confusion of the situation was getting deeper.

"Well, what do you think? Doesn't that sound reasonable?"

"Who is this guy?" J. C. asked, beginning to believe she might be on to something. "Did you happen to catch his name?"

"No, I don't know what his name is."

The fact that guy had been so close so many times and she still didn't know who he was instantly dampened her mood.

"He never said his name?" Garret asked, not wanting the trail to get cold.

"No, he never introduced himself and I never asked him what his name was. I told you, he was weird and I didn't want to have a conversation with him."

The high she was on a minute ago was quickly evaporating. If she had only known the importance of obtaining the man's name while she was aboard the plane, she would have figured out some way to get it. Without it they had reached another dead-end.

"J.C., I think we ought to put a private investigator on this. If that creep is staying in the same hotel with Nicole, she could be in danger. If somebody was tailing him, and he tried to go near her room again, we'd have him. Do you think you could give a good description of him, Nicole?"

There was a measure of concern in Garret's voice. If some maniac was running around out there, he wanted to be sure Nicole wasn't going to be in harms way.

"I can try, but if your private investigator was any good, couldn't he just get the passenger list from the flight to Chicago? If he checked the seating chart, his name should be easy to find because he was sitting right next to me," she said as she looked at him innocently.

Garret felt foolish for not thinking of that himself and he looked sheepishly at J.C. Apparently, his concern for Nicole's safety had gotten in the way of his common sense. J.C. couldn't help it, he burst into laughter. His laughter helped to relieve some of the tension that had been building up since the conversation had begun.

"That's a good idea, Nicole. Why don't we get a hold of Davis, he's worked well for us in the past. We'll need someone who is going to come up with some quick results. I guess we had better hang around until he can get here, just in case he needs more information from you, Nicole. When he's squared away with that information, we can take off and Garret can handle the rest," he was dialing the phone while he spoke.

They went over all the facts with Davis as soon as he arrived. Nicole was impressed at how thoroughly he searched through the information. As she handed over all of the evidence, he went over each piece with a fine-toothed comb. Feeling very comfortable with his ability to handle the situation, Nicole finally began to relax a bit. Davis was a 'take-charge' kind of guy. Although he had a pretty good sized frame, his appearance was kind of plain which probably helped him to blend in with the crowd. That was a necessity she was sure he needed with his particular occupation.

With the situation under control, J.C. and Nicole headed for the beach. The sun was high and the air was warm. It was a beautiful day to spend at the ocean. They drove in silence, each left to their own thoughts; both thinking about the string of events that had lead up to that morning. After they had driven for a while, a large wooded area came in to view. J.C. turned down a long, dirt road that was shadowed by tall trees and slowed the car to a crawl.

"Have to take it easy through here. Lot of potholes, but I'm afraid if I have it paved, it would just invite trouble. Even though the land is posted, it only stops the honest guy from entering."

J.C. was busy watching for the next hole as he spoke.

"It's very nice out here; I assume you own this land?" she questioned as she watched how well he maneuvered the car around.

"Yeah, I've had it for a long time now. Someday I want to build a house in the clearing just ahead. Just haven't found the time to get it started."

They were approaching the clearing when J.C. pulled the car off to the side and shut if off. He popped the trunk and took a blanket and a picnic basket out and closed the lid.

"Comin'? We have to walk in from here, it's not far."

He reached for her hand as she got out of the car.

It surprised her that he was offering his hand. Confused by his actions, she didn't know how to read him; it was like yesterday never happened. He was so congenial and understanding today, just the opposite of yesterday. Finally she couldn't stand it any longer, she had to say something. Was this some kind of trick or was he really just being nice? There was no way she was going to let him make a fool out of her again today. She let him stand there with his hand extended for a second before she spoke.

"J.C., I really don't know what's going on here. I don't want to say anything to upset you or make you angry with me; but I want to make sure we're on the same page here. Yesterday you were cold and calculating and you treated me rather crudely. Today, however, you've been amazingly the total opposite. I don't get it. What has happened in twenty-four hours to make you behave so differently? Excuse me for being so blunt; but if I get right to the heart of things it makes it easier for me."

She hoped she hadn't stepped over the line, but she liked this side of him. She didn't want an hour or two to go by and have the other J.C. come storming back in.

A low, throaty laugh erupted from J.C. Boy, did I deserve that, he thought. He was glad Garret wasn't there to witness her speech. He would have been on the ground, rolling with laughter, yelling, 'give him some more!'. Nicole hadn't said anything humorous and she was quite annoyed by his laughter. She didn't find the situation funny at all.

"Nicole, I'm not laughing at you. Believe me. That was quite a speech, though. You do go right for the juggler. I admit I acted like a prick toward you yesterday, and I truly apologize. Garret had already given me a rundown on your qualities and I didn't believe a word he said. I had to find out for myself whether or not I could trust you. What I put you through, and I humbly apologize for that, I had no idea, was enough to gain respect and trust from anybody, including me. Garret's been my only friend for so long, and it would be an honor to consider you as one. Now, if you will forgive me, and take my hand, we'll go down to the beach. Then you can take that damn recorder of yours out, and we will continue with this interview. Deal?" he asked her as he extended his hand for a second time.

Yesterday had been a most unpleasant ordeal for Nicole. If it had helped her to get this interview with J.C., she had to guess it had been worth it. The places he took her back to yesterday was ground that she would never tread on again with anyone, interview or not! Smiling widely, Nicole locked her hand in his. She could handle a friend like him; it sure was a lot better than being his enemy.

They walked to the edge of the clearing and J.C. stepped aside and let Nicole go through first. When she got to the other side she was astonished by the sight. There was a wide, open beach that stretched for miles. The rushing waves were crashing onto the shore with a soft, pounding noise. The foam lapped at the sand, pushing it aside, uncovering all the treasures hidden just beneath the surface. The blue sky blended so smoothly into the water, it made the horizon look endless. The cool breeze carried a mist of salty moisture and a relaxing aroma that could only be found by the ocean. It was truly beautiful.

"No wonder you like to come here, it's amazing, J.C."

Her eyes were lit up like a child's. She had forgotten how tranquil it was to be at the ocean. The fact that it was a private beach and they didn't have to share the beauty of their isolated splendor with anyone else didn't escape her.

"I have some of my best thoughts here. I've done a lot of wheeling and dealing right about where you're standing. Of course, I just put the thoughts together here; I finish the paper work back at the office. But on the other hand, if I brought my clients out here, they'd be so mesmerized, I could probably close my deals a lot faster. Be more to my advantage too. Maybe I should consider changing my strategy. What do you think?" he asked as his eyes twinkled with mischief.

"Something about that sounds very under-handed, J.C."

She laughed at the thought of some of his prestigious clients wandering through the waves in their Brooks Brother suits. The easiness between them felt so good. What a difference a day makes, she thought. He put the basket down with the blanket and took her hand again. They walked down the beach, wandering in and out of the water. The waves would come up and lap at their feet and then pull away, leaving the sand wedged between their toes. They talked easily of how the drilling on J.C.'s land started, how he met Garret, what made him start his investment company. They talked for hours. Finally, they both gave into hunger and started back up the beach to the picnic basket. When they got situated on the blanket and got the food ready to eat, J.C. grew solemn.

"Nicole, turn the recorder off for a while, please. I want to show you something."

He gazed at her so earnestly.

"Sure, no problem, J.C.," she replied and reached over and hit the 'stop' button.

Whatever it was he wanted to say, he certainly had her full attention.

"Yesterday, when we were sharing information about our childhoods, I wasn't completely honest with you. I didn't tell you the whole truth about my mother's death," as he spoke, he handed her a fragile, yellowed paper.

It was all folded up; like it was something he always carried around with him. She carefully undid the folds, making sure not to tear the paper. It was really hard to get it open, the paper was so old and delicate. She continued to work carefully because somehow she knew that the piece of paper was very precious to him. When she finally got it opened, she began to read:

> *My Dear, Wonderful Justin,*
> *There can be only one reason why you would be reading this letter, and for that, I hope you can forgive me. Words cannot begin to tell how much I truly love you. The hardest choice that I have ever had to make is obviously over. The last thing I ever wanted to do is to leave you alone, but I fear I have run out of choices. I have faith that you will overcome this disaster and you will take all our hopes and dreams and make them your own. I will always be with you in your heart, as I take you in mine.*
>
> *I can vividly remember when I was in the hospital, the day you were born. The doctor placed you in my arms, and I thought, what a precious little Miracle we have created. In that instant, I felt an overwhelming sense of devotion to you. All I ever wanted was to protect you, watch you grow and to fill your little heart with so much love. You brought me so much joy. It was you that kept me going, you were my strength. It was worth getting out of bed, just so I could watch you greet the morning with your incredible smile. You were the sole reason for my existence. As I watched you grow into a young man, my heart could have burst with pride. You were so strong, so full of life and compassion. The vow I made to you, as a baby, was to protect you. And I failed, so miserably. I can not take that chance again. It pains me to have to tell my son why I'm committing such a tragic act, but I know you won't be able to accept my death without an explanation. Justin, I am with child. Although this should be a delightful time for us,*

it has condemned me to my fate. There is no way I could deliberately bring a defenseless little being into the hell that we live in.

It has been hard enough to watch you suffer all these years. In my heart, my dear son, I know you will understand and hopefully forgive me. I love you to the end of this earth. Grow stronger, make me proud,
  Your Loving Mother

When she finished, she carefully folded the letter back to its original state. There were no words to describe how she felt. It was difficult to picture how a young man would possibly react to a letter so profound. J.C. had been so young when his mother died. Nicole turned her head toward him as she studied his profile. What an awful burden he had carried on those shoulders. As he stared out at the ocean, he looked as though he were a million miles away. She was willing to bet she was the only one who had ever seen that letter. Garret may have, but her intuition said no. His mother's words carried such a personal message; she wondered why he shared the letter with her. Did he have to bear his mother's secret alone? It was no wonder he hated his father so much. It wasn't just his mother's life that ended way too soon; he destroyed his only sibling too. Harboring that information would have prevented him from being able to lash out at his father with it. What a cross to bear for one so young.

She didn't want to make J.C. uncomfortable by staring at him, so she turned her head back toward the ocean. He had made the right choice to bring her here. The ocean had a healing effect on the soul. How long would one have to sit by the ocean to heal a wound as deep as J.C.'s? It was amazing what they had accomplished in the last two days. They had shared their private horror stories; starting out as enemies, they had managed to become friends. There was a strong feeling that her friendship with J.C. would be deeply fierce and unconditionally long. Knowing one thing for sure, that she was willing to go the distance, she stood up and extended her hand to him.

"Come on, Boss," she used Garret's term of endearment. "Time for a walk."

They walked in silence for the longest time. There didn't seem to be a need for words. As the sun started to set, it looked like a big ball of fire suspended in mid air, the orange glow bursting over the sky. It was a breath taking sight, a beautiful closure for the day. Before long, they had gone a long way down the beach. J. C. knew it would be getting dark soon, so they turned around and headed back toward the blanket. He finally broke the silence.

"I figured I owed you the truth, after yesterday."

He was referring to the letter. The sound of his voice was tender and mellow.

"You didn't owe me anything, J.C., but I'm glad you showed it to me."

She knew this was going to be a delicate conversation, so she chose her words carefully.

"J.C., did anyone else know that your mother was pregnant? Did anyone else see the letter?"

He didn't answer for a few moments. Knowing that it was a hard subject for him, she didn't push him, either.

"No, no one knew. About the baby or about the letter. I was the one that found her body. I don't think she meant for me to be the one to find her. Nicole that was indescribably the most horrid thing a man could go through."

He had to take a moment to compose himself before he could continue.

"After we had taken care of her body, I went to my room and laid down on my bed. I was completely numb; I couldn't believe she had left me there, alone. I shoved my hands up under my pillow, above my head; I always used to lie like that. That's when I found the letter. She had hidden it under my pillow. After I thought about it for a while, I guess I understood why she did it, but it took a long time to forgive her for it."

"Didn't the coroner find the baby when he examined her?"

She just couldn't fathom the fact that no one knew that she was pregnant.

"There was no autopsy. There was never a question of foul play, so the sheriff ruled it a suicide. So, there was no need for one. She was buried with her secret, just as she wanted it to be. You're the only other person who has ever read that letter. And that's the way it will always be."

"J. C., why did you let me read it, tell me the truth."

She knew there was something more he wasn't saying.

"Yesterday, after you told me about Bobby, you said it felt good to finally say it out loud. I could see the pain you were going through as you spoke; but yet, you said it felt good once you had finally told the story. Nicole, this pain is old, and it's heavy, and I wanted to get it out, too. You were brave enough to do it in front a complete stranger. I knew I could do it in front of a friend. And I do feel better, like a weight has been lifted from my shoulders. I thank you for that, my friend."

He leaned over and gave her a hug.

"We need to get going, they'll be sending a search party out after us."

They both started picking up the remains of their picnic. Nicole folded the blanket and J.C. picked up the basket. They were in no hurry to get back to the car. They were each branding their own special memories of the day. It was one of those rare days, the kind that only come along once in a blue moon. The ride home was pleasantly quiet. The stars twinkled brightly in the evening sky. It was hard to believe that J.C. was the same person she had met yesterday. Who would have thought there could ever be warmth in those cold eyes of his? After hearing his story, she had no reason to wonder why they were so cold. She remembered hearing someone say 'if you think you've had a hard life, just walk a mile in someone else's shoes.' She fully understood the meaning of that statement now. Her childhood didn't seem so bad after learning about his.

TEN

It was late when Nicole and J.C. returned from the beach. Garret was nearly out of his mind from worrying. J.C. never gave it a thought to call him until they were about half way home from the beach. When he finally called him from his cell phone, it was to arrange a meeting in the hotel dining room. They had been so involved with J.C.'s letter, and getting past yesterday's events, neither one had given a second thought to the other problem. J.C. wanted an up-date on the situation. Davis had been out all day trying to uncover leads and they were sure Garret was doing whatever he could. Hopefully someone had some kind of information for them. Parking the car in the hotel parking lot, he walked with Nicole into the lobby.

Nicole turned to J.C. and said, "I'm going to check for messages before I freshen up for dinner. I'll meet you and Garret in the dining room in half an hour, O.K.?"

What she really wanted was a quick shower to wash the salty film from her skin.

There was only one message waiting for her at the desk. Waiting until she got on the elevator before she opened the folded paper, she leaned wearily against the wall and read it. It was from Gloria, wondering why she hadn't called in. The day had moved so swiftly and time had gotten away from her; she had completely forgotten to call the office. Absentmindedly she looked at her watch knowing full well it was too late to call the east coast. Still, all in all, it had been a very productive day. It was on her agenda to find out if there were any women in J.C.'s life and who they were, but the jolting news about his mother had taken precedence over everything else. Again, she ran out of time. Maybe they could fit it in after dinner. The time Sam had allotted her was screaming by her, way too fast. It was as plain as the nose on her face that there was a lot more going on than what she was already aware of.

She wondered how Garret had made out with Davis, the private investigator. Well, she'd find all that out after her shower.

J.C. went right to the dining room. Garret was already seated with Davis enjoying a cocktail when he sat down. Ordering himself a tall, iced tea, he never drank alcohol because he didn't like the influence it had over a person.

"Where's Nicole?" Garret asked, "I thought she was joining us."

The fact that J.C. was alone made Garret wonder if they had spent another bad day together.

"Oh, she'll be down. She's probably starving, but she wanted to freshen up before dinner. We walked all day, hardly had a bite to eat. The ocean air always leaves me famished. I could probably eat a whole steer about now."

Something about J.C.'s tone was different. Garret couldn't put his finger on it though. As he stared at him for a moment, he thought he even looked different. There was kind of a glow about him.

"What did you find out, Davis; did you get the guy's name? Were you able to find out anything about who he is or where he came from?"

"No, J.C., I can't get that information until tomorrow morning. I did get the guest list from the desk clerk," he gave a little chuckle. "Seems as though he's got a little crush on your reporter. Didn't take much to get the list after I mentioned her name. Wish they were all that easy! I'm going to check one against the other as soon as I get the seating chart. But for now, I'm going to stake out Nicole's room tonight. Just to be on the safe side. From what Nicole told me this morning, I think she's got the right guy. We just need to find out who he is, and what he wants."

J.C. nodded in approval as he took a long draw from his tea glass.

"Well, if you guys don't need me anymore, I'm going to scout out a safe spot to watch her room from," he was getting up from his chair as he spoke.

"O.K. Davis, we'll be waiting to hear from you. No matter what time you get any information, you call. Day or night, got it?" J.C. replied with an authoritative tone.

"Yeah, no problem," Davis answered as he headed toward the door.

"Did you guys have a good day?" Garret asked, now that Davis had gone.

He couldn't believe how much he was looking forward to seeing her again. Feeling like a teenager on his second date, the anticipation of her arrival to the table was just about killing him. He kept glancing toward the door waiting for her to appear.

"Yeah, we did. You were right, Garret, she does get under your skin. What a wonderful person she is. I like her, I like her a lot."

J.C. smiled fondly, remembering what a good day it had been. Garret felt a pang of jealousy and he immediately felt guilty for it. There hadn't been a smile like that on J.C.'s face in…he didn't know when. Come to think of it, he'd never seen one like that before. Garret was beginning to experience very selfish feelings when it came to Nicole. He didn't like being stuck with Davis today while J.C. was off on a picnic, having a great time. This could be the woman he might want to spend the rest of his life with. Unfortunately, his loyalty to J.C. made him hold his feelings for her at bay. If she made his friend that happy, like it or not, he'd back off. In all the years he had known J.C., there was never any woman he had shown any interest in, after Elizabeth. Except, of course, for sexual purposes. Why did he have to pick this one? But, if she was the one who put that sparkle in his eye, so be it. He'd be the odd man out; he'd try to be, anyway.

Nicole entered the dining room as though on cue. She had thrown a plain, emerald jumpsuit on, fluffed her still damp hair, and headed downstairs. She never needed any make-up, a little mascara, a little lip gloss, that usually did the trick. The rest was just natural beauty. The emerald color in the suit made her eyes come alive. Quite a few heads turned as she headed to the table to join the men. They stood up in unison once she neared the table, both unable to take their eyes from her. Garret's stomach was doing little flip-flops.

"Good evening, gentlemen, I trust I haven't kept you waiting too long?"

Squeezing J.C.'s shoulder as she passed, she gave a sweet smile to Garret and took her chair. Garret didn't let the show of affection get past him. Again, the pang of jealousy hit the pit of his stomach. Again, the guilt followed. He didn't quite understand what was going on and he certainly didn't know how long he was going to be able to handle that. Jealousy wasn't something he had ever had to deal with and he didn't want to have to deal with it over his best friend.

"Well, have I missed anything?"

The waitress came over and she ordered a diet coke.

"Did you talk to Davis? Have we gotten any more information?"

Looking at both men, she waited for an answer. As Garret searched her face for that forlorn look she wore yesterday, all he saw was excitement dancing in her eyes. There seemed to be a certain glow about her, too. Just how good of a day did they have, he wondered? Jealousy swallowed up every other emotion he had at that very moment. He really didn't trust himself to speak, but J.C. just sat there waiting for him to fill her in.

"There won't be much he can do until morning but, he is going to watch your room tonight though. Other than that, it's been pretty quiet today."

For me anyway, Garret thought to himself. Obviously, from the glow you two are sporting, you had a pretty great day. Nicole picked up on Garret's somber mood. Thinking that it wasn't usually like him to act that way, she wondered if something was bothering him. She hoped that he would cheer up and join in the festive mood she and J.C. were sharing.

"I still don't get this baby thing. A baby named Rae Anne. Where is the connection? What are we missing?"

She was more or less talking to herself. J.C. reached over and delicately touched the top of her hand, as if to get her attention.

"You want to order something to eat? I am famished. We never did eat much of that picnic lunch."

J.C. was unusually chipper. Such cheerfulness was definitely out of character for him. The whole scene was almost making Garret gag. He felt like a fourth leg in a three legged contest, it just didn't fit in and neither did he right now. There seemed to be some kind of bond between the two of them that he couldn't penetrate. How could they seem so close after spending just one afternoon together, especially after the day they had yesterday? It just wasn't adding up. There wasn't much he could do tonight, Davis had everything under control. So, he was going to skip dinner and let them have some space. The thought of it was just about killing him. It seemed like the more he wanted to let go of his feelings for Nicole and be happy for J.C.; the more upset it made him, because he couldn't have her. He hoped that she wouldn't come between them. He had to make sure he wasn't the one that made her come between them.

"I'm kind of tired, so if you'll excuse me, I think I'm going to skip dinner and head home. Tomorrow sounds like it's going to be a full day, so I think I'll hit the sack. You two enjoy your dinner."

He pushed his chair away and stood up, hoping selfishly, that their meal would stink.

"Oh, won't you stay, Garret? We haven't seen you all day. We won't keep you out late. We all could use a good night's rest."

Nicole was pleading with him to stay, but she could see it wasn't doing much good.

"Ya'll have a good night."

His knew his tone was a little too short, but he couldn't help himself. The way she kept saying 'we this' and 'we that', Christ, it was like they were already married. He just needed to get out of there and get some fresh air.

"Garret didn't seem himself tonight, J.C.; do you think there's something bothering him?"

Nicole was concerned about him. That certainly wasn't the easy going person she had met yesterday.

"He'll be O.K., he's just not used to so much excitement," was how J.C. dismissed Garret's irrational actions. "Ya know, when you told us what that guy said, about the baby, I thought he might be talking about my mother. But then, I knew it couldn't be that. No one else knew about it. So, I don't know what to think."

They stopped talking long enough for the waiter to take their order.

"You know J.C.; it was your turn today, to tell me about your sweethearts and you didn't do it. Even though you did share some very personal information with me, you still have to tell. Those were your rules remember?" Her eyes were sparkling with mischief. Even though she was teasing him, she still expected him to come through with the information. After all, it was only fair!

"You don't have your tape-recorder hidden in there anywhere, do you?"

It was quite obvious that there was no room to hide a tape-recorder. The suit fit her like a second skin and it looked good that way.

"No, but I do have a good memory, so start talking," she laughed as she leaned back in her chair and waited for his story to begin.

"Actually, I only had one love in my life too, Nicole."

He was using a very light tone, one you would use when talking with a friend. It didn't seem to bother him, either, that she brought up the subject.

"Her name was Elizabeth Bordoe. She was an exquisite looking woman. Well, she wasn't quite a woman yet, but it doesn't feel right to call her a girl. We had one big problem though. Bartholamuel Bordoe, most people called him Buck, hated the ground I walked on. Her old man tried his damnedest to keep us apart. Eventually, I guess it worked, but I truly loved her. It was hard on her because she would have to sneak out to spend time with me. We'd meet in the park, down by the river. Things started getting pretty serious after a while, or at least I thought so. I was going to ask her to marry me. I was from the wrong side of town for old Buck. He was hooked up pretty tight in the political arena. Guess he didn't think it would help his career, with me hanging on the arm of his little girl."

"What happened, why did you two part?" Nicole asked as she reached for a piece of celery from the veggie dish on the table.

She hadn't realized how hungry she was until she sat down.

"I wish I could tell you that. She was supposed to meet me at the park one night. After we, ya know…had been together," he was stammering to get the words out.

Nicole couldn't suppress a giggle, he was actually blushing.

"This is hard enough without you adding any special affects," he reprimanded her, teasingly. "But seriously, after that happened, I wanted to ask her to marry me. It was the right thing to do, and I was madly in love with her. When she met me at the river that night, I was going to propose to her. I had spent every cent I had on the best ring I could buy, and I waited and waited, but she never showed. I went to our spot every night for the next month. Nothing. I kept trying to find another way to get in touch with her, but her old man had made that virtually impossible. Then one day I was having lunch at the dairy bar in town when I overheard two of the local gossips talking. They said she had gone to Europe to school and wouldn't be coming back for a long time. I figured it was probably her daddy's doing, but at that point I didn't care. She said he'd never keep us apart and I guess I foolishly believed her. That night I went back down to the river, took that diamond ring out of the box, and gave it the biggest toss I could. I thought that would get her out of my system. Didn't work. I still have dreams about her."

He put his arms down in front of him as the waiter approached with his meal.

"Thank you," he said politely, as the waiter put his food in front him. He waited until he placed Nicole's food down and walked away.

"She literally broke my heart. Poor Garret, he took the blunt of it. The only way I could get her off my mind was to work like a dog. He was right there with me. I worked that poor guy to the bone, but he never complained." He leaned forward in his chair; a real serious look came across his face and he asked, "Tell me, Nicole, how could she just leave me like that? She said she loved me more than anything. How could she just go away and never let me know why? I could never figure that out."

He sat back in the chair and released a little sigh.

"I guess I'll never know. Anyway, I haven't been able to fall for anyone else. Maybe it's because I'm afraid of getting burned again. Maybe she was my only chance at knowing what love is. Who the hell knows? Let's talk about something else," he said as he began to get a little mellow-dramatic. "Hell lets eat. I'm starving."

The smile came back to his face and he dove into his food like he hadn't eaten in a month.

They talked through dinner and they laughed a bit. They were really enjoying each other's company. It was a lot different being with Nicole than being with Garret. Not that he didn't enjoy being with Garret. It was just different, being with a female. There's no way he would ever open up to a guy like that. It had been kind of nice remembering Elizabeth for a moment. It still gnawed at him every now and then about where she ended up and who she married. He often hoped she had been plagued with the same questions about him. It didn't seem right that he should suffer alone. Time flew by and it was midnight before they knew it.

"I better let you get upstairs. It's been a long day. I really enjoyed it though, thank you Nicole," his eyes had a warm glow to them as he spoke. "I'll walk you to the elevator."

"Good night J.C.," she said as she gave him a kiss on the cheek and entered the elevator doors. "See you in the morning."

Nicole could feel the exhaustion creeping into her body. Although physically she was whipped, mentally she was charged to full voltage. Where could Elizabeth Bordoe have disappeared to? If she did love J.C. as much as he said she did, why did she suddenly vanish? There was definitely something more to that story. As she started to get undressed, she thought about Davis being somewhere outside of her room. She would rest a lot easier when Davis got that seating chart tomorrow. Maybe they could find this guy and get some answers.

As Nicole was getting ready for bed, her thoughts wandered back to J.C. It had to be heart wrenching to lose the two women he loved most in the world. No wonder he came across as bitter and cold. Even though he had led such a rueful life, some how he still managed to come out on top. He must truly be a man with a powerful constitution and she had to admire him for that.

Before climbing into bed, she walked over and glanced out the peep-hole in the door. No sign of Davis. It was still comforting to know he was out there somewhere, even if she couldn't see him. Maybe she could finally get some sleep. She climbed into bed and turned out the light. As soon as her head hit the pillow, she was down for the count. But not for long. A loud thumping noise woke her from a sound sleep. Looking over at the alarm it was 4:15 by the red glowing numbers.

"Not again! This is getting real old," she said out loud. "What in the hell is going on out there?"

Throwing the covers back, she charged across the room. Just then, a huge thud sounded against the wall outside. Frightened by the noise, she jumped back away from the door. It sounded like someone was coming right through the wall. There was an awful ruckus going on in the hallway so she ran to the phone and called the front desk.

"Yes, this is Nicole Bentley on the seventh floor," she whispered. "Something frightful is going on outside my room. The noise woke me up, but I don't dare look out there. It's too close to my door."

She sounded so alarmed; the clerk said he would send security up right away. She waited by the phone, just in case, until the noise subsided. When it was finally quiet, she snuck over and took a peek out of the peep-hole. The security guard was talking to a big man who had his back to her. He was holding onto another man by the collar of his shirt. The big man turned slightly and she noticed it was Davis. Davis started toward her door with the other guy in tow. Just then, he knocked on the door.

"Nicole, it's Davis. Let me in so I can call J.C. We've got our man."

With one eye glued to the peephole, she was watching his face as he spoke. Unlocking the door, she stood behind it while Davis ushered the other guy in. Agilely tossing him into a chair, he told him to sit there, and not make a move. Then he went to the phone. Nicole stepped out from behind the door and immediately felt shivers going up and down her spine.

"It *is* you!" she yelled as she stared into the face of the man from the plane.

"Yeah, J.C., we got him. I caught him trying to shove another envelope under Nicole's door. I don't know, I haven't opened it yet. O.K., we'll wait here for you."

Nicole had gone in to dress while Davis used the phone. When she came out, he was opening the envelope.

"You want me to make some coffee, Davis?"

She didn't know if she was using his first name, or his last name. Davis was the only name they had given her.

"Yeah, that would be good," he replied, only half paying attention to what she even said.

"What's this mean to you?" he asked, as he handed her the piece of paper.

RAE ANNE IS BARTHOLAMUEL'S GRANDDAUGHTER was all it said.

"Nothing, absolutely nothing," she replied with a bewildered look on her face. Turning to look at the man in the chair, she asked, "What does this mean?"

With a blank stare on his face, he just sat there without saying a word.

"Miss Bentley just asked you a question, Jason. Don't you want to answer the lady?" he asked giving him a swift kick in the leg.

The point on Davis' shoe had connected with a hard blow, but he still didn't get an answer.

"This is Jason Deveroe. Do you know him?" he was asking Nicole while he glared at Jason.

Raising his foot to give a vicious kick to the other leg prompted Jason to finally answer.

"Bartholomeuel Bordoe's granddaughter, figure it out for yourself, tough guy!" was the only reply he gave.

"How does Bordoe have a granddaughter?" a booming voice asked from the doorway. "He's only got one daughter, and she and her husband don't have children," J.C. finished, as he and Garret charged into the room.

So J.C. did search until he found her. The little snake forgot to mention that piece of information, Nicole thought to herself.

"That's right. He only has one daughter, but he also has a granddaughter. That information is a hundred percent legit. That's all I'm saying. If you want to know anything more, a lot of green backs will buy you some good information," he smugly replied.

"Why you little," Garret crossed the room in three steps; his hands were about to go around Jason's throat.

"Back off, you big oaf. If you touch me, I'll have the cops down your throat before you can blink an eye. You've got no right to keep me here. I've done nothing wrong."

It was quite obvious that he was pretty scared of Garret, even though he was trying to hide it. Crouching down as far into the chair as he could get, he had his arms above his head as if to protect his face.

"He's right, Garret. Don't touch him."

J.C. didn't want Garret getting into trouble over some little jerk.

"Stalking someone is against the law," Davis replied as he walked over and stood in front of Jason with his hands on his hips. "Now why have you been following her?"

"You give me five thousand dollars, and I'll tell you everything you want to know," as he spoke, he was looking right at J.C.

"I'm not giving you shit. Now get the hell out of here. If I catch you hanging around Nicole again, you won't have to worry about calling the police. There will be a bunch of them standing over your dead body! Now get the hell out of here," yelled J.C. as his face turned a dark shade of scarlet as anger mounted toward the idiot sitting in the chair.

"O.K., O.K., hold it for a second," Jason spouted nervously.

If he didn't get to talk to Nicole, the whole plan would be ruined. So what about the money? It would have just been a bonus anyway. The story was what he really wanted.

"I'll talk to her, alone. No one else. That's the deal."

"No, she's not going to be alone with you. No deal."

J.C. didn't trust the little bastard.

"All right, hang on a minute," Jason was stalling so he could think.

Looking over the men in the room, he didn't really like his choices. The guy they called Davis had already given him a hell of a kick in the leg, the damn thing was still throbbing. The other guy was as big as the Jolly Green Giant; he didn't want any part of him. The only one left was J.C., and he didn't think he would be any bed of roses either. Trying to think of a quick solution, he knew he was running out of time.

"I'll meet you and her at your office at 10:00 today. It will be safer talking there. Just the three of us. I don't want those two guys around me," as he spoke, he was pointing at Davis and Garret.

J.C. looked over at Nicole with his eyebrows raised waiting for her to make the call.

"O.K., but this better be worth it," she said, scowling at him.

"Oh, it will be worth it. You can count on that!"

He was inching toward the door. He couldn't wait to get the hell out of that room.

ELEVEN

After everyone cleared out of the room, Nicole dropped onto the sofa in exhaustion. There were still a few hours remaining before their 10:00 meeting with Deveroe. It was time to call Sam and let him know what was going on. It was already the second of July and she needed more time. What she needed right then though, was some coffee and a long, hot shower.

When she finally wandered out of the bathroom all the signs of fatigue had vanished. After another cup of coffee, she was ready to conquer the day. First thing on the agenda was to call the office. Dialing the familiar number, she waited for Rose to answer.

"Good morning, this is Rose. How may I help you?"

Responding with a voice that was always so crisp and clear, Nicole thought for the millionth time how perfect she was for the job.

"Hi Rose, this is Nicole. Is Sam in?" she asked.

"Nicole, where have you been? We've been worried sick! Is everything all right?"

The high pitch in her tone was a dead give away that she had been worried about her.

"I'm sorry I haven't called in before now, Rose. You wouldn't believe what's going on out here. But right now I really need to talk to Sam. He can fill you in later."

There was an impatient tone in her voice and Rose picked up on it right away.

"O.K., I'll get him on the line right now," she replied, switching the call over to Sam's office.

"Nicole on line one, Sam. It sounds like it's pretty urgent," she informed him over the intercom.

Sam pushed the button for the speaker phone. He was going over a report with Gloria and he didn't want to tie himself up with the phone at his ear.

"What's going on out there, Red?" he asked, nonchalantly.

"All hell has broken loose out here, Sam. I'm going to need more time. A guy named Jason Deveroe has been following me. We just caught him outside my room this morning."

Although she was talking fast, Sam caught the undertone in her voice. Immediately he grabbed the hand receiver so he could talk privately with her.

"Who the hell is Jason Deveroe? Who caught him outside your door? Just what exactly is going on out there?"

When it came to Nicole, Sam had a real soft spot. She was more like a daughter to him than an employee. If anything happened to her there would be hell to pay.

"Are you O.K., Red?"

"I'm fine, Sam, really."

Hearing the urgency in his voice was enough to let her know that he had been worried. Even Sam's long arm of protection couldn't reach her there, but the thought of him still trying to keep her safe from harm made her smile. He may act like a bulldog, but when it came right down to it, he was nothing but a big, old pussycat.

"Let me explain what's been going on so far."

Filling Sam in on all the events that had happened with Deveroe up until then, she finally reached the point in the story about the meeting.

"Sam, something hot is boiling underneath all of this. I want to see it through to the end. I think that article about the donation was just bait. Deveroe is hiding something, but he seems awfully anxious to meet with me. When he tried to set up a meeting alone with me, J.C. wouldn't go for it. There's something he wants to tell me and he sure has gone through a lot of trouble to get this far. Hopefully, I'll find out who this baby Rae Anne is and where she fits into the puzzle. But I'm going to need more time. What do you say, Sam? Can I have it?" she pleaded with him.

There was a long silence at the other end of the line. There was no way he could say no! But he would make damn sure nothing was going to happen to her while she was there. Finally Sam's voice broke the silence.

THE COVER STORY

"O.K., Red, you can stay. But, you be damned awful careful. You keep in touch with this office, do you hear me?"

His voice was gruff as he barked those orders at her. Then, on a softer note he added, "And good luck."

She hung up the phone and dialed J.C.'s office to let Tami know that she would be ready in one hour and could she send someone over for her? Nicole was hoping Garret would pick her up. Maybe she could find out why he was so ornery last night. After she finished getting dressed, she decided to go down and get a bite to eat. Stopping at the front desk, she asked the clerk to send whoever arrived to pick her up over to the restaurant. When Oliver arrived at her table she was just finishing a bowl of fruit. Garret didn't appear to be with him. Feeling a little disappointed, she grabbed her things and walked out to the car.

Nicole and J.C. were waiting in his office when Jason Deveroe finally arrived. After going over the scene from earlier that morning, Nicole had already figured out that Jason wasn't a heterosexual. The little things he did and the general way he conducted himself gave it away. The way he cowered when Garret went for his throat, not that anybody else wouldn't have been afraid of Garret; but it was the way he scrunched up and held his hands in front of his face. The tone of his speech was a dead give away. Not that his sexual preference made any difference to her, she just noticed those kinds of things. It did make her wonder if J.C. had come to the same conclusion.

Jason looked very nervous when Tami ushered him into the office. As he stepped over the threshold his eyes darted quickly around the room to see if Garret or Davis were hiding somewhere. When he saw that the room was clear, he visibly relaxed a little bit. Nicole didn't want to waste any time, but she did want to start right at the beginning.

"Deveroe," she used his last name as a little intimidation tactic. "You're the one that sent me the newspaper, aren't you? You knew about the donation, didn't you? What made you think I would bite on the story? What was your role in all of this?"

Rifling one question after another at him, she wasn't giving him a chance to answer any of them.

"Whoa, slow down, Red!" J.C. exclaimed, trying to calm her down.

It was difficult for him to keep up with her questions. Spinning around so she was face to face with J.C., a look of confusion clouded her face. There was only one person who called her Red, and that was Sam. Where on earth had he gotten that name from?

"He called me right after you talked to him. You must be a pretty special person to him," he was referring to Sam. "He threatened me with bodily harm if anything happened to you. I took that very seriously!"

J.C. watched as her expression transformed into a warm smile.

"That figures. Sam thinks he's my guardian angel, but trust me, he sure doesn't look the part," she added, and turned back to Deveroe. "Now where were we? Let's start with the newspaper. Did you send it to me?"

If they wanted to get any information, it was imperative that she slow down and ask one question at a time.

"Yes, I sent it to you. And, to answer your second question; yes, I knew about the donation."

No one had offered him a chair, so he stood there feeling rather awkward. It didn't appear that anybody really cared how he felt or whether or not he was comfortable.

"How did you know about the donation?" J.C. asked him, he was quite curious to hear his reply because he still didn't know where the leak had come from.

"It's really a long story," Jason stated.

Knowing the other two, the ones that he considered the goons, weren't around to hurt him, he was beginning to act a little cocky.

"Well, we have a long time, so out with it," J.C. said with a sneer.

It was getting harder not to let it show how perturbed he was getting with the man and his line of bullshit.

"Well," Jason was taking his sweet time to answer him. "It all started with you," his attention was focused on J.C. "I wanted to expose some information I thought you might be interested in. So I came here, to your office. I happened to be standing outside the door to that other office," he was pointing toward Tami's office. "The door was open, and I heard you talking to your secretary. You were giving her instructions for a letter you were sending to the shelter. I could hear every word you were saying from where I was standing."

THE COVER STORY

"Show me," J.C. interrupted him, his anger was mounting. "Show me right where you were."

If Jason could get vital information from lurking outside a doorway, J.C. wanted to know exactly where he had been standing. If that's how the information had leaked out of the office, he'd have to do something different with the security system. Knowing all along that there had to be an explanation for that horrible mix-up, he just never expected it to be so easy to pilfer such private information.

Jason led them to the entrance door of Tami's office. Just outside the door was a general parking lot. While the door was still open, Jason stepped outside and leaned up against the wall. J.C. and Nicole had followed him outside.

"This is where I was standing," he said as he pressed his body tight against the wall, close to the door, demonstrating his prior actions to J.C.

J.C. stepped back inside and looked out, but he couldn't see Jason's body. As he moved around inside the office, he still couldn't see him. There was no way, from any point in that office, that Jason could be seen. That concept really bothered J.C.; he would have to do something about that situation. Vital information flowed through their offices on a daily basis. If it was that easy to eavesdrop, then other people could be doing exactly what Jason had done. Making a mental note, he'd definitely have to address the problem with his security team.

"O.K., get back in here. Now, continue, what happened next?"

J.C. had his arms crossed over his chest. At this point, he was scowling profusely at Jason and acting as if it was his fault for the flaw in his daily operation.

"As I was saying, I heard you give her the address for the shelter in Pennsylvania," his look indicated he was talking about Tami. "I had followed several of Nicole's story lines; she has done a lot of human interest work. The location of her office worked well in the equation, New York City is not far from Pennsylvania. I knew if I could get to her with the news of the donation, she'd follow up on the story. All I had to do was get your name on the cover letter that went to the shelter; I knew the rest would be easy."

"Yeah and how did you manage to get my name on that letter?" J.C. asked, his temper was rapidly rising, but curiosity was keeping it at bay.

"I bribed one of your guys in the mail room so he would give me the envelope. When I got it, I added your name to the paper and copied the address. It was as simple as that," finishing his little confession, he had a pretty smug look on his face.

J.C. was so furious; he wanted to wipe that look off his face with a fist. Unfortunately he couldn't because he wasn't done with him yet. Thinking of the good, quality people he had on staff, how could this little pissant have bribed one of his employees?

"How much did you give this guy?" he yelled at Jason, his temper was getting harder to keep in check.

"It's not how much I gave him; it's what I gave him."

Demonstrating to J.C., he stuck his tongue out, ran it leisurely across his lips and slightly raised his brow. Rolling his eyes slowly while his tongue moved sensually across his lips, he gazed right into J.C.'s eyes with a wanton glow.

"What the hell does that mean?" he said in a thunderous voice. When Jason didn't answer him, he turned to Nicole, "Well, what the hell does that mean?"

Nicole walked over and whispered in his ear, "He's gay, J.C. Now do you know what that means?"

J.C. let out a yelp, like someone had struck him and exclaimed, "Ah, jeez. That is disgusting!"

It looked like he was going to be physically ill.

"Tami!" he yelled and she came scurrying into the office. "Find out who the pervert was that he bribed and fire his ass immediately. Go, right now!"

Tami darted by him, hoping she was moving fast enough for his approval. The anger J.C. was feeling was very evident. Finally, he knew where the leak had come from. If she could find the right person, it would be much better for his sake if she was the one to terminate him. He might not like the way J.C. would handle it.

"Why are going to fire him? Just because he might be gay?" Jason asked sarcastically.

"No, I'm firing him because he screwed with my mail," yelled J.C.

"And pardon the pun?" mumbled Jason.

"Get back in my office and let's get the rest of this over with," he turned to Jason and added, "And I don't want to hear anymore of that gross shit, do you hear me?"

Nicole had to put her hand over her mouth to hide the smirk she was trying to avoid. Seeing J.C. get so worked up over something most men crave, under normal circumstances of course, struck her funny chord; but she sure didn't want him to see her laughing. She was quite sure he wouldn't see the humor in it.

They all went back into J.C.'s office and Jason continued to relinquish the information he harbored to gain his revenge. It was a little uncomfortable to talk about at first, but he told them about the affair with Charles and how he got dumped so he could run for Mayor. Although J.C. was listening intently, he couldn't believe what he was hearing. Even though he had never met Charles, he did know that he was Elizabeth's husband, so how could he possibly be gay?

Next, Jason focused on Bartholamuel's bogus marriage. The explanation of how Buck married for the family money lead right into revealing his mistress, Charlotte Evans. J.C. figured that Jason had no reason to lie, but he sure had enough incriminating information on old Buck. It wasn't hard to figure out that he had married for the money, but J.C. didn't know anything about the mistress. It was unbelievable that Jason just continued on, how much more did he know about those two families?

Because the ball was rolling along so well, Jason went to straight to Charles' and Elizabeth's failing marriage. The truth came out that Buck had arranged that whole, horrid mess. Jason watched for any kind of reaction to register on J.C.'s face as he continued with the saga. At the mention of Elizabeth's name, J.C.'s eyes had grown very cold and his jaw was set as if it were made of stone, but he quietly listened as Jason rambled on. Feeling the hair on his body stand up when Jason repeated the fact that Elizabeth had to be drugged to walk down the aisle, J.C. didn't know how much more he could listen to. Proud of the reaction he was getting from J.C. with all the little secrets he had already released, Jason was getting really anxious because he had saved the best for last. Finally, he told J.C. about Rae Anne.

"Did you know J.C., that Elizabeth had a baby girl?" he asked, watching J.C.'s face very carefully as he spoke. The finale was what he'd been waiting for and he wanted to witness the complete unraveling of the powerful man before him, so he finished with, "Her name is Rae Anne."

J.C. looked at him with contempt pouring from his eyes. At that very moment, he felt a great hatred building up inside for that man. Hell, he wasn't even a man; he was nothing but a little fairy.

"What the hell are you talking about?" J.C. bellowed at him, with fists balled up at his side and doing everything in his power to keep them there.

"What's even more, Charles and Elizabeth never even consummated their marriage. I know that for a fact. So, who do you think sired that little girl? Who do you think her daddy is, J.C.?"

The knife was inserted and he gave it a little twist with every word he used. First, he could see the doubt registering on J.C.'s face, and then the confusion. Finally, he could see the light was dawning and he had witnessed it all! If J.C. had given him the money he asked for, he probably would have told the story in a more compassionate manner. All he really wanted was what the end result this little visit would cause, but with the treatment he received, as far as Jason was concerned, J.C. deserved all that and more.

"I don't believe you, you little bastard, you're making that up." J.C. screamed at him.

As he was yelling he could feel his chest tightening up. The blood was rushing to his head, causing a horrendous, pounding sensation. The tension he felt across his chest made him feel as though his heart was being crushed. If Elizabeth had been pregnant and he was the father, she would have told him. There was no way she would have kept that from him, she couldn't have been that cruel. J.C. began to shake with anger toward the piece of scum standing in his office. Jason foolishly stood there with that smug look on his face again. There was no way J.C. was going to listen to any more of his bullshit; it was time to wipe that smug look off his face. As he started toward Jason the only thing he could see was the color red.

When Nicole finally came around from the wave of shock Jason had just put her through, she saw what was going to happen. There was no way she could let J.C. near Deveroe, he'd kill him. Doing the only thing she could think of, she stepped in front of J.C. to block him from Jason. In the spare of the moment she didn't know if that was the right move to make, but she knew she had to make some kind of move.

THE COVER STORY

"You had better get out of here while you still can, Mr. Deveroe. I think you've provided us with more than enough information."

J. C. was still coming toward him. Jason wanted to savor the moment a bit longer, but the look on J.C.'s face put a fire under his ass. It was better to get out while the getting was still good. After all, he had accomplished what he had come for and with great pleasure, too! The rest was up to Nicole; he had faith that she could handle the rest of the story without him. It wasn't in his best interest to stay with that maniac coming after him.

Nicole couldn't believe what she just heard. Never mind about her, what about poor J.C.? Standing there as white as a sheet, he looked as though he was going to collapse.

Nicole ran to the door and yelled, "Tami, find Garret and get him over here now!"

Grabbing a hold of J.C., she gently guided him to the sofa. The poor man looked like he was about to come unglued. Just as she got him settled, Garret barreled through the door.

"What the hell happened to him?" he asked, as he headed over to J.C.

Kneeling down beside him, he waved a hand in front of his face and got absolutely no reaction.

"Nicole, what happened to him? Where did Jason go?"

Nicole filled Garret in on the whole sordid story, telling him how cruel Jason had been when he gave him the news of Rae Anne. It was her belief that J.C. might be in shock. The realization of the whole story must have finally sunk into J.C.'s mind and he wasn't handling it very well.

"Where is that little son-of-a-bitch? I'll tear his head off and shove it down his neck," Garret screamed, he was as angry at Jason as J.C. had been.

Nicole was so glad she had shagged him out of there. There would have surely been a murder if he had stuck around. If J.C. hadn't killed him, Garret certainly would have.

"He ran out of here like his ass was on fire. I think he realized his battleship mouth had gotten his rowboat ass in deep shit. I don't think he'll show his face around here again. J.C. was headed toward him with nothing but red in his eyes. There was no way Jason was stupid enough to let J.C. get a hold of him."

Nicole glanced over at J.C., wondering how long he was going to be out of it.

Wandering absentmindedly over to the window and staring out at nothing, something J.C. had told her came back to mind. If Elizabeth had suddenly disappeared, supposedly to Europe, she could have been pregnant. The baby could have been born abroad before Elizabeth returned home. If that was truly the case, then where was Rae Anne? Why wouldn't she have told J.C. about her pregnancy? If she really loved him like J.C. said, it would seem as though he would have been the first to know. There were still an awful lot of unanswered questions. As the idea popped into her head, she turned to Garret to share it with him.

"Garret, we've got to go to Texas. That's where all of the answers are and we've got to go as soon as possible."

"What are you talking about? What answers?" He looked at her like she had flipped her lid.

"O.K., let's say Elizabeth really did have a baby. That's very possible; she did disappear for quite a long time. Question number one—why didn't she tell J.C. she was going to have his child? Let's go with the possibility that she couldn't get to him. Obviously her father didn't want her to associate with him right from the beginning, so that's a good possibility. Question number two—what happened to the baby after it was born? J.C. knows that Elizabeth and Charles don't have any children. We know that she couldn't have given her away. The reason being, the baby had a name, Rae Anne. You don't name the children that you give up for adoption; at least I don't think you do. Also, Jason said that Buck had a granddaughter. There is no way Buck could claim her as his granddaughter if an adoptive family was raising the child, right? So that means Rae Anne must be around there somewhere. They wouldn't call the child his granddaughter if she was adopted by someone else. They would have kept the whole ordeal totally hushed-up, wouldn't you think? I think I need to talk to Elizabeth myself. We need to go to Texas."

It just made sense that Garret should agree with her. Even though it was a long shot, she knew the answers had to be there. Maybe they should take Davis with them to do the leg work that they couldn't do without getting caught. The next thing was to get all of this past J.C. Garret was still trying to digest the theory Nicole had sprung on him. The points she presented were good ones; there was a possibility she could be right.

"Maybe you're right. Can you imagine how J.C. will feel if he finds out he's had a daughter all this time? To make matters even worse, he's never even known about it?" Garret stated as he was staring off in wonder.

"Don't talk about me like I'm not in the damn room!" J.C.'s thunderous voice startled the two of them so badly, they both jumped when he spoke.

"Sorry, J.C.," Nicole said. "We didn't know you were back among the living. How are you feeling?"

"Like I took a hell of a fall from a very high building. I heard what you said Nicole, about going to Texas. I think it might be kind of dangerous. If there's a kid of mine walking around in Dalton, someone has taken a lot of pains to make sure I don't know about it. What makes you think you can waltz right in there and just yank that information out from under their tight asses?"

For a man that didn't smoke, he sure felt like he could use a cigarette.

"I know it might be a little risky, J.C., but Garret will go with me for protection. We should take Davis too. Given his profession, he must have ways of extracting information. We'll be very careful," she said, realizing she hadn't officially asked Garret to go with her.

Maybe he wouldn't go. Then she'd be up shit creek without a paddle.

"Garret, you will go with me, won't you?"

Those beautiful, green eyes were pleading with him to say yes. How the hell was he supposed to say no to that? The situation was making him crazy. Of course he wanted to go with her; he wanted to go to the end of the earth with her. All day long he had spent missing her. What if he spends all that time with her and gets even more attached? How will he be able to just hand her over to J.C. when they get back? The thought of being alone with her was more than he could stand. While his head said 'no, don't go' his heart was saying, 'are you out of your mind, of course you're going!' Guilty feelings filtered into his conscious for thinking of himself instead of J.C., but he couldn't help it.

"Yeah, I guess I could go," he answered, hoping they didn't hear the catch in his voice.

Trying to speak as nonchalantly as possible, he couldn't prevent that giddy little noise from escaping his throat. Just the thought of having Nicole all to himself was making him as nervous as a man standing at the altar.

"There's always a big fourth of July doings every year. They have a community picnic, and a big parade. If Charles is running for Mayor, he'll be there campaigning. We should be able to get a look at everybody in town at that one outing," he suggested, trying to make a true effort to keep his mind on the business at hand and not on Nicole.

"I'm going too," J.C. decided with a stubborn look spreading across his features.

When he heard the words J.C. had spoken, Garret could feel his heart fall right into the pit of his stomach. Trying to keep a straight face, inside he was dying, he didn't want J.C. to go to Texas with them. The anger he felt was wrestling with his guilty feelings and he was terribly afraid that the anger was going to win.

"You can't go, J.C.," Nicole pleaded. "If you show your face, you'll give the whole plan away. No one will talk to me if you're around. Come on, use your head, don't be so damn stubborn. You can't go. We'll keep you posted every hour if that's what it takes, but you can't go."

The match was pretty even when it came to stubbornness, but he would ruin everything if he went. Garret was silently rooting for Nicole. Of course, it was for selfish reasons; but still, he wanted the victory to wind up in her corner.

J.C. was quiet for awhile. A stubborn look would cross his face every now and then, but still, he remained silent. If they had only had gotten more information out of that asshole, Deveroe. Realizing that the reason he left was to save his own life, J.C. knew that it was impossible to get blood from a stone. If he let them go, was there a possibility that Nicole's safety would be in jeopardy? The probability of that was slim; she would be in good hands with Garret. How could he not let them go? What if he did have a daughter out there somewhere? How could Elizabeth do that to him? It would be too easy for the love he felt for her to turn to hate if this whole story were true. How could he have loved a woman who couldn't even tell him that she had birthed his child? Not knowing if the story was true was killing him. If he really wanted to get to the bottom of this mess he would have to let them go to Texas, without him.

"O.K.," he said with a sigh of defeat. "You guys can go ahead. I'll stay here and wait. Davis is definitely going with you. You have got to promise that if there's any trouble, you have to come right back. I don't want anybody getting hurt over this. Do you hear me?" he was looking directly at both of them as he spoke.

"You got it, Boss," Garret replied, feeling a little guilty for being so overjoyed, especially since it wasn't the right occasion for it.

"What about you, Red? Do you agree?"

"Yes, J.C., I agree," she was getting used to him calling her by Sam's nickname.

Garret couldn't quite figure out where the name 'Red' came from. Why was J.C. calling her by that name? It sounded just a little too comfortable for his taste and he wasn't sure that he liked it. There would be plenty of time to check it out because he was going to have Nicole all to himself for a least a day or two! Even though they were going to Texas for serious business reasons, he tried to hide the smile that was bursting to spread across his face.

TWELVE

It felt so good to wake up feeling absolutely refreshed. Nicole slowly rolled over and stretched her body out like a lazy cat looking to get its belly rubbed. It felt so good to get a full night's sleep but she just wasn't quite ready to get up. It was the first time in days that she felt totally relaxed. Lying on her back, she watched as the blades on the ceiling fan kept going round and round. The pattern had a hypnotic effect making her eyelids feel very heavy. Just a few more minutes, she thought, and drifted back to sleep. It wasn't until the phone rang before she woke again.

"Hello," she said in a low and gravely tone.

"Did I wake you, Nicole?" J.C. asked in surprise.

"No," she hesitated, struggling to clear the slumber cobwebs from her eyes. "Yes, I'm lying. I didn't realize I had fallen back to sleep," she sheepishly replied.

J.C. chuckled a little and said, "I'm really sorry I woke you. Garret and I are down in the dining room and Davis is on his way. I think we should discuss the agenda before you guys take off for Texas. We need to put a solid plan of operation into place. If the three of you go off half-cocked, who knows what will happen? How soon can you join us?"

Lying back on the pillow and closing her eyes, she calculated a time table in her head. Sam would be expecting her to call and given the time difference, that should be done soon.

"Give me a half hour, forty-five minutes," she said, as she was thinking out loud, "I need to call Sam. Then I'll grab a shower and get dressed. I don't think I can make it any sooner."

"That's O.K., we'll have some breakfast. We can get started without you. Davis isn't here yet, either. Come down as soon as you can."

Nicole gave Sam a quick call. Excitedly she summed up yesterday's events and told him what their next step was going to be. Warning her again to be careful, he disconnected. Jumping into the shower, she quickly dressed and headed for the dining room.

When she got to the table, all three men were present. Pulling up a chair, she sat down quietly and listened to the conversation already in progress.

"So, Davis, it won't be any problem for you to go to Texas over the holiday?" inquired J.C.

"You might think it's a problem when you get my bill; but no, it's not a problem for me," he said, smiling at J.C. "What's the closet airport to Dalton and what's the lay out of the town? I think it's best if we stay at two different motels. That way, we won't draw any attention to the fact that we're all together. Garret and Nicole can stay right in town. I should stay on the outskirts. I'll be less noticeable there," he explained.

"There's a little motel called The Rambling Rose about three or four miles outside of Dalton. That's a pretty decent place. Garret and Nicole can stay at the Stonewall Inn, right in the heart of town. Beaumont's the closest airport and we'll get the rental cars from there. I'll have Tami take care of all those details when I get back to the office. It will be about an hours drive from there."

The waiter came by with more coffee and Nicole ordered some fresh fruit and an English muffin.

"Obviously, Rae Anne isn't a little child anymore," she piped in. "When was the last time you saw Elizabeth, J.C.?"

J.C. hadn't thought about Rae Anne being older; in fact, he was still thinking in terms of her being a baby. Nicole's statement threw him for a loop for a moment. After composing himself, he contemplated her question for a moment. It didn't take him long to come up with the answer. "The last time I saw Elizabeth was sixteen years ago."

It was hard to believe that much time had gone by.

"That would make Rae Anne about fifteen years old then," Nicole replied, making the correct calculation.

How could someone hide his own daughter for fifteen years? His own flesh and blood. The war between love and hate waged its battle for J.C.'s heart as he recalled Elizabeth's sweet face in his mind. It was hard to believe that such a picture of innocence could commit such a vile act. At that moment, hatred was getting the upper hand. Nicole could see the pain registering on J.C.'s face, so she quickly started the conversation again.

"If Donovan is campaigning for Mayor, he'll be busy shaking hands and patting baby bottoms. Maybe I can get Elizabeth alone for a few moments. Garret, you can point her out to me, can't you?"

"Yeah, that shouldn't be a problem. I'm sure her appearance couldn't have changed that much in sixteen years."

"I'll find out where this Charlotte Evans lives," interrupted Davis. "If she's been Buck's mistress all these years, she must have some knowledge of the family secrets."

The plans were starting to come together pretty well. The waiter brought Nicole's breakfast; she hadn't realized how hungry she was until he had set it down in front of her. Picking up a fork, she stabbed a piece of watermelon and popped it in her mouth.

"That bastard Buck has got to be at the bottom of this," snarled J.C. "He had the money and the power to hide my daughter from me. I bet he never thought I'd have the money and the power to get her back!"

It would be a pleasure to take Bartholamuel Bordoe down, piece by piece, if it came to that. Then a horrible thought came to him. What if his daughter didn't want him? What if she was happy where she was? Would she reject him? That was something he didn't think he could handle.

Rae Anne Evans was anything but happy. At one point in time she had hoped that her mother would miraculously change into a loving, caring person. Hope went to the way side as she lived in constant fear of her. Charlotte Evans was a cruel and abusive woman. Nothing Rae Anne could do met with her mother's approval. Even though she was a straight 'A' student, she would find something about her work to constantly criticize. Of the handful of friends that she did have, Charlotte didn't like any of them and refused to allow them to visit their home. Participation in after-school events of any kind was unheard of; which made Rae Anne feel like a prisoner in her own home.

Even the ugly clothes that Charlotte insisted on dragging home from the second-hand shops couldn't conceal the beauty that she was really blossoming into. The boys at school stopped to take a second look at the long legged, sleek looking, doll that seemed to have appeared from no where. With curly, blonde hair and striking, blue eyes, she looked nothing like her mother. Although she was well proportioned, when she looked in the mirror all she saw was a tall, drink of water.

Charlotte was jealous of Rae Anne's natural beauty, so any chance she got to make the poor girl self-conscious, she took it. Most of Rae Anne's clothing did come from second-hand shops and thrift stores. The majority of outfits were ugly but she couldn't complain or she would get the back of Charlotte's hand across her face. It seemed as though they were always at least one size too large or last years fashion.

"There," she could hear her say, "You've got plenty of room to grow! No sense wasting good money on clothing for a growing young girl."

Ironically, Charlotte wouldn't be caught dead in a second hand piece of clothing, but Rae Anne was too afraid of her to point that out. One of the classes that were offered in school was home-economics. One morning Rae Anne decided to approach the teacher about learning to use the sewing machine. It was like second nature to her when she sat down and threaded the needle to do a practice run on a piece of scrap material. With her teacher's help, she started bringing a lot of her clothing in and restyling the outfits so her wardrobe was a bit more fashionable and her clothes actually fit. Charlotte didn't seem to notice, but then again, she didn't do any of the laundry.

Charlotte raved about her hairstylist while Rae Anne had never stepped foot inside of a salon. The only thing that saved her from a bad hair cut was the natural curly hair. When Charlotte got done lopping off hunks of hair here and there, Rae Anne would spend hours in the bathroom with a pair of scissors, trying to straighten out the mess she had made. How could God have been so cruel to her, giving her a mother like that? When she was younger, she often fantasized that she was given to the wrong family at birth. Praying that someday her real family would realize the mix up and come to rescue her was the only thing that kept her going. When she grew older and that fantasy didn't work for her anymore, she thought life must be playing a brutal joke on her.

Rae Anne was in the bathroom one morning looking at her reflection in the mirror. Slowly turning her head from side to side, she couldn't see anything that remotely resembled her mother's features. Naturally, she assumed that she must have gotten her looks from her father. Finally mustering up enough nerve to question her about it, Charlotte's tone cut the air like a sharp knife when she said that her father was dead and so was that subject.

Rae Anne was so lonely; she almost hated her very existence. Knowing that other kids in school had wonderful relationships with their mothers, she could never figure out why she seemed to be such a burden to her own. When she got home from school, the list of chores was always posted on the refrigerator. After changing clothes, she'd whip through the chores, get supper started and finish her homework. Charlotte never had to lift a manicured finger.

Everything was different when Uncle Buck was around. Then Charlotte would fawn over her as if she really did love her, which was very confusing for poor Rae Anne. When Uncle Buck was at the house, Charlotte would promise to take her to the movies, or tell her that they would go shopping together. Then when he left, Charlotte's promises seemed to vanish into thin air. Things would go right back to normal. And normal was awful.

Life was at least bearable when he was around. When he came through the door, he would shower her with hugs and kisses and usually she'd find a hidden gift in a coat pocket. Every year on her birthday when she made a wish before blowing out the candles; her wish was that Uncle Buck would marry her mother so they could be a family. With Uncle Buck around all the time, maybe her mother would love her more. At least love her a little bit, that was a better way to put it. For some reason she never got her wish. Several times she put a bug in his ear about it and he would just smile at her sweetly and say 'Oh, maybe someday, little angel'. It hadn't happened yet and somehow she got the feeling it never would.

It really didn't matter anymore because Rae Anne was making plans. On her eighteenth birthday, she was getting out of that hell hole. Wherever she decided to go, it would be as far away from her mother as possible. There was no way for her to know that one of her fantasies was going to come true.

With the plans well in order, the foursome decided they had covered everything they could foresee. Tami was taking care of the flight plans. Davis was packed and ready to go, he would be the first to leave. Nicole and Garret would follow on the next plane out. As Nicole headed up to her suite to pack, Garret left with the understanding that he was coming back to pick her up. Pulling up in his own personal car, Garret drove Nicole to the airport so he could have her all to himself. Taking the limo meant that he would have to share her attention with Oliver, the driver, and he wasn't willing to do that.

Missing the morning rush hour made the traffic bearable on the way to the airport. As soon as they received the boarding passes, they were ushered onto the plane. When they got settled into the seats, Nicole mulled over the latest events in her mind. Trying to fit the pieces together seemed almost impossible. It was hard to imagine how J.C. was feeling at that moment, talk about your life crumbling down around you.

"Penny for your thoughts," Garret said, interrupting the silence.

"Oh, I was just trying to put myself in J.C.'s shoes. Jason Deveroe sure did unload a lot of information in his lap. When he told J.C. that Elizabeth's father had drugged her before the wedding ceremony, you should have seen his face."

Nicole absentmindedly sucked in a breath as a flicker of J.C.'s expression ran through her mind.

"You're kidding me, Nicole! Why on earth would a father drug his own daughter on her wedding day? What kind of monster was he marrying her off to?"

As he sat there shaking his head in disbelief, his eyes opened wider when another thought occurred.

"What kind of mother would allow that to happen? I should have been there when that discussion took place. That little jerk never would have walked out of there on his own," Garret growled as he worked himself into a lather.

"That's exactly why Jason didn't want you there. There was several times that J.C. wanted to take a poke at him himself. I had to give him credit though. Keeping it together had to be tough, but Jason was still harboring details he was more than willing to share. If J.C. had lost his temper at that point, he never would have found out about Rae Anne. Jason knew exactly what he was doing by saving the most important information and using it for the finishing touch. I think he actually enjoyed watching J.C. come unglued. I thought it was pretty shallow on his part to take out his revenge on an innocent party."

The stewardess stopped in front of their seats and offered a beverage. Nicole decided on a diet Pepsi and thanked her.

"Getting back to the wedding, I guess the reason they drugged Elizabeth was so they could get through the ceremony without her bolting. Jason made it sound like it was an arranged marriage and she definitely had no part in the arrangements. Hopefully, if I get a chance to get her alone, I can get some answers to those questions. I know J.C. would like to know why he was never informed about her pregnancy, especially if he was the father. Out of all the information Jason threw at him, I think her pregnancy bothered J.C. the most, which is understandable. That poor man has got to be swimming in a pool of grief right now. Just the fact that he's got all that information in his possession and can't do a damn thing about it has got to be nearly killing him."

"Yeah, it doesn't sit well with J.C. if he's not the one in the control seat. Believe me, I've witnessed that a time or two. I remember when Elizabeth disappeared. It was the only time I ever saw J.C. drink, didn't take much to get him loaded either. There was no way he could even stand up but, he was going over to old Buck's place and 'shoot the son-of-a-bitch', I believe were his exact words."

Garret laughed at the memory of hearing J.C. slur as he spoke those words.

"Thank goodness, he passed out before he could get to the front door. The next morning he was sicker than a dog. It was the first and last time he ever drank. That was when he decided to work like a mule to ease the pain. Boy, I felt sorry for that man. Guess that's why I shied away from any serious relationships myself. Love couldn't be worth it if it made a person hurt that badly."

Garret had made an opening, but he didn't know if it was really the appropriate time to bring up her private life. On the other hand, the opening was right there. If he didn't take advantage of it right then, would there be another opportunity to question her without making a fool of himself? If he kept questioning his reason, he wouldn't be asking her anything. Instead of continuing the argument he was having with himself, he decided to just ask.

"What about you, Nicole, is there someone serious in your life?" he questioned, not really knowing if he wanted to hear the answer.

"No, actually there isn't, Garret. I'm way too busy to bother most of the time. New York is a very hard place to meet a nice guy. I'm not saying that they aren't out there. It's just very hard to tell from the packaging on the outside, what you're getting on the inside! And I don't have the time to read labels."

The sweet sound of laughter filled the air and it made her eyes sparkle. Garret was hanging onto every word.

"I was engaged a long time ago, but it worked out rather badly. I guess that experience has made me a little leery about relationships, too."

It came as a big surprise to her that she had mentioned the engagement, it just kind of popped out. That was a subject she never brought up. Maybe it was the fact that Garret made her feel so at ease. Maybe it really was a healing thing when J.C. forced her to tell about her past. Whatever it was, it was a good feeling to let those words slide out of her mouth without wincing afterward.

Garret was elated when Nicole said she wasn't serious about anyone. However, there was still one thing bothering him that he wanted to clear up.

"Nicole, why did J.C. call you 'Red'?"

The question had been on his mind since the word came out of J.C.'s mouth. Where did the name come from? Had they grown so comfortable with each other that they felt they could use pet names?

Nicole laughed softly, remembering her first reaction to J.C. calling her by the nickname Sam had given her.

"My boss calls me that. Sam phoned J.C. and threatened him to make sure nothing happens to me; he's really a sweet man. That's the nickname he's called me by since the first day he hired me," as she spoke, she was smiling fondly at the memory. "He must have used it when he talked to J.C."

"That's nice," he said, feeling like a jerk for thinking that J.C. had pinned a nickname on her.

It wasn't like him to jump to such conclusions; but he had never known the feeling of jealousy before. Of course, he hadn't known Nicole before, either. It made him feel a bit guilty to harbor such feelings against a good friend.

What was this woman doing to him? Damned if he knew, but smiling shyly to himself, he had to admit he really liked it! The more time he spent with her, the more he wanted her for himself. There had been so many years spent at J.C.'s disposal, not that he had minded it, but he had never met a woman who had this kind of affect on him. It was hard to believe that this was happening to him. Is this how J.C. felt about Elizabeth, only more intense? If that was the case, could this situation only get worse? What would become of him if she decided she wanted J.C. and not him? What would happen to his heart when she left for New York? Not even wanting to think about it, he pushed those thoughts far from his mind. Just enjoy what time you have now, he resigned to himself as he leaned back in his seat.

Turning his thoughts back to their earlier conversation, Garret still couldn't imagine what kind of monster Elizabeth's father had married her off to. This had to be one bad character if the bride-to-be had to be drugged to make sure she made it down the aisle.

THIRTEEN

Charles Donovan III was, indeed, a bad character. Maybe he was born with a bad seed that prevented him from being anything but trouble. If there was a fight in the school yard, you could bet that when they got the bottom of the pile, Charles was always somewhere in the stack. A dark cloud loomed over him no matter where he went. If he was walking down the street, most people would step aside to let the shifty looking thug pass by. It didn't take long for him to become the black sheep of the family; his entire life was based on a series of lies and manipulations. The fact that he was his father's namesake was a grave disappointment to the Donovan family.

Charles' mother was a stern, militant type woman. Running her household, including her husband and her children, with an iron glove, her demands were to be immediately carried out, and her word was final. Anyone who believed in the philosophy of 'spare the rod and spoil the child' was a darned fool in her opinion. Charles was a constant thorn is his mother's side and she rode him hard. Getting into trouble must have given him some sort of perverse pleasure because the more she rode his ass, the more grief he gave her. Constantly at battle, Charles was always left in defeat.

As a result of their on going conflicts, Charles developed a deep resentment for his mother. The older he got, the deeper the resentment spread. Lashing out at any female that had any kind of authority over him, they all reminded him of his mother, whom he hated. By the time high school graduation rolled around, he could have cared less if every woman that existed fell off the face of the earth. There was absolutely no use for them, and definitely not in a sexual way where he was concerned.

When Charles entered law school, there was no way he was prepared for the type of self-discipline it would take to succeed. Knowing he could never make it on his own, it didn't take long to find friends in dark places. With their help, and his money, he still barely managed to scrape by. Nearly giving up hope of ever passing the bar exam, he finally skimmed by on the eighth try.

Having friends in dark places had more advantages than getting help with grades. People familiar with science would state that a person is born with the gene that decides whether or not they are heterosexual or homosexual. Hatred toward woman installed by the loathing of his mother was Charles' reasoning for his homosexuality. The secret places he could now frequent supplied him with all kinds of sexual pleasure without the worry of being exposed. Being accepted in the underworld offered many other benefits if you had the money to pay for them. Besides the constant supply of male whores, recreational drugs were as easy to come by as candy in a dime store. What really impressed him was the addiction of possessing power that only money could buy.

What should have been one of the best days of his life turned out to be one of the saddest for Charles when he finally passed the bar. After a long night of celebration he returned to the apartment to find a letter waiting. The Bitch was summoning him home because his father was ill. Even though he was finally a full fledged lawyer and a grown man, there was still some kind of hold she had over him and he couldn't believe he was going home. Not knowing how it could be possible, he hated his mother even more.

It was worse than ever living at home after having so much freedom. Losing the ability to feed his healthy, sexual appetite whenever the urge struck took its toll on his disposition and brought on a burning desire to find a job. As luck took a turn for the better, he entered the Bordoe Family Firm.

Bartholomeuel Bordoe was one of the most recognized citizens in Dalton, Texas. Charles couldn't believe his good fortune of landing such an outstanding position. Of course, that position came with strings attached. Buck, Bartholomuel's name of choice, had checked Charles' background thoroughly before inviting him to join the firm. There was a need for someone with connections he could count on. Someone who could get the job done discretely. What he really needed was someone to do his dirty work. From the information he obtained from having Charles' investigated, he knew he had the right man. Charles took care of any matter Buck gave him; never asking any questions, just doing what he was told. There was never any controversy and the law never showed up on the firm's doorstep. Buck's problems always seemed to disappear without a hitch. That's how he knew Charles was doing his job properly. An even bigger stroke of luck came when Buck called Charles into his office one day.

"Sit down Charles; we need to have a discussion."

Buck was sitting behind his massive desk pulling smoke from a Cuban cigar. Pointing toward the humidor, he offered one to Charles. Declining the offer he took a seat in the wingback chair opposite Buck.

"I have a major problem, Charles. After giving it a lot of thought, I'm inclined to believe that you could help me out. It's a very delicate matter, so the information I am about to give you will never leave this office. Am I clear on that?"

Buck stopped talking and waited for Charles to reply.

"You know that's not a problem, Buck. It's never been one before."

Charles waited patiently to hear what the next line of dirty work was going to be. Buck went on to explain how his daughter, Elizabeth, had gone and gotten herself knocked up by some white trash rancher. Sending her away to a convent to have the baby, he hoped that the problem would be contained until he could figure out what to do. The local people thought she was in Europe attending school, which would explain her disappearance. However, the Sisters at the convent have informed him that Elizabeth has been trying to smuggle letters to the son-of-a-bitch, even though Buck had forbade her to have any contact with him.

"The baby is due in another month. Now, to get to the root of my problem; I fear she will try to run off with him the first chance she gets. That will not be acceptable. She doesn't know it yet, but I've already made arrangements to take the baby away from her…that's another matter we'll discuss at a later time…that should take some of the wind out of her sails. This is where you come in, my friend. I have given this a lot of thought and I'm quite sure it just might work! If she were to marry as soon as she comes home, there would be no where to run. Even he's not going to want her if she is wed to another man. The bottom line is, you want a partnership in this firm, and I want a husband for my daughter."

Buck grew quiet as he watched Charles' facial expressions like a hawk.

Charles was trying to remain calm; but his heart was hammering in his chest so loudly, he wondered if Buck could hear it. Sweat slowly seeped from his pores threatening to expose his nervous state to his soon-to-be father-in-law. Faking a sneeze, he pulled a handkerchief from the breast pocket of his shirt and wiped his nose and quickly dabbed at his forehead before stuffing it back in the pocket. Satisfied that Charles most likely wouldn't turn him down, he continued.

"I know this is probably not the way you expected your wedding day would come about, or how you thought you'd choose your bride. But, this is a very important matter to me. I don't expect you to give me an answer right away. Tomorrow morning will be soon enough," having finished on that note, he waved his hand signaling that Charles was dismissed.

Before he could reach the door, for insurance purposes, Buck added, "But, if you choose not to marry Elizabeth, you'll never make partnership in this firm."

Charles' shaking hand finally found the doorknob, but he was sweating so profusely he could barely turn it. Strolling down the hallway as normally as he could manage, when Charles finally reached his own office, he stepped inside and leaned heavily against the wall. It had been a fear that his knees were going to buckle and send him reeling to the floor before he reached his destination. Buck had no idea he was handing him the world on a silver platter. Never having any interest in women and marrying Elizabeth purely for status-quo would mean he'd never have to perform any husbandry duties. It would be just like a business arrangement. Finally, he could have it all. A partnership in a firm that he wouldn't have dared dream of, a beautiful wife to escort to the social functions, and best of all, a permanent tie to bind him to the Bordoe standing in the community. What more could anyone ask for?

This wedding may even put him back in good graces with his own family. Not that he really cared how they felt about him. Knowing how badly his old man's health was failing, getting back into good graces might mean getting his name back into the will. Not that he needed the money, but he was entitled to it. That bitch of a mother would never leave him anything and he knew that for a fact!

Charles wanted to run back into Buck's office and shout at the top of his lungs, 'Yes, I'll marry your daughter!' Not wanting to stir up any suspicion in the old man's mind, he figured he had better wait until the given time limit. That day had certainly turned out to be the best day of his life. It would be interesting to see how the old man was going to approach Elizabeth with the marriage plans. Charles had never even spoken to her. If the old man wanted Elizabeth to marry Charles, her opinion in the matter wouldn't count. That line of thought made him snicker to himself. Buck sure knew how to run his household! Too bad his old man couldn't have taken lessons from him. Buck would have put his mother in her place in a hurry. Just as Charles had plans to keep Elizabeth in her place.

FOURTEEN

It came as no surprise when Charles announced that he would take Buck up on the offer to marry his daughter. The big rush to take care of the wedding plans was set into motion. Buck calculated the time before Elizabeth could return home and set the wedding date for one week following her arrival. Unfortunately he couldn't give her the lavish wedding he had always dreamed of. Not knowing what her reaction to this whole ordeal would be, he thought it was best to limit the spectators. Just a small family gathering would have to suffice. The next thing on the agenda was to take care of the legal matter concerning the baby. For that particular business he sent for Charles, the new partner in his firm. When Charles arrived, he took his usual seat across from Buck.

"I want you to draw up some papers stating that I will be the legal guardian for this child when it is born."

Buck was busy lighting a cigar so he missed the jaw-dropping response that came from Charles. He had known they were going to take care of the baby issue at some point, but he would never have guessed what Buck had in mind. Keeping silent, he knew it would only annoy Buck if he asked any questions.

"Sometime in the future we'll take care of adoption papers, but for now, this is the way we will handle it."

Buck leaned back in his chair at that point, blowing cigar smoke toward the ceiling as if he were thinking about what his next words were going be. Actually adopting the baby wasn't something he wanted to do right away. Giving it a trial run with Charlotte to see how she would handle being a mother was what he really wanted to do before that kind of paper work was drawn up. If things didn't work out the way he hoped, he'd have to rethink the whole situation. Better to be safe, than sorry. After all, this was his grandchild's life he was mapping out. Although it had been Charlotte's idea to raise the baby, she had never had children of her own. Buck didn't know if his mistress could handle that kind of responsibility.

"I want the baby taken away from Elizabeth right after the delivery. That will give her a couple of days to get used to the situation before she comes home. I don't want to inform her about the wedding plans until the day before she leaves. The shock over the absence of the child should still be fresh, so she won't put up too much of a fight. By the time she ends up coming around, the wedding will be over. If she never gets a chance to see the baby, she won't know what she's missing out on. That's how I want things handled. You got that Charles?" Buck stated, swinging around in his chair to see if he had Charles' full attention.

"I'll get things taken care of right now," Charles replied and closed the folder he had been taking notes in. When he stood up, he added, "Anything else, Buck?"

Buck just shook his head indicating that he was through. Heading for the door, Charles was still in a state of shock, he couldn't believe what he had just heard. It seemed as though Buck was being quite hard on Elizabeth. Considering all she'd been through, she had to be in frail condition already. This plan of Buck's had better not push her over the edge. It wasn't his idea to get married in the first place, but he certainly didn't want a wife that had to reside in the loony bin.

Two weeks later, Buck got a phone call from the convent. Elizabeth had delivered a seven pound, eight ounce baby girl at 12:03 a.m. They were left with strict instructions to call at the time of birth, but the Sisters felt it was much too late. The call didn't come until the first light of dawn, which was at 5:00 a.m., to inform him that baby had been born. Buck called Charles and they whisked off to the convent to retrieve the little girl before Elizabeth had a chance to see her.

Unfortunately, they were a little too late. When Buck was escorted to Elizabeth's room, the sleeping baby laid upon her mother's chest. Elizabeth had dragged herself out of bed in the middle of the night and found the child in the nursery. As she gently picked up the little bundle and cuddled her to the chest, her motherly instincts kicked in full bore. Considering the pain she was in, she carried the sleeping cherub back to the room as gently as she could manage. Before contemplating going back to sleep, she counted the babies fingers and toes and gently touched the peachy fuzz on her head. When she was satisfied that she was a perfect little girl, she laid the baby on her chest and fell soundly asleep. That was how her father found the two of them. Buck was irate. Tip-toeing over to the sleeping pair, he gently pried the baby from Elizabeth's arms.

Passing her over to the nurse he whispered, "Get the baby out of here and ready to travel. Believe it when I say, someone is going to pay for this!"

Then he sat down in a chair by the corner and waited for his daughter to awaken. It was a while before Elizabeth began to stir. As she yawned and slowly pried her eyes open, her hands instinctively went to her belly. After feeling the unusually flat surface, she remembered bringing the baby back to the room. When she tried to sit up too quickly, a searing pain shot through her abdomen. Trying to find the baby, her eyes darted all over the room and then she spotted her father.

"Oh, Daddy isn't she beautiful?" she asked, her voice still groggy from sleep.

Still trying to locate the missing child, she remembered falling asleep with her while she was on her chest. Where could she possibly have gone to?

"Where is the baby? Did one of the Sisters take her?" When she got no response from her father, she asked again. "Daddy, where is my baby?"

Buck stood up and walked over to the foot of the bed. Looking down at his daughter for a long moment, he finally spoke.

"Elizabeth, we've taken the baby from you. I think it's best if you give the baby up for adoption. We've found her a good home with married, loving, parents," as he spoke, there was a strong emphasis put on the word 'married'. "They will take good care of her. You will disgrace this family even more if you bring that child home. It's all been taken care of, so now you can get some rest."

Buck stepped away from the bed assuming that because he gave an order, she was automatically going to follow it. There was no way he expected her response.

"Noooo," she cried out sounding like a wounded animal. "You can't take my baby. You can't. She's all I have left. You can't take her away!"

THE COVER STORY

Elizabeth tried to get up from the bed. The sobbing was so hard her whole body was heaving; she needed to find the baby. Buck moved quickly to the side of the bed. Grabbing her by the shoulders, his strong hands held her down on the mattress. Fighting him as best she could, she slapped at his arms and face and even tried to kick him. There wasn't anyway to break free, he was just too strong for her in the state she was in. Sister Mary-Catherine came running when she heard the howling noises erupt. When she saw how disturbed Elizabeth was, she ran to get the doctor. The doctor gave Elizabeth a powerful sedative that knocked her out immediately and he guaranteed it would last for hours. It would be long enough for Buck and Charles to get the baby and all of its things away from the convent. Elizabeth didn't know it then, but she would never see her baby again.

Still in a numbed state from the sedative, she finally awoke. The blank stare she wore made her look distant, unfocused. Occupying the corner chair where she had found him that morning sat Buck. Even though she wouldn't look at him, she could feel his vast presence in the room.

"How are you feeling, Elizabeth? I was beginning to worry about you."

Although Buck's voice was gentle, the sound of it sent a shudder right through her. Hoping he would just go away, she wouldn't answer him.

"I know you're upset, Elizabeth, but everything will turn out just fine. Wait and see."

Moving out of the chair, he walked to the foot of the bed so he would be clearly in his daughter's view. Elizabeth looked right through him as though his huge frame wasn't even there. The fact that she was disregarding him was beginning to piss him off. She might as well snap out of it, he thought, nothing was going to change. The doctor said she could leave at the end of the week. Deciding he'd rather not come back to this drab place, he might as well tell her about the wedding plans while he was standing right in front of her. It would serve her right for ignoring him.

"When you get home Elizabeth, there's going to be a wedding," he stated and still it didn't get a response from her, so he added, "It's going to be yours."

Elizabeth kept staring straight ahead, acting as if she didn't hear him.

"One week after you arrive home, you will marry Charles Donovan III. We'll have a little backyard ceremony, just our immediate family and his.

Charles hasn't thought much about a honeymoon, so we can leave those details up to you."

Staring at her intensely, he still could not get her to respond.

"Fine, have it your way and don't say a word, but those plans will not change."

With that, he turned on his heel and walked out of the little room. When he was halfway down the hall, he heard a loud, sobbing, 'Nooooooo' coming from the direction of her room. For some odd reason that made him smile. Sister Mary-Catherine came running at the sound of the noise. Buck grabbed her by the arm to stop her before she could reach the room.

"Get the doctor and have him give her a prescription for a mild sedative. Keep her on it until it's time for her to come home. Don't leave her by herself for any reason until her departure from here. I have given her some information I don't think she cared to hear and I don't want her to harm herself. Got that?"

Buck released her arm only after she nodded her head 'yes'.

When Elizabeth came home from the convent, she was despondent. Absolutely no one could get through to her. Buck was a little worried that she wouldn't be able to go through with the wedding, so the doctor told him to cut down on the sedatives he had been pumping her with. Two days before the ceremony was to take place, Elizabeth started to come around. It was just the calm before the storm because on the morning of her wedding, she went into complete hysterics. Buck called for the doctor and he came directly over. It took three people to hold her down while he gave her a shot of a sedative that would numb her until the wedding was over. Buck figured it was the only way to get her down the aisle, and he didn't care what happened after that. Charles' would inherit the problem then and Buck knew that Charles would prevent her from doing anything that would embarrass either family.

The only way to get her down the aisle was to guide by the arm and hold her by the waist to keep her steady, but the wedding still took place. No one seemed to notice that she gave no response as the Reverend asked her if she would take Charles as her lawfully wedded husband. It was just easier to skip over the rest of the parts that required a response from her and finally, the ceremony was completed. Elizabeth had a husband, and Charles had a partnership. With the blessed event finally over with, Buck could relax a little bit. Charles was the one that was in for the rollercoaster ride.

Surprisingly enough there were no hysterics in store for Charles. In fact there was no honeymoon either, which was fine by him. If he was ever expected to share a marital bed, that would have been the time for it. So he was just as happy that his wife didn't plan one. Elizabeth didn't plan anything, she just simply gave up. There was no baby, no Justin, and no life. There was only one emotion that she displayed and that was the unbridled hatred for her father and Charles.

FIFTEEN

When their flight arrived in Beaumont, Texas, true to J.C.'s word, Tami had a rental car reserved for them. It was a clear, sunny day but the temperature had already soared to 95 degrees and was still climbing. After retrieving their luggage and locating the car, they headed north on route 96. Driving along the highway, Nicole watched through the window as they past several sprawling ranches, rich with grassy feeding pastures. The herds of Brahman cattle grazed lazily as though the heat didn't affect them in anyway. Southern enchantment paved the miles as fields of cotton sprinkled the brown earth and groves of beautiful Magnolia trees stood tall and proud. It was a quiet, peaceful ride and within an hour, they had reached the Dalton city limits.

Maneuvering down one of the side streets with ease, the car came to a rolling stop in front of a sprawling hotel. Far from anything that Nicole had pictured in her mind, the Inn was wonderfully southwestern in style; it resembled a grand hacienda with its graceful archways that were spruced with fresh flowers. A spacious reception area offered all the comforts of home with an overstuffed sofa and a reclining chair that faced a large, flat screened TV. In the middle of the floor was the most gorgeous winding wrought iron staircase. French doors on the back wall opened up to a brick paved courtyard lush with trees and tropical greenery. As they checked in, something that really impressed Nicole was how friendly the people seemed to be. New Yorker's were always in much too big of a rush to offer ample hospitality. Making a mental note she decided to try and be more courteous when she got home.

The rooms were just as magnificent as the rest of the inn. Waiting for the porter to arrive with the luggage, Nicole wandered out the French doors onto the balcony. Leaning against the wrought iron rail that surrounded the alcove, she looked across the tree-lined street at a splendid view of the park. A hum of noise buzzed from the street below and the sound of birds chirping came from somewhere in the thick foliage of the trees. A knock on the door pulled her from the sanctuary of her perch and she crossed the room to let the porter in. Quickly placing the bags in front of the armoire, he slid quietly out of the room so Nicole could unpack.

After getting settled in, she decided to find Garret. There was no sense in wasting the rest of the day so if they could go out and explore, the land marks might help to develop the story in a more credible manner.

"Garret," she called to him when she finally found him on the veranda taking in the view. "Take me on the tour. Show me the ranch where you and J.C. drilled for oil. I want to see the park by the river and where you grew up. Show me everything!" she said in a voice full of excitement.

Even though he'd been in California for some time Texas would always be his home so it thrilled Garret to be her personal tour guide. Getting back into the car, they headed out of town toward J.C.'s old ranch. Passing by The Rambling Rose along the way, Nicole found herself wondering what Davis was up to. Peering out of the window as they rode in a comfortable silence, she was fascinated by how flat the land was around her. Unlike New York's hills and mountains, when she looked out across the terrain she could see for miles. When they came to the beginning of a vast grazing range corralled with a bobbed-wire fence, the car began to creep along.

"Right up here on the left is J.C.'s old ranch." Garret explained as he rolled the window down to get a better view.

The gaping hole sucked in a rush of heat that instantly swallowed the cool air in the front seat.

"It's a cattle ranch now; I don't think the oil wells produce anymore. I think J.C. found a streak of luck that was meant just for him. I would say that after all he'd been through that he deserved it, too. If you look to the right of that big barn, you can see the old oil rig is still standing."

Following the direction that his finger was pointing, Nicole could see an old machine that looked almost like a ride that might be found at an amusement park. A big, steel arm stretched above the ground horizontally with two oval disks attached to the one end. The arm was centered on what appeared to be a tripod base, but it was difficult to see any more of the machine because it was so far from view. There wasn't a chance of getting closer without actually driving on private property so he put the window up and slowly drove on.

As they continued, Garret pointed out different land marks that he thought Nicole might be interested in. It was so relaxing to drive on the country roads with so little traffic and he was definitely enjoying the company. Every now and then he'd make turn here or there, it wasn't long before they came upon another ranch. Finding a spot to pull over, he stopped the car and shut the engine off. Glancing out the window at the vast fields, it appeared that the cattle fence went on for miles and miles.

"This is where I grew up," he said with a bit of nostalgia lacing the words.

At the end of the driveway sat a large house done in brick veneer with a covered porch that wrapped around on both sides. Several splendid Oak trees offered plenty of shade to the enormous, green lawn. Along the edge of the property ran a long, irrigation ditch dividing the yard from the fields. Nicole tried to picture Garret with his brothers playing football in the front yard or sitting lazily on the wooden swing that hung by chains from the rafters of the porch.

"After my folks died, my brothers sold off the land and moved out of Texas. I never had any interest in the place, ranching just wasn't for me. I don't even know who owns it now. When they sold it, I had already relocated to California."

Absentmindedly he reached for the keys in the ignition and started the car. Taking one last look around, he heading back in the direction they came from.

"Do you miss being in Texas Garret?"

Nicole thought she had detected a little sadness in his eyes as they left the ranch.

Giving the question some thought, he finally answered, "I guess what I really miss is the smell of fresh, baked pie filling my nostrils after coming in from a hard days work. Or the fried chicken my mother would rustle up on Sunday afternoon. It was the one day we'd all sit down together for a home cooked meal so she'd spend hours in front of the stove cooking." Glancing over at Nicole, Garret chuckled as he continued, "No matter how hard she'd try, she'd still end up with flour plastered in her hair or on her cheeks. I guess it's the family oriented things that I miss. Just seeing the old ranch reminded me of her. Most of the time I don't really give it much thought."

As Nicole listened to him weave his touching childhood memories, she wondered for the hundredth time what it would have been like for her to look back fondly on a memory. Just one good one would have been nice. Thinking about it made her feel sorry for the lost little girl inside and it made her sad knowing there wasn't anything she could do about it.

"Well, this is the park by the Neches river," he told her as they pulled into a spot and parked the car.

Laying his arm across the back of the seat, he turned to look at Nicole.

"You want to get out and take a walk down by the river? I don't know about you, but my legs sure could use a good stretch"

All the traveling had definitely cramped his long legs, but taking a walk was actually more of a ploy to spend more time with her.

"Sure, that sounds like a splendid idea!" Nicole said excitedly, welcoming anything to take her mind off her current thoughts. "Is this the same park that I saw from the balcony of my room?"

"As a matter of fact, yes it is!" Garret replied as he walked around the front of the car to open her door.

The park was superbly groomed and quaint, wooden benches were scattered along the concrete walkway that led to the river bank. Water rose and splashed as it cascaded from a large fountain in the center of the park. Bronzed Confederate Generals stayed on their mighty concrete horses while they reared on their hind legs as if ready to charge into battle. Taking care not to miss anything, they wandered slowly down the path to the river bank. When they finally reached their destination, the river was so calm, the reflection from the water looked like a huge mirror. Mighty Oak trees lined the banks with their branches sprawling over the water offering plenty of protection from the sun.

As they stood at the rivers edge looking down into the smooth pool, Nicole gazed at Garret's reflection in the glassy water. That is a picture that belongs plastered on the side of a bus for a blue-jean ad, she thought. The all-American male, bare chest glowing in sun drenched sweat, long, lean, legs perfectly filling the denim material right to the seams; she could picture it,

Garret standing with his hands on his hips, wind blown curls all astray, intent brown eyes staring off into the distance.

As she continued to study the reflection, it was amazing how small she appeared next to his large frame. However intimidating his presence may be to a stranger, it still astonished her that she felt so utterly comfortable with him. Apparently Garret had stood still long enough while she ogled him from the watery, looking glass. Jerking her back to reality when he took her by the hand, they continued to stroll down the trail. This must be a Texan thing, she thought, remembering that she had held hands with J.C. while they strolled on the beach.

Garret couldn't believe how bold he felt, just grabbing her hand that way. Half expecting her to pull it away, he was totally elated when she just continued to walk without missing a beat. Being with her made him feel like a teenager again and he loved that feeling. It would have made him extremely happy if the day could go on forever.

Nicole's hand looked tiny enveloped inside of Garret's huge one, but she liked the protective way that it felt. As they walked on heading up toward the square, the quiet, peacefulness of the river bank dissipated. Golf carts loaded with banners and decorations were scattered all over the square. Dozens of people were laboring to get tents and make-shift booths into place while flags of every size and shape were being displayed all around them.

"Texans must take their independence day very seriously," she observed. "There's going to be quite a shindig here tomorrow, isn't there?"

All the commotion going on was making quite an impression.

"If we weren't here on business, Nicole, you'd really enjoy yourself. I'm sure it isn't as grand as the Macy Parade, but it sure ranks up there. The whole park is turned into a festival with games and food booths of every kind. The aroma alone would make your mouth water. Everybody turns out for the parade, even good ole Uncle Sam! Clowns wander through the crowds giving away balloons and American flags and tossing candy to the kids. It really is a very pleasant event."

As he spoke, his eyes lit up and his expressions made it look as though he were a little boy, trapped in a mans body. Just watching his emotions transform with such excitement made Nicole burst in laughter.

"I tell you what. We'll come back another time when we have no business to take care of, when we can just have some fun. Then you can show me how Texans really celebrate the Fourth of July," she teased him.

"I'm going to hold you to that, Ms. Bentley," he tossed at her.

The suggestion that there might be another time in the future that they could spend together was enough to make him weak in the knees. It would be like Heaven on Earth if she really meant it. The sun was starting to set and the air was finally cooling off. Nicole's stomach started to rumble in a subtle way to remind her it would like something to eat. If she was feeling hungry, she knew Garret was probably starving.

"Why don't we rustle up some chow, cowboy? I'm absolutely starving!"

It was getting late and she wanted to make sure she was well rested for the day to follow.

"Then I think I'll find my way to my room. I want to make sure I'm very alert for tomorrow's assignment," she said as she slung her arm through his and they headed back to the car. Garret didn't want the day to end but he knew they had serious work ahead of them so he gave in to Nicole's wishes.

There was a little Mexican restaurant down the street from the Inn that looked very inviting. Deciding to give it a try, they sat on the patio and ordered some food along with something to drink. Although it was quite spicy, the food had very good flavor. Chattering while they sipped their drinks and waited for the food to digest, the conversation finally came around to Rae Anne.

"Who do you think she'll look like, Garret, her mother or her father?" she asked, curiously.

"Does it really matter? She'd be a beauty if she resembled either one," he said, sitting lazily back in the chair as he rolled a tooth-pick around on his teeth. "It would probably be better for all those involved if she had her mother's temperament. Could you imagine a female version of J.C.?"

A soft, melodious laugh spilled from Nicole. Garret enjoyed the sound of her laughter and especially liked the sparkle that emitted from those beautiful eyes. In fact, there wasn't one thing he could think of that he didn't like about her. It was too bad they couldn't have met under different circumstances. Maybe this was fate, though. If he hadn't met her here and now, maybe he never would have had the opportunity to know her at all.

"What does Elizabeth look like?" asked Nicole, the curiosity caused by this phantom woman was mounting. "Was she pretty?"

"You know, I haven't seen her in a while, but from what I remember, she was a real beauty though. I can understand why J.C.'s heart was broken. It really is a shame they didn't end up together, especially now, with Rae Anne in the picture." Taking the toothpick out of his mouth, he leaned forward in his chair and looked earnestly at Nicole. "I can't, for the life of me, figure out why she didn't tell J.C. about the baby. That's the one thing he's going to have a hard time forgiving her for, if he ever can. I don't think I could."

The more Garret thought about what Elizabeth did or didn't do, the angrier he became. Throwing his hands in the air as if to express his anger, he continued, "Hell, he thought he didn't have any family left. Now he finds out he's had a daughter for fifteen years. Nicole, you know there's going to be hell to pay and I don't know who's picking up the tab yet. You can bet I don't want to be in their shoes."

Garret was right. When they had left, J.C. had been in a decent mood. Unfortunately, there was going to be a lot of time to spend by himself and there was nothing to do but think about the situation. What else could he do? When he had his fill of thinking about it, he would definitely want to do something about it. There wasn't a chance she would want to be in that person's shoes either. But where did the real blame lie? Was it Bartholomuel that dealt the nasty hand of cards? Could Charles somehow be behind this charade? What about poor Elizabeth? Garret had a good point, too. Where was her mother when all this was going on? There were still so many unanswered questions. The only prayer Nicole had was that she could find Elizabeth alone at the festival. Somehow she had to get her to talk. Maybe luck would be on her side when she finally got to meet with her. For the sake of the story, but really, more for the sake of J.C., she had to hope that Elizabeth would open up to her.

SIXTEEN

It was a glorious day for the Fourth of July celebration. When Nicole awoke, the sun was streaming into her room. It took her a moment to realize where she was, but when she did a broad smile crossed her lips as she slid her hand under the goose down pillow and pulled out the five Worry Dolls. Entering the room the night before, she found the duvet cover had been turned down on the king sized bed and a magical box of Worry Dolls had been placed upon the pillows. Instructions were left to place one doll for every worry she had under the pillow in order to awake the next morning worry free. Even though she wasn't aware that she had a superstitious bone in her body, it was such a delightful folklore she couldn't resist following the directions that had been provided with the box. Besides, she believed they needed all the help that they could get so she stuck one doll for her, one for J.C., one for Elizabeth, one for Garret and one for Rea Anne under the pillow before turning out the light. There was nothing in the instructions about who was supposed to remove the dolls so she quickly shoved them back under the pillow to avoid any bad luck.

    Jumping out of bed like a little kid, she ran over to the window and peered out. On the street below the town's people were buzzing around getting ready for the big day. The street had been transformed into a colorful sea of red, white and blue. Sorting through the small pile of clothes in one of the drawers of the armoire, she looked for something that would be cool and managed to come up with a pair of denim shorts and a tank top. Not wanting to miss out on anything, she hurried into the bathroom, took a brief shower and quickly dressed. When she got downstairs Garret was standing in the large reception area. Looking as though it was a scene taken from a western movie; he was surrounded by a bunch of men all clad in cowboy hats, just shooting the bull. Nicole walked up and gave a radiant smile to the group of men.

"What are you talking about?"

As though his gaze held a magnetizing effect when she glanced up, her eyes locked onto his, mesmerizing her. Silence filtered over the moment as they just stood there, looking intently at each other. Finally, Garret broke the silence.

"A reality checker. Is that one of my jobs now?"

A broad smile had spread across his face as he continued to look down, not wanting to take his eyes from her.

Just then, Elizabeth strolled by them apparently heading toward one of the park benches. Damn my luck, Garret thought.

As he poked Nicole in the ribs he pointed toward her and said, "There's Elizabeth, sitting over there on that bench by herself."

Nicole looked around until she spotted her. Elizabeth sat with her back straight and her shoulders squared. Every inch of her appearance whispered elegance and fine breeding to anyone that might be looking at her. Although her beauty was breathtaking and her actions delivered a regal performance, her eyes held the same empty look as J.C.'s had when she first saw him.

Drawing a deep breath, Nicole whispered to Garret, "Wish me luck. I'm heading over there."

Slowly walking toward the park bench, she intentionally stalled for a moment at a booth that was selling Mexican spices; not wanting to appear as though she was deliberately heading toward Elizabeth. When she finally reached her destination she glanced at the empty seat next to her.

"Hello!" There was no response to her greeting so Nicole asked, "Is anyone else going to use this bench or are you alone?"

"I'm always alone," she said in a flat, empty voice.

"Do you mind if I sit?" Nicole asked and flashed a friendly smile toward her, but Elizabeth kept her gaze straight ahead.

"Suit yourself," she replied in the same flat voice.

"I'm Nicole Bentley."

Extending her arm to offer a handshake was fruitless because Elizabeth didn't attempt to acknowledge the gesture, nor did she answer right away. When she finally did speak, there was no enthusiasm in her voice at all.

"I'm Elizabeth Donovan."

THE COVER STORY

From across the street, a short, heavy man waved at Elizabeth. It seemed to take a lot of effort on her part, but Elizabeth managed to wave back.

"That's my husband," finally turning to look at Nicole, her voice held a twinge of disgust as she spoke, "He's running for Mayor."

After sitting there in an uncomfortable silence, Nicole didn't think that Elizabeth would engage in any kind of small talk. Not wanting to waste any more precious time, she decided to just jump in with both feet. The most she could do would be to get up and walk away.

"I know, Elizabeth. I'm a reporter from New York. I write for a magazine there and I'm doing a story on J. Collins Savage."

When no recognition registered in her eyes Nicole decided to try again. Afraid that the name Savage might be confusing her, she chose to leave it off.

"J. Collins?"

Elizabeth held her silence as she mulled the name over in her mind.

As a spark ignited in her dull eyes and the words barely escaped her lips, she asked, "Justin, Justin Collins?"

Surprised by the emotion that suddenly flickered in Elizabeth, Nicole rushed forward taking advantage of it before she withdrew again.

"I'd like to ask you some questions if you've got a minute."

After witnessing her dull demeanor, Nicole imagined that she had more than a minute to spare; it was more like a whole lifetime. Elizabeth started to respond; but at that moment, her husband started across the street toward her.

"Not here, not in front of him. Meet me at the river bank after the parade. Now please leave before he gets here," as she quickly spoke, her eyes never left the man that was scurrying to reach them.

When he finally stopped wheezing and caught his breath, he asked, "Who were you talking to, sweetheart?"

Stepping closer to the bench he extended his arm for her to take.

"It was nobody, and I'm not your sweetheart," she spat at him.

Dutifully she rose and took his arm, purely for show. As they walked, the flood gates opened on Elizabeth's memories. When she entered the house, her father was waiting for her.

"Where the hell have you been?" he bellowed at her.

"I've been with Justin, Daddy."

Swiftly he reached over and back-handed her across the face. The stunning force of the blow sent her reeling to the floor.

"I thought I told you, I don't want you with that poor, white trash!"

As he bent over her in an intimidating manner, he was close enough to nearly spit the words in her face.

"Now stay the hell away from him."

"I will not stay away from him. In fact, I'm going to marry him, and you can't stop me!" she yelled defiantly at him.

Even though she was deathly afraid of him, Elizabeth was still livid.

"The hell I can't," he said as he raised his hand above his head ready to strike her again.

"He has to marry me," she yelled, hoping to stop the hand from swinging. Afraid to look him directly in the eye, she averted her glance to the floor and said in a much softer voice, "Because I'm pregnant."

As he slowly lowered his shaking hand, in a seething tone, he asked, "What did you say?"

Tears were gathering in large pools and spilling effortlessly down her cheeks. Fear from her father's wrath began to sink in and she could barely understand him because he had his teeth clamped so tightly together in anger.

"You heard me," she said in a shaky voice.

The words she had spoken escaped in barely a form of a whisper. The confidence she had been filled with just minutes ago had evaporated and seeped from her body.

"Why the hell hasn't that yellow bellied son-of-a-bitch been over here to ask for your hand in marriage then?" Buck yelled as his facial color flushed to a deep crimson.

"Because he doesn't know it yet," she cried out in defeat.

Realizing that her last words had given him the upper hand in the situation, he quickly took advantage of it.

"Then he never will. Get upstairs and pack a bag."

The icy, cold look of pure hatred her father displayed at the mere mention of Justin's name made Elizabeth run up the stairs taking two at a time to pack a bag. Afraid that if she didn't do as he said, he would have one of his goons do something horrible to him. It wouldn't do her any good to run to her mother. After displaying one of her acts of defiance, her mother declared that Elizabeth's performance was a replica her of father's actions and she washed her hands of her sometime ago. Believing that his blood seemed to run deeper in her soul, there was nothing her mother could, or would do for her ever again. Elizabeth had always thought her mother was a bit crazy, so it hadn't mattered much when she had suddenly began to shun her. Now she wondered if she behaved that way on purpose, just to survive a life with the brutal man that was her husband.

Having been born and raised as a Southern Baptist, it took her by complete surprise when they pulled in front of the Catholic Church. Only then did she realize what her father was up to; he was sending her to a convent until the baby was born. It never crossed her mind that she would never see Justin again. The Sisters helped carry her bags into the convent while her father gave explicit instructions that she was to have no visitors or send nor receive any mail. Locked away in a prison paid for by her own father, Elizabeth might as well have been in Hell.

Although her father told the Sisters that she was not to have any contact with Justin Collins, she tried in various ways to reach him. One time she dropped a letter out of a second story window to the gardener. The foolish old man brought the letter back into the building and gave it to Sister Mary-Catherine, one of the strictest Sisters in the order. That got her two weeks of solitary confinement. It never occurred to her that she could be so miserable in a place where people came to find solace and peace. The donation her father made to the church must have been substantial for them to keep such tight reigns on her behavior.

Committing suicide had even crossed her mind, but she hadn't wanted to harm Justin's baby. The little being growing inside of her was the only thing she had left of him. When she got out of the convent, she was taking her baby and going to find Justin. If he would have her, she didn't care what her father thought of her. The only way she could survive in that place was to think of the three of them becoming a family after the baby was born.

Just when she thought things couldn't get worse, her father put the baby up for adoption before she was even released. Elizabeth nearly had a break down with all the screaming and crying, but he was relentless and she never saw her little girl again. Ashamed and feeling totally defeated, she didn't know how she could ever face Justin again. How could she possibly explain her disappearance when proof of the baby no longer existed? Why would Justin even want her? All her worries were needless because her father had taken care of that, too. Before her return to Dalton, he had announced the engagement and the wedding followed shortly after. Elizabeth felt as though she died a little more every day. There was nothing left to live for.

The sound of Charles' voice brought her back to present.

As he led her by the elbow to another bench he said, "We'll watch the parade from here, honey."

It absolutely sickened her when he addressed her with terms of endearment. The loathe she felt for Charles almost equaled the feelings of hate she expressed toward her father.

Not having been to one in a long time, Nicole found herself actually getting excited about the parade. Finding the perfect spot by a tree to sit and watch, she sat crossed-legged and waited like a child for the parade to begin.

"Well, aren't you going to tell me what she said?" Garret asked as he plopped down beside her.

Leaning back on his arms, he stretched his long legs out in front of him and lazily crossed them at the ankles.

"Charles was across the street so she couldn't say anything. As soon as he spotted her talking to me, he rushed over to see who she was with. Before he could get to us she told me she didn't want to talk in front of him and she'd meet me by the river after the parade. I don't know how she'll get away from him; he never took his eyes off from her when I was sitting there. I don't think she likes him very well. It was sort of evident the way she snarled out that he was running for Mayor."

"Why wouldn't she like him?" Garret asked, somewhat confused. "That is her husband and they have stayed married for all these years."

"Well, for one thing, he's gay. For another, she's never slept with him."

Those were a few things that didn't get discussed when they filled Garret in on what Jason had told them.

"What?" Garret couldn't hide the fact that he was shocked. "Where did you get that information from?"

Nicole figured that would be the reaction from a lot of people when they found out the news.

THE COVER STORY

"Jason told us. Apparently they carried on an affair for five years. That was how we figured out that J.C. was Rae Anne's father. According to Jason, the marriage had never been consummated."

"How could you just leave that part out, Nicole? That's like the meat of the story. All you gave me were the potatoes," he looked at her disappointedly.

"I thought I told you everything. I was confused. I couldn't believe the things I was hearing myself. I didn't do it on purpose, Garret. What would I gain by hiding that from you?"

The information wasn't left out on purpose and now he was making her feel guilty about it.

"So now you know quit your bellyaching!" she said as she gave him a little swat so he would lighten up.

"Wow, if that's true, I guess I wouldn't like him very much either."

Garret shook his head in disbelief. The disappointment was soon forgotten; there was no way he could stay mad at Nicole. Besides the fact, he was trying to digest the information Nicole just filled him in on. Who would have thought? Charles…gay?

The parade was about to start; they could hear the marching band from down the street. What a spectacular show that stretched out before them. There were dozens of beautifully designed floats and marching bands with majorettes. The fire company and the police department participated by marching down the street in full uniform. A Jazz band played, followed by a fashion float for the Miss Texas contestants. There were clowns and Southern Belles and an Uncle Sam figure on stilts. It was remarkable the effort the people had put into the day. Nicole enjoyed every minute of it and didn't want to see it end. When the parade had fully passed them by and the people started to mill around the square, she grabbed Garret's hand and brought him to the path that led to the river.

"I'm going down and wait for Elizabeth. If she gets away from Charles, keep an eye on him. Try to keep him away from us. If you can't, then come and find us before he does. Let us know he's coming, O.K.?"

Waiting for him to acknowledge before she turned toward the path that led to the river, she wondered how Elizabeth was going to disappear without Charles. Walking at a quick pace, she pictured J.C. and his mother running along the banks. When she reached the river bank, it was easy to imagine how two young lovers could get carried away in such a romantic setting. Totally lost in thought, she didn't realize it when Elizabeth came up behind her.

Giving a startled jump, she turned to her and said, "Gosh, you scared me!"

"I see that," Elizabeth said dryly as she looked out across the water, probably thinking about some of her own special memories. Finally she asked, "What did you want to talk to me about?"

"I don't know how much time we have, Elizabeth, so can I be frank with you?" she asked, hoping she would be cooperative.

Slowly she shook her head yes, but doubt clearly registered in her eyes.

"Good, then let's get started. Why didn't you meet J.C. down here the night you were supposed to?"

At the mention of J.C.'s name tears welled in Elizabeth's eyes. Hesitating to speak, she didn't know whether she wanted to tell Nicole any of the past. It was a complete stranger standing in front of her and she didn't know if she could be trusted. Nicole could see the uncertainty in her eyes, but there wasn't much time; she had to get to her.

"Elizabeth, I know you don't know me from Eve. All I know is that J.C. loved you very much. In a very short time he lost the two most important women in his life. One he had to put to rest, but you just disappeared into thin air and he searched for you for a long time. The question he asked me was how could you confess to love him so much and then leave him without a trace? Your disappearance unraveled him completely. If it weren't for his friend Garret, he might not have made it through the whole ordeal. It would soothe him a great deal if you could just enlighten him with the truth. It won't heal the wounds, but maybe it could set things right between you," she spoke with sincerity. The tears were welling up in her eyes again so she hurriedly continued, "Elizabeth, I'm here for J.C., Justin, if you will. Please trust me enough to tell me, why didn't you meet with him that night?"

As her shoulders started heaving, the tears promising to spill over her lashes started to fall. After she sobbed quietly for a moment, in a weak, soft voice, the truth started to spill from her lips.

"I wanted to, truly I did. I loved Justin more than anything in this world."

In a useless effort she tried to dry her eyes, but the tears kept coming. Pausing for a moment, she tried to compose herself.

"My father caught me coming into the house that night," as she continued, the sadness of the story reflected in her eyes. "I had been with Justin and I was starry-eyed and full of confidence, being with Justin did that for me. When my father demanded to know where I had been, I told him and it resulted in a huge fight. That's when he told me I could never see him again. When I refused to obey his orders, he slapped me across the face and told me again that I was never to see him. I still disobeyed, and that very night, he sent me away."

Tears were rolling down her face. Finally she stopped talking and made an effort to wipe them away.

"It felt like I was sent to a prison, I missed Justin so much. There was absolutely no way to contact him. I tried to sneak a letter to him but when the Sisters found out, I received a harsh punishment. I was confined in the House of the Lord, but it was like living in Hell."

It was quiet for a moment before she spoke again.

"How is Justin?" she asked, softly. It was impossible to hide her fondness for him, it reflected in the expression she wore on her face.

"Not any better than you, Elizabeth. Even after all this time, he's never loved anyone else but you. Every night for a month straight he came down to this spot and waited for you to show up. When you didn't come, he was beside himself with worry. It wasn't possible for him to believe that your father could keep you apart."

Letting her mull that over in her mind, she wondered if she should go on. It seemed so cruel to have such delicate, personal information coming from a total stranger, but there was so little time to ease into it. In as soft a gesture that was manageable she pointed out across the water.

"There's a diamond ring in the bottom of this river somewhere. After purchasing it, he couldn't find you so that he could give it to you. It was his intention to purpose on the night that you didn't show up."

Nicole was going to continue until she heard this pitiful wailing noise.

"Stop," she cried. "Stop, don't tell me anymore."

Elizabeth was sobbing so hard, her whole body was trembling. Nicole put her arms around her and let her cry. It was probably wasn't the first tears she had shed since the miserable incident had happened. Every effort spent trying to pull herself together would cause her to cry even harder. Nicole felt so sorry for this woman. It wasn't her intent to make her even more miserable or to cause her so much grief.

"I'm so sorry Elizabeth. We can stop if you want to. I can't put you through this," Nicole said as she searched for a handkerchief.

"No, it's O.K., I can go on. I wasn't going to tell you this, but I think Justin has a right to know. The reason my father sent me away," she hesitated to catch her breath. "I was pregnant with Justin's child, and he didn't even give me a chance to tell him that he was going to be a father. My father took advantage of the fact that Justin didn't know it yet and sent me away that very night."

As she looked out across the river again there was so much pain in her eyes.

"What happened to the baby, Elizabeth?" asked Nicole, using a cautious manner. There was a vital need to know if she had any idea about what was going on with Rea Anne.

The tears started to flow again, only this time not as hard.

"My father sent me to a convent. After I had the baby," she tried to continue but the sobbing became worse, "He, he…made…me…put her up…for adoption."

It was hard to make sense of her babbling but she was so upset and could hardly get the sentence out.

"I never saw my little girl again." Trembling again as she spoke, "I suppose it was just as bad for Justin, never even knowing that he was a father. It will be impossible for him to forgive me; I can't manage to forgive myself. My life was over when they took that little girl from me. There was nothing more to live for after losing Justin, and my baby."

About that time, Garret was racing over the knoll.

"He's coming," he panted as he bent over and took a deep breath of air. "Charles is coming. You've got about five minutes."

"O.K., Garret, keep watch," she pulled Elizabeth off to the side.

"Nicole, tell Justin about the baby. I was so ashamed of what my father did, I knew I couldn't face him. When I came home, he had a wedding planned for Charles and me. I had no choice. Tell Justin I love him and I know I always will. Please tell him," she was pleading with Nicole.

The least she could do was to try and make things right after all these years.

"I'll tell him. I promise. We'd better go now. And thank you, Elizabeth. You shouldn't have had to go through that," she said softly as she gave her shoulder an affectionate squeeze.

"Yes, yes I did," she quickly replied and turned to walk in the opposite direction that they expected Charles to come from.

Nicole hated what she planned next, but unfortunately found it necessary.

"Elizabeth," she called to her before she was out of sight. "Do you know who Rae Anne is?"

Elizabeth shook her head no and before she could move again, Nicole hollered, "Ask Charles who she is."

Elizabeth shook her head 'yes', indicating she would, and hurried on.

"Come on Garret. We need to get out of here," she said in a low voice, grabbing his hand to head in the opposite direction of Elizabeth.

"What did you do that for?" Garret asked, his eyes widening in disbelief.

"Do what for?" Nicole inquired as she watched her footing while they hurried along.

"Why on earth did you ask Elizabeth who Rae Anne is?"

Waiting for an answer, he stopped short.

Yanking strongly on his arm, she tried to get him going again.

Irritated by his actions, she smartly retorted, "I can walk and talk too. Can't you Texans?" Turning back around, all she heard was a grunt, so with a frustrated sigh, she added, "I asked her because she doesn't know who Rae Anne is."

Stopping again totally confused, Garret looked at her in disbelief, "How could she not know who her own daughter is?"

"Because her father made her give the baby up for adoption! The only opportunity she had to see the child was once, right after she was born. J.C. is right; Buck has got to be behind this. I was trying to find a way to get her to ask Charles about Rae Anne. Maybe we can use him as bait to get to Buck."

"Jeez, Nicole, how much more information did you forget to tell me?" Garret asked with a hurt tone creeping into his voice.

"I didn't know that myself until I asked Elizabeth. Now come on, Garret, we've got to get out of here."

As she spoke she was pulling on his arm, again. All she wanted was to get behind some cover before Charles got to the river bank.

Charles stood at the top of a knoll watching as the two of them scurried away. From his position, he was able to get a clear glance at their faces, but neither of them looked familiar. There was no worry; he would find out who they were and what they wanted. When they were out of sight, Charles chased after Elizabeth. There better be some answers for me, he thought, and she had better be quick about producing them!

SEVENTEEN

When Charles finally caught up with Elizabeth, it was evident that she had been crying. Who the hell were those people she'd been talking to? What could they have said to make her cry? It surprised him that her eyes were moist from a sentimental outburst; he thought the only emotion Elizabeth had left was hatred.

"Elizabeth," he called to her in a tone that was very short. "Who was that woman you were down by the river with?"

It didn't surprise her in the least that he had seen them talking. Nothing ever got by Charles, he was always spying on her.

"None of your business," she said in a flat tone.

"You may as well tell me, dear. You know how I have a way of finding these things out," he said as he squeezed her arm a little tighter than was necessary.

Elizabeth yanked her arm away with force that she didn't even know she had. It had been tiring to live a lie with this man; a man she never had any feelings for, except maybe for contempt. Drugged so they could get her to walk down the isle, she never even agreed to marry the man. It was all her father's doing; it was because of him that she was stuck in a lousy, loveless relationship. The only reason she hadn't fought it was because she had been so ashamed that she had gotten pregnant in the first place. It was bad enough that she humiliated her family, but getting pregnant out of wedlock had hurt her father deeply. But what about her feelings, didn't they count? When her father took her baby away, it nearly destroyed her. She didn't care anymore. Not about her father, not about Charles. As soon as Nicole informed Justin about the baby, her conscience would be clear. It was her only wish that she could have been brave enough to do it long before now.

When the opportunity arose she was going to pack her things. With a sizeable trust left by her grandmother; there was more than enough money to provide a life of comfort. Leaving Dalton was going to put this miserable charade behind her. The thought of escaping Charles and the horrible life she existed in made her step begin to feel a little lighter. It was a wonder she hadn't thought about leaving a long time ago.

"I'm waiting for an answer, Elizabeth! Who were those people?" he asked as his tone started to get nasty.

For the first time ever, he didn't scare her at all.

"Find out for yourself. While you're asking around, find out who Rae Anne is, too."

When he heard the familiar name, Charles stopped short in his tracks and in a stunned tone he asked, "What did you say?"

Looking at her in complete shock, small beads of sweat broke out across his brow. Standing there watching him squirm, she was quite surprised at his reaction. Who could this person be? The name sure stirred up a lot of reaction in Charles.

"Who is Rae Anne?" she asked again, now that her curiosity was totally peaked.

"Where did you hear that name?" he asked, a tremble catching in his voice.

Knowing she couldn't have pulled the name out of thin air, it was probably those two he had seen by the river that questioned her about it. When it was clearly apparent he wasn't going to tell who Rae Anne was, she turned around and continued to walk. Charles was bent over trying to get some wits about him so his head would clear when he saw her walking away and damn near stumbled trying to catch up with her. Someone was stirring up a whole lot of trouble and he had to get to the bottom of it, but first he was taking Elizabeth home. There wasn't any reason to allow access to anymore information than she already had. It bothered the hell out of him that he had no idea how much information that was.

"Come on, I'm taking you home," he grumbled as he grabbed her by the arm. "I've got some errands to run. You'll be more comfortable at the house."

THE COVER STORY

It didn't bother her in the least that he was going to leave her alone. In fact, if he wasn't going to be around she could start packing some of her things. Taking a deep breath, she could almost smell freedom in the air! It was definitely turning out to be a real Independence Day for her.

Taking the long way around the park to avoid Charles, Nicole and Garret finally made it back to the car. Looking around the parking lot, neither one of the Donovan's was in sight.

"I'm going to call Davis and have him meet us at The Rambling Rose. We need to get together to compile our information," Garret was pulling his cell phone from his pocket as he spoke.

"There's a phone in the rental car," Nicole said. "I'm going to call J.C. He's probably going out of his mind waiting to hear from us. Can I have the keys, please?"

Garret reached in his pocket extracted the keys and handed them to Nicole. Just then, Davis came on the line. Nicole walked over to the car and let herself in. Inserting the key into the ignition, she turned the engine over and started the car. It felt like it was a hundred and fifty degrees inside so she cranked up the air. Pushing the buttons on the key pad, she waited for the connection to go through.

"Hello, Tami, is J.C. in?" knowing it was a silly question when she asked it, the phone was probably sitting in his lap.

"Hi, Nicole, yes he is and he's been waiting anxiously for your call. I'll switch you right over."

"Hello," he abruptly spoke when his voice came on the line, the tension was obvious.

"Hi, J.C., I'm sorry to have kept you waiting for my call. It's the first chance I've had to get to a phone," she apologized and felt badly for leaving him on pins and needles all this time.

It wouldn't have done any good to call him any earlier; there wasn't any information to give him until now.

"I want to give you the run down on what we have so far."

Nicole continued to tell him about her meeting with Elizabeth. Starting right out with Buck hauling her off to the convent after their fight, she continued with Elizabeth getting into trouble for trying to contact him by a letter. When she told him about her crying when she mentioned the engagement ring being in the bottom of the river, she could still picture her shaking with grief. Finally, she agreed with him that Buck had to be behind the whole scheme with Rae Anne. When she finished, she gave him the message from Elizabeth.

"Before we split, she made me promise that I would tell you about the baby. She said you had the right to know that you were the father, but, J.C., she doesn't know about Rae Anne. Buck made her give the baby up for adoption and she doesn't even know about her existence, that, I'm sure of. When we were parting at the river, I asked her who Rae Anne was. There was absolutely no reaction, she just shrugged her shoulders. I know she doesn't know, so I told her to ask Charles about her. I'm hoping we can use him for bait."

It was really quiet at the other end of the line. J.C. was still trying to absorb everything Nicole had just told him.

"Are you still there?" she asked in a worried tone.

"Yeah," J.C.'s voice sounded rough. "I'm still here."

"J.C., Elizabeth wanted me to tell you she still loves you, said she always will."

The tone in her voice had softened when she pictured Elizabeth's delicate silhouette as she was saying the words. Nicole glanced over and saw that Garret approaching the car. Opening the driver's door, he slid quietly into the seat trying not to interrupt her conversation

"Davis is waiting for us," he mouthed the words to Nicole.

"Is there anything else, J.C.? We're going to meet with Davis at The Rambling Rose," she concluded.

"No, keep in touch," when he finally spoke, his voice had been barely audible.

Nicole knew she unloaded some heavy information on him. A lot of emotional baggage that he had packed away was going to come to surface and he'd have to take some time to figure it out.

Charles walked Elizabeth home; they only lived a block or so from the town square. Getting into the blue Cadillac, he headed straight for the Stonewall Inn. Assuming that's where the two strangers would be staying, it was the first place he was going to look.

THE COVER STORY

On the drive to the Inn, it didn't take long for Charles to connect Jason to the whole sordid ordeal. How could he have been so stupid to confide in his former lover? If they found out about Rae Anne, did that mean Jason had spilled his guts about their relationship too? Knowing full well that the information he was sharing could come back to bite him in the ass; he shouldn't have let him walk away. What he should have done was to dispose of him permanently; but it hadn't been easy for Charles to let him go at all. Jason had no idea how hard it was for Charles to tell him good-bye; he was the only person that had brought him joy his whole miserable life. Trying to act as casual as he possibly could that last day, he just didn't want Jason to know he was dieing inside. If the relationship had continued and he did become Mayor, the town was so small, someone would be sure to dig up the little secret. Buck would have killed them himself if he were to find out.

There was no way that Charles would even consider telling Buck he didn't want to run for Mayor, mostly because he couldn't come up with a reason good enough for Buck to buy into. There was so much at stake that he had no choice but to do what was expected of him. So, he let go of the one thing that had ever meant anything to him. Instead of thinking with his head, he thought with his heart and let Jason walk away instead of being carried away in a body bag. Look where that had gotten him, right in the middle of a hornet's nest. Worst of all, he knew damn well that nice guys always finish last, that was the reason he never acted like one. First things first, he had to find out who that woman was.

The big, blue Caddy stalked the parking lot trying to find a spot to accommodate its oversized frame. Squeezing into a vacant hole that wasn't nearly large enough to allow exit or entrance from the truck on the right side, Charles slammed the gearshift into park and hit the passenger door of the vehicle on the left side while trying to extract his cumbersome body from the car. Using the courtyard entrance to avoid looking conspicuous, he stood at the wooden case filled with colorful pamphlets that were on display to entice the tourist to visit the local attractions. Not wanting anyone to see him asking questions, he waited until the lobby was clear before approaching the desk. Waddling up to the counter, he finally got a chance to ask if the two people he described from memory might be staying at the Inn. As luck would have it, one of the desk clerks thought he had recognized the woman from an old issue of *Who Are the People* magazine. Excited to the point of almost wetting his pants, Charles asked the clerk if he could see the magazine. Carrying on to Charles that he had been the one to discover they had a celebrity, of sorts, staying right at the Inn, the clerk bent down behind the counter, shuffled through some papers and came up with the copy. Sure enough, there she was, pictured on the second page. The caption under the photograph identified her as Nicole Bentley, field reporter.

"Yep, this is definitely her," Charles said as he studied the photograph. Looking back at the clerk, he asked, "You wouldn't know who the gentleman is that is accompanying her, would you?"

"No sir, I don't believe I have ever seen him. Sorry, I can't help you with that one." he replied.

"Could you tell me what kind of vehicle they are driving?"

"No sir. That would be against company policy sir."

Charles knew that he would probably have to pay for anymore information so he reached in his pocket and folded a fifty dollar bill in half and slid it on the counter.

"Maybe this will help to jog your memory," smiling while he spoke, he pushed his hand closer toward the young man.

Picking fat, stubby, fingers just high enough for the lad to see there was a bill beneath his palm, he watched for a reaction. When the clerk shook his head 'no' he reached in the other pocket and pulled out a folded hundred dollar bill and placed it on top of the fifty.

"Who's going to know?" he asked as he glanced around the empty lobby as if to prove that no one else was there.

Temptation was lurking in the young mans eyes, but he wasn't convinced yet that it would be O.K. to give out the privileged information. Once again Charles put his hand in his pocket and withdrew another hundred dollar bill. This time the clerk couldn't resist and snatched up the three bills before Charles had a chance to change his mind. Looking around the room closely to be certain no one was watching the kid fumbled through the registration cards. When he found the right one, he got a piece of paper and wrote down the model of the car and the license plate number. Folding it in half and sliding it across the counter, again he looked around before he handed the information over to Charles. Nodding his head as a token of thanks, he turned around and headed out the door.

Unfolding the paper and reading its contents while walking to the car, he couldn't believe his good fortune. The next step was to figure out what kind of plan to come up with. Sooner or later he had to call his father-in-law and tell him the news. The old man was going to explode. Deciding that there was no point in waiting around, he picked up the phone and dialed the number. The shit was going to hit the fan so he might as well get it over with.

"Buck, it's me, Charles." He wasn't looking forward to having the conversation and he sounded a little stressed when he spoke, "Can you talk?"

"Just a minute," Buck said as he went into his library and closed the door.

Picking up the phone, he waited to hear the click from the receiver in the living room.

"O.K. Charles, what's got your short's in an uproar?" Buck asked, curiously.

"We've got a problem, a big one. There's a reporter in town from New York City. Somehow she got Elizabeth off by herself after the parade. I don't know what kind of information she gave her, but Elizabeth was crying when I finally caught up with her. She wouldn't tell me what they were talking about; but she asked me about Rae Anne," he quickly recapped the events for him.

"What did you say?" yelled Buck in a thunderous voice that bounced off the library walls.

Charles had to hold the receiver away from his ear the voice was booming so loudly.

"How do you know she's a reporter?"

Buck was irate with his son-in-law; he had never known him to be so careless.

"Why on this green earth did you let Elizabeth go off with her? What the hell does she know? How could you be so damned stupid?"

Charles tried to answer the questions as Buck fired them off at him, but he couldn't get a word in edgewise. Finally he waited until line was quiet and then explained the situation.

"I went to the Stonewall Inn and I found out from the desk clerk who she was. The name is Nicole Bentley and she is traveling with a real, big guy. I don't know who he is and neither did the clerk. I didn't let Elizabeth go off with her, she just disappeared. I think they had a meeting spot prearranged. I was across the street doing some campaigning when I saw the reporter talking with her earlier in the day. As soon as I saw her sitting on the bench, I got over there as fast as I could, but she had already left. Elizabeth wouldn't tell me who she was. When I realized she had disappeared after the parade I thought something was up. When I finally found her down by the river bank, she had been crying. The other two had taken off but I got a look at them before they got away. I don't know what she knows, but she did ask me who Rae Anne was," he carried on as a fearful tone took over in his voice.

"Where's Elizabeth now?" growled Buck.

"I walked her home so I could do some investigating. They're driving a green, Buick Skylark; I have the license plate number, but the car wasn't at the Inn. I scoured the parking lot after the desk clerk gave me the information, they're not here and I don't know where they are."

"You find them fast and you do something about this situation. If they find Rae Anne, it's all over. If they find her, you're over, you got me?" Buck promised him and was dead serious when he hung up on Charles.

When Garret and Nicole pulled up to The Rambling Rose, Davis was outside waiting for them. They were all famished so they decided to meet at a nearby burger joint to discuss business while they ate. As a measure of precaution they took separate vehicles. A shaded picnic area behind the building rendered the privacy they needed, so after they ordered they brought the food outside to eat. Between bites of the burger, Nicole told Davis about meeting with Elizabeth.

"I wouldn't be surprised if Charles and Buck were in on this together. When I was sitting with her on the park bench, as soon as he noticed that she was talking to a stranger, he darted across the street. She told me she wouldn't speak in front of him and wanted to meet by the river bank after the parade. It was a good thing that Garret was on the look out because it wasn't long before he found us. I did manage to speak with her for a while before he interrupted us though. It seems as though Buck immediately sent her to a convent when he found out she was pregnant. There wasn't time to tell J.C.

and she was forbidden to have any kind of contact with him. Charles had to know what Buck was up to because the wedding took place right after she was released from the convent. By that time, the baby had already disappeared and I don't think that even Buck could make all that happen on his own. Elizabeth has no idea who Rae Anne is."

Diving into the rest of her food, Nicole decided that Davis could have the floor so she could eat the rest of her lunch while it was still warm. Having some pretty exciting news of his own, he explained that he had tailed Buck for hours yesterday. Tailing him finally paid off when he led him to Wayland. It was a neighboring town located about an hour east of Dalton, convenient enough to drive daily if he wanted, but far enough away to keep the lid on a secret, if he had one. When Buck pulled into the driveway of a cozy little house, a young girl practically flew out the door to greet him.

"She was probably about fifteen or so," Davis was saying. "The best part is," he hesitated, taking a deep breath, trying to build the suspense. As he could see the excitement rising, he added, "She had to be Rae Anne."

That was all the comment he offered as he watched the pair sitting on the edge of their seats. Looking first at Davis and then back at Garret, she couldn't stand the anticipation any longer.

"How do you know, Davis? Come on, tell us." Nicole knew what he was doing, but she was too excited not to be reeled in.

"Because," he said, hesitating for yet another moment, "She was the spitting image of J.C.!"

"Oh my God!" Nicole cried out, taking a quick breath as she leaned back on the bench.

"No kidding!" Garret gasped as he tried to imagine how his friend was going to react when he finally got introduced to his daughter

They were quiet for a few minutes as they tried to picture a female version of J.C.

Garret came to his senses first. If anyone even had a clue about the search for Rae Anne, they would probably try and whisk her away. There was no way that Garret was going to take the chance of losing track of her. Not when they had come this far.

"Davis, you go back to that house. Keep a close watch on Rae Anne. Wherever she goes, you go. Don't let her out of your sight."

"That shouldn't be too hard. The only two places she has been since I've been watching the place is home and to a little flower shop down the road. I think she works there. I'll take care of my end. What are you guys going to do?"

"We'll see if we can find Charles, maybe he took the bait we gave him." Nicole replied as she stuffed the last of her burger in her mouth.

It wasn't like her to clean her plate and she still didn't know how she crammed all that food in her face. Especially after the breakfast she ate. There must be something in the air in Texas! Afraid that if she kept eating like that, she'd look like a hippopotamus by the time she left for New York.

Little did they know that instead of doing the hunting, they were about to become the hunted. The slip of paper pertaining to the license plate number was sitting on the seat and Charles had been scouting around for the green Buick since he had gotten off the phone. Riding around for about an hour gave him plenty of time to think the situation over, he was pretty sure that he had everything figured out. If Jason did tell them about the love affair and they did confront Buck and there was no doubt in his mind that they wouldn't, there was nothing stopping them from giving him that information too. Life for Charles would be literally over. After giving it some deep thought he came to the only conclusion there was, the two of them would have to have an accident. Someone would have to run them off the road and kill them. There wasn't time to find someone else to do the dirty work; this time he'd have to take care of it himself. The job had to be done properly because his life virtually depended on it.

Nicole and Garret left the burger joint and headed back toward town. Deep in discussion about the strategy they were going to follow, they failed to notice the blue Cadillac that slowly passed by. It was still oblivious when the car pulled a 'U' turn in the road behind them and started to chase the Buick down. When Garret finally looked out of the rearview mirror, he observed a blue vehicle swiftly coming up behind them. It seemed to be picking up speed, as though the driver wanted to pass. When he glanced in his mirror again, the car was directly on the rear bumper.

"What the hell?" just as the words left his lips, the car lunged forward as though it had been hit from behind.

THE COVER STORY

It was a good thing they were wearing the seatbelts because the force of the cars connecting sent Nicole and Garret flying forward. Seconds later they heard another crushing noise as the car behind them rammed at the bumper again.

Tired of being a sitting duck, Garret hollered, "Hang on Nicole."

Pushing harder on the accelerator, the speedometer began to read sixty-eight, sixty-nine, seventy, and soon it was reading eighty-five, but the car behind them was still hot on their trail.

"Who is that?" Nicole screamed hysterically, "What is the maniac trying to do?"

"I don't know, but I think he's trying to run us off the road! Hang on Nicole, he's coming up fast."

Garret was trying desperately to keep the car on the road. When the other driver got almost beside them, he swerved the car over and collided with the Buick forcing it onto the shoulder. Stepping on the gas and correcting the wheel, Garret managed to get the vehicle back on the road. Still the Cadillac charged after them again. Practically standing on the gas pedal, Charles floored it to catch up to the Buick again. The two cars were almost hood to hood when he started to jerk the wheel causing the Cadillac to shift into the other lane.

"Hold on tight, Nicole," Garret yelled as he slammed the brakes on just as the other car was about to collide with them.

The rear end of the Cadillac just caught the front end of the Buick. The impact of the hit sent the Cadillac into a heated tail spin. Spinning out of control, it circled around four or five times before it went careening off the side of the road. Picking up momentum as it went down a small incline, it finally came to a screeching halt when it slammed head-on into a tree.

As they jumped out of the car at the same time, they could see the airbag going off as they ran toward the accident. As the bag went off the driver's head was shoved back against the headrest. The force was so strong that it snapped the headrest completely off. There was no movement coming from the front seat of the car. As they peered through the window it was quite evident based on the twisted angle of the head to the neck that the driver's neck was broken in the impact. Garret cautiously pulled at the door trying to pry it open. When there was no movement or sound coming from the body, he instinctively placed his fingers on the neck to feel for a pulse. There was none to be found so he gently tipped the head back away from the airbag. Staring at him through empty eyes was Charles Donovan III. Nicole took a deep breath and looked at Garret.

Yanking the cell phone from his pocket he dialed 911 and gave the operator the status of the accident. After giving them the location he mentioned that the driver was already dead so there was no rush. Then he dialed the number for J.C. It was high time he came down here and helped them out. They made a promise that if there was any danger they would contact him immediately. What could be more dangerous than being run off the road by a maniac? The whole situation was spinning out of control. J.C. knew he'd end up down there sooner or later. The company jet and a pilot had been on stand-by since day one. It would take him less than an hour to get there and Garret and Nicole would meet him at the airport.

On the way there they tried to reconstruct what might have been Charles' plan. Either he got some information out of Elizabeth, however doubtful that seemed, or he had been snooping someplace else. Maybe Jason had contacted him to gloat about the confrontation with J.C. That didn't seem likely after the frightened way he acted when Garret and Davis were in the same room. Besides the fact he had to know that Charles would kill him if he knew he opened his mouth. There wasn't anyone else that knew why they were there. Unless, of course, he had taken the bait about Rae Anne and he was smarter than they gave him credit for. Just having her name spoken in public after fifteen years of hiding probably scared the crap out of him. How did he find out who they were and why had he tried to run them off the road? Obviously, he wanted to either scare them, or eliminate them completely. They continued to debate the issue all the way to the airport.

When they arrived to pick him up, J.C. was already impatiently waiting for them. A carry on bag was all he had so they didn't have to claim any luggage. Walking out of the terminal towards the parking lot, Garret quickly filled him in on the car chase that Charles had led them in. When they spoke on the phone he had already informed him about the death.

"Why do you think he tried to run you off the road?" asked J.C.

"Well, we gave it some thought on the way over here. Elizabeth must have asked Charles who Rae Anne was; that was our bait. She really didn't know about the baby, J.C.," repeated Nicole, wanting to reinforce the fact. "We think he probably called Buck to inform him that we knew about Rae Anne. Our theory is, Charles must have figured out that we got the information about Rae Anne from Jason. If Jason told us about the baby, he could have also told us about their love affair. If we went to Buck claiming that we knew about Rae Anne, there was a strong possibility that we would tell him about Charles and Jason's relationship, too. It didn't matter what drastic measures it took to keep our silence. If we got to Buck before he got to us, his life was over anyway."

"That has a logical ring to it. But now we've got to confront Buck. There's been a big lapse in time since Charles put him on alert, he could already be making plans to take Rae Anne out of the area."

J.C. was starting to get nervous. The chance to finally see his daughter was so close; he didn't want to risk losing it now.

"Davis is watching Charlotte's place. We told him not to let Rae Anne out of his sight," Garret added, seeing a look of relief wash over the other mans face.

"J.C., I think we should split up," Nicole interrupted. "You and Garret can go to Buck's; I need to get to Elizabeth's house. The poor woman doesn't even know yet that Rae Anne exists and she was just as much a victim of circumstance as you were. It's only fair that she should know the truth, too," Nicole retorted while her eyes were pleading with him to understand. "We don't know that she's even been informed of Charles' death, either. I don't think she should be alone at a time like this."

"You're right," he replied, after giving it some thought. "Someone should tell her. Meet us at Charlotte's when you can."

"Both of us, right?" Nicole asked as she held her breath waiting for his answer.

"Yes, both of you," he sighed. "We'll just have to deal with all the garbage later. Right now, making sure Rae Anne is O.K. is the most important issue we need to take care of. It would be better if we took care of that together."

He never thought he would be saying 'together' and meaning him and Elizabeth. It wasn't clear on how he would deal with the other issue when the time came, but right now, he couldn't worry about it. It was important to get to Buck before he could put any plans that might have come up into motion.

"Thank you, J.C.," she said, as she was backing over to the car. J.C. and Garret would have to rent another car to take to Buck's, she was going to take the Buick.

EIGHTEEN

    Thinking about the phone call he had just received from Charles, Buck paced back and forth across the ornate carpet in the library leaving a tell-tale path where his feet had trod. It was bothering him something fierce that things were going on that he had no control over. Being a man with unquestionable power, situations that deemed him defenseless just didn't happen. No matter how hard he tried to the juggle the facts around, he couldn't make the connection with the reporter, Nicole, to Rae Anne. Things just weren't adding up at all. There were only three people that knew of Rae Anne's existence, three that knew the history behind Rae Anne's existence, and that was him and Charles and Charlotte. It just wasn't possible that the reporter could have gotten any pertinent information. Charlotte wouldn't have breached the knowledge of how Rae Anne came to be with her; there was no way she would do anything to cause the child harm. After all, she loved her and raised her as her own daughter. There was no doubt in Buck's mind where Charles' allegiances lie; because of the nature of his duties in the firm, he had proven that loyalty time and time again. Fifteen years had flown by since he brought that little angel home. Managing to keep her existence a secret for so long, he assumed that things would continue just as they had in the past. Hell, he had raised the kid right under her own mother's nose, if no one had discovered who she was then, why were they snooping around now? The thought of losing his only grandchild after all these years deeply disturbed him.

    Just to be on the safe side, he decided he better get Rae Anne away from the danger Nicole's presence was causing. Buck picked up the phone and dialed the number to Charlotte's house.

    Without bothering to say 'hello' he started yelling into the receiver, "Take Rae Anne and get the hell out of town."

It wasn't unusual to just start yelling and screaming at her when he called, but as she listened to him rant and rave this time, it was the urgency in his voice that frightened Charlotte.

"What's going on, Buck?" she asked, with frustration creeping into her tone. "Where do you want me to take her?"

"I don't care," he continued to scream into the receiver. "Just get her out of town. No...better yet, get her out of Texas!" he said as his voice continued to escalate. It sounded like he was very agitated, right on the edge of being out of control and it frightened her even more.

"What the hell is going on, Buck?" she pleaded with him for an answer.

"There's a reporter digging around in town asking all kinds of questions. Somehow she found out about Rae Anne. I can't figure out where she got her information from, but it's only a matter of time before they find her. Pack enough things to hold you over for a couple of weeks and get her out of the state. Right now, Charlotte, you hear me? I'll get in touch with you when things have calmed down. Now get going!"

Knowing Charlotte would do as she was told; he slammed the phone down in the cradle. Continuing to pace the library floor in an effort to pull a viable plan together, he paused for a moment in front of a life-sized portrait of his wife, Grace. As he stared at the picture of the woman it seemed as though he had been married to forever, a nasty sneer settled on his face. It would be easy enough for him to blame the wife he hardly knew for the mess he was in. Whenever something didn't go Bucks way, somehow the fault managed to drop directly in her lap.

As he quickly moved away from her eminent glare, his thought was that he should have left her a long time ago. There was only one reason the wedding had taken place to begin with, it was so he could get his hands on the family's old money. Marriage to Grace Heartly Bordoe had been a bitter disappointment for Buck. Hoping to produce a house full of sons and providing him with only one daughter just proved what a pitifully weak person she turned out to be. After the delivery of his little girl, lovely Elizabeth, Grace moved into her own room and wouldn't consent to even sleeping with him again, let alone consider having any more children. The relationship fell apart soon after the marital duties ceased, but Elizabeth remained the apple of his eye.

Then his sweet girl got mixed up with that heathen, Justin Collins. It broke his heart when she told him she was carrying his bastard child. To punish her for her sins, he sent her away until the birth of the baby. Immediately after the delivery, he told Elizabeth that he had already put the baby up for adoption. There was never a chance that Buck would allow strangers to raise his grandchild, but Elizabeth had never known he kept little Rae Anne for himself.

There wasn't a man alive that didn't need a sexual release and if Buck couldn't get it at home, by God, he was going to get it some place else. All the release he would ever need was found when Charlotte Evans got her digs into him. A group of men from Dalton were attending a political convention in Las Vegas. Everyone knew his reputation with loose women so one of his colleagues set him up with the company of Charlotte for an evening, hoping that somewhere down the line it would earn a special favor. It wasn't like she was really a hooker, she was just *very* available.

Buck's idea of a good time was a little off-color but Charlotte didn't seem to mind the strange, erotic demands and they hit it off immediately. The thought of going home to an empty house, it seemed empty even though Grace still resided there, after spending four glorious nights with Charlotte was almost like a death sentence. Much to his surprise, it didn't take a whole lot of persuasion to get her to relocate; so kind of like getting a new puppy, he brought her along. There was no need for an extravagant place to set up housekeeping, a room with a large bed to satisfy his sexual urges was all that concerned him. There was a nice little apartment available in Wayland, which was the next town east of Dalton, and the rent was very reasonable. Money wasn't an option, but he didn't like to part with anymore than was necessary. It was an easy commute so he could be there whenever the need to be pleasured struck.

The affair had gone on for seven years before the birth of Rae Anne. To Buck's delight, it had been Charlotte's idea to raise the baby as her own. That little scheme bought a big piece of Buck's heart, but he had no idea that she only made the suggestion for security reasons. The arrogant manner in which Buck had conducted his whole life kept him from seeing the truth about Charlotte's interest in him. The purse strings, however tight they may have been, were the only strings she cared about. Given his naivety of the situation, he thought she would love his granddaughter as much as he did.

When the baby came along, things took a drastic change. To guarantee the comfort of his little Rae Anne, he had purchased a quaint little house for the three of them. Bank accounts were set up in Charlotte's name to ensure that his granddaughter wouldn't want for anything. It was about an hour commute from Dalton to Wayland, but he made the trip as often as he could. It was worth the drive to see his little angel's face light up when he came through the door. He thought the world of that child. After all the time he had spent watching her grow up and taking care of her welfare, no one was going to take her away from him; he just wasn't going to allow that to happen.

After establishing his own empire, built with his wife's money of course, deep down he knew he should have gotten a divorce. Knowing that under the circumstances he couldn't grant her wish, it nearly killed him when Rae Anne would whisper in his ear 'marry Mommy, Uncle Buck. Then we can be a real family'. Maybe when this mess was all over that's exactly what he would do. There had never been a loving relationship with his wife and it would be enjoyable to spend his later years with Rae Anne constantly by his side. Maybe he could persuade her to become a lawyer and take over the firm. There would be some aspects that Charles would continue to oversee; he didn't want her involved in the dirty end of the business. Besides, Charles handled all of that too well to have him give it up.

Buck didn't know it yet, but that chance to marry Charlotte and for the three of them to become a family was never going to happen. As soon as she placed the phone back into the receiver, the impact of what was going on hit her just like a smack in the face. It took a minute or two to pull herself together and then she ran to the desk and yanked out the bank books. The register for the checking account read a balance of seven thousand dollars. Adding that to the one hundred and twenty thousand dollars she managed to pilfer into a savings account made a fairly decent amount of cash to get away with. Buck would blow a gasket if he knew how much of his money she had stowed away. Even though she wished the total was increasing larger, she had worked like hell to get the meager amount that was staring her in the face. Little Precious needed this and Little Precious had to have that, nothing was too good for his little angel. If Buck had ever known Rae Anne was wearing second hand clothing, he would have strung Charlotte up by the neck with a second hand rope.

It wasn't as if she had free reign with the deposits he had made into the account every week. The checkbook was gone over with a fine tooth comb every Monday evening and explanations for every nickel she had spent were expected. There weren't many ways for her to hide money, so she had to resort to whatever means she could. It took a while, but she finally realized that whatever she purchased for Rae Anne was never questioned. It became a ritual to shop for new clothing for the kid and after Buck reviewed the receipts, she'd take the clothing back to the store and get cash refunds to squirrel away. Thank goodness he didn't have an eye for fashion or it would have been obvious that all the receipts for salon visits belonged to Charlotte but were passed off as Rea Anne's. It was easy to spend a quarter of the amount of money that was recorded as new clothing for a complete wardrobe at a second-hand shop. It was pretty hard to tell the difference between a good haircut and a bad one with the curly mop of hair that covered the kids head so she decided it was just as easy to cut it herself. The savings on the extra cut enabled her to get a manicure on a weekly basis.

Knowing full well that a day like this would eventually come and given the fact that no one else had ever looked out for her welfare, it was time she took the initiative to look out for herself. There was no walking away empty-handed this time. If the kid hadn't come along leaving Buck in need of someone to care for her, he probably would have ditched her a long time ago. They always did, some just sooner than later. The end had finally come; but this time it was her turn to do the leaving. The thought of Buck's slobbery, wet lips smothering hers nearly made her hurl. The perverted little quirks that he acquainted with normal sex sometimes made her sick to the stomach. It was no wonder his wife quit sleeping with him; he clearly had no idea how to properly make love to a woman. Charlotte was almost glad it was over. Twenty-two years of sleeping with Buck had been like a prison sentence. Somebody just handed her a 'get out jail free' card and she was going to use it; she wasn't hanging around to thank anybody for it, either. Charlotte was more than willing to ditch the kid as it had never been in the plan for her to become a parent. The sound of Rae Anne calling her 'Mother' was just like somebody running fingernails down the center of a chalk board, they both sent shudders up her spine.

Carefully planning her escape, the first step was going to the bank and taking a withdrawal on all of the money from both accounts. Then she was coming back to this shabby little house and pack everything that would fit into the car. By the time Buck figured out what was going on, she would be long gone. If she wanted to get out of the house before Rae Anne returned from work she was going to have to hurry. Glancing at the clock and calculating the time, she figured there was about three hours left before her shift ended. Charlotte was glad she had encouraged her to get a job at the flower shop down the street, even though it had been self-motivated to get the girl out of her hair.

If Buck found out what she was doing, there was no doubt that he would literally kill her. In a lot of ways it felt as though he already had. All Charlotte wanted to do was take what little pride and what little self-esteem she had left and enjoy life for a while. Buck's money was going to make all of that possible.

Figuring the business at the bank wouldn't take long, it upset her that the manager wasted precious time trying to talk her out of withdrawing the money. When he wouldn't listen to reason, she finally burst into a fit of hysterics which caused a terrible scene. To avoid a disaster, he quickly handed over the cashier's check along with the amount of cash that was requested. Charlotte checked her watch as she came out of the bank. Damn it, she thought, when she realized she wasn't going to make it back to the house before the kid got out of work. There was no way around it; she was going to have to deal with Rae Anne.

All those years of raising someone else's child hadn't been easy, but she knew that taking care of that kid was the only way she could hold onto Buck. Not that she really wanted Buck; all she had wanted was the security that Buck's money could give her. When she told him that she would care for her, she never dreamt in a million years that taking on Rae Anne would end her freedom. It felt like she had been a caged animal; she couldn't come and go as she pleased with a kid around. Everyday she resented Rae Anne more and more for it. If Buck would have at least allowed her to have some friends, she could have spent more time away from Charlotte. Buck was afraid that the other children's parents would start asking questions that there were only hidden answers for. So, Rae Anne and Charlotte were stuck together all day, everyday, except for the time she was in school. Charlotte went out on a limb and tried to get Buck to send her away to a boarding school, but there was no way he would have his little angel sent away for so long. The monotony of it all had taken its toll on Charlotte and she began resenting Buck, right along with his granddaughter.

The trouble in Buck's little paradise couldn't have come along at a better time for Charlotte. Ready and willing to run, she was eager to get away and live like she deserved to. If she was careful, the money she had stashed would last for quite some time. The fine lines nesting on her face was proof enough that she wasn't getting any younger and finding another sugar-daddy wasn't going to be so easy. Besides, she had her fill of the 'Buck's' that had come and gone in her life, enough was enough.

The car was nearly loaded when Rae Anne came through the door. Noticing that the trunk was stuffed with suitcases as she walked by the car, she rushed into the house to see what was going on.

"Mother," she hollered from the living room.

The southern endearment 'mama' was never allowed to be used because Charlotte hated that even worse than she hated being called 'mother'. Ignoring the voice calling out to her, Charlotte came out of the bedroom with a jewelry box in her arms. It was pitiful that she had to beg Buck for each little piece she owned, which meant that the contents of the box weren't taking up too much room. Considering how hard she had worked for the meager haul, it was going with her. It was the last of the things that needed to be loaded into the car. If that bank manager hadn't held her up for so long, the scene that was about to take place with Rae Anne could have been avoided.

"Mother?" when she spoke her name it was more in the form of a question.

What the heck was going on and why were the bags packed and loaded in the car? Charlotte hadn't told her to pack anything and she certainly wouldn't be going anywhere without her. Looking at Charlotte, her eyes reflected total confusion.

"Don't ever call me that again," she snapped at the girl. "I'm not your damn mother. Never have been, never will be."

Charlotte's confession totally stunned and bewildered the young girl standing in front of her. Eyes widened with fear and tears beginning to form in the corners, Rae Anne couldn't seem to find her voice.

"Where are you going?" she finally managed to ask.

"It's really none of your business," Charlotte snapped back at her.

"What about me?" she asked in a whisper. "Is Uncle Buck coming to get me?"

Charlotte had never left her alone before and she was beginning to get frightened at the aspect of staying by her lonesome in the empty house.

"He's not your uncle," as she spat the words, she looked at Rae Anne as if she were mentally challenged. "He's your grandfather, you stupid kid."

Speaking the last words that she would ever have to say to Rae Anne, however cruel they may have been; she walked out the door leaving her in a pool of tears.

"Maybe I shouldn't have been so hard on her," she said to herself as she slid into the driver's seat of the car. "After all none of this was her fault."

It's a little too late to be feeling sentimental toward the kid, she thought. Let somebody else deal with her for a change; thank God it wasn't her problem anymore. It really didn't matter anyhow because in a few hours, she would just be another bad memory.

Davis had watched the whole scene from his post and was surprised when Charlotte pulled out of the driveway alone in the vehicle. Turning his attention back toward the house, he saw Rae Anne standing in the doorway watching the back of her mother's car disappear while crocodile tears streamed down her face. It was obvious from the way the car was loaded that once Charlotte left, she had no intention of coming back. Davis found it hard to believe that anyone could be that coldhearted to leave a child alone when she was clearly that upset. Pulling his cell phone out, he called J.C.

"Where are you J.C.?" he asked, careful not to take his eyes off from Rae Anne.

"We're just about a mile away from Buck's house. What's going on?"

Davis related everything he had witnessed to J.C. and asked what he should do to comfort his daughter. It was against his better judgment to leave her alone while she was crying like that in the doorway.

THE COVER STORY

"Oh jeez, how could that bitch do that to a child? Can you go over there, Davis? Tell her someone will be there shortly. Please be gentle and try not to scare the shit out of her; but don't tell her anymore than you have to. Nicole's gone over to inform Elizabeth about Rae Anne. They're going to meet us over to Charlotte's when she's done. I don't plan on being at Buck's too long. Just long enough to set the record straight. We'll be there as soon as we can."

"O.K., I'm headed over there right now." Davis hung the phone up and got out of the car, not quite knowing how he was going to handle the situation. The child was terribly distraught and he was a total stranger to her. It didn't seem right to Davis that the poor kid was caught in the crossfire of circumstances that were clearly going to cause her more distress before it was finally over. Trying not to frighten her anymore than she already was, he walked slowly up the driveway. Rae Anne cautiously watched him take every step; a look of fear was starting to register in her eyes.

"Rae Anne," he spoke softly and had called her by name before he got too close; thinking that if she realized that he knew who she was, then maybe she wouldn't be so afraid. "I know you don't know who I am; my name is Davis and I'm not going to hurt you. I was sitting across the street when I saw your mother leave a few minutes ago. I know you're upset and I don't think you should be alone right now. Some very special people are going to be here shortly to take care of you. I would like to keep you company until they get here, if that's alright with you. We can stand right out here if you like."

Keeping a steady pace he reached the doorway where she stood and watched as she slowly gave him the once over. When it occurred to her that he wasn't going to harm her in any way, he could visibly see some of the tension leave her body. Finally she spoke.

"She's not my mother," was all she said.

A deaf person could have easily detected the sadness in her voice.

NINETEEN

Having first hand knowledge of the accident, Nicole assumed that someone probably had notified Elizabeth that her husband had been in a fatal car wreck. Going on natural instinct it was likely that she would be at the hospital identifying Charles' body. Stopping at a gas station to get directions, she checked there first but no one had seen her. There couldn't have been a bigger surprise that Elizabeth was at home, apparently packing her belongings. Walking up the porch steps and peering through the window, she saw that there were several boxes and a suitcase piled on the living room floor. From the bulging contents of the boxes, it appeared as though she had been at the project for some time. Stepping away from the window and moving toward the door, she gently pushed the button to ring the bell. Elizabeth appeared from the other room looking calm and collected.

What if no one had notified her of Charles' death, Nicole wondered. It certainly didn't look as though she'd been crying and there was no revealing evidence that she had even been upset about anything.

"Hi, Elizabeth, may I come in?" Nicole asked softly.

"Nicole, what a nice surprise!" she exclaimed as she pulled the door open and stepped aside allowing her to enter. "As you can see, I have just started packing some of my belongings, but I could certainly use a break."

Cocking her head to one side as if she were confused about something, she asked, "Elizabeth, you do know that Charles was in an accident, don't you?"

"Yes," she replied as she gently shook her head, "What a pity."

Nicole stared at her in disbelief. Acting so nonchalant as though it was just some stranger that died in that car accident and not the man she had been married to for fifteen years, she didn't even show the slightest hint of remorse.

The anger that was usually displayed when his name was mentioned seemed to have evaporated right along with the man's life. It was strange, very strange.

"Well, that's not why I'm here," she said as she shifted her shoulders a little bit, trying to shake off the weird feeling that filtered over her. "Unfortunately, I do have some more disturbing news for you."

It was too bad they couldn't have discussed the information about Rae Anne under better circumstances. It seemed as though every time Elizabeth had to get a dose of bad news, it was Nicole who had to deliver it.

"Sit down; I'll get us some iced tea," Elizabeth said, motioning for her to take a chair as she turned toward the kitchen to get the beverages.

"I'm sorry, but we don't have time for tea, Elizabeth." Taking a deep breath as if it were going to give her the courage to continue, she began speaking. "I apologize for having to do this to you again, but I have some things to tell you. They aren't pleasant and because we have such a small window of time here I have to give this information quickly. Please forgive me for being so blunt, but I'll start from the beginning. A man named Jason Deveroe met with me and J.C.,…umm, pardon me, I meant to say Justin,…umm,…I'm sorry."

The right words just wouldn't come to her. For a moment her mind was in a stupor as she tried to figure out how to present the information without making if feel as if it were another punch in the stomach. Realizing there was no gentle way to say the words she just spouted them out.

"There's no easy way to tell you this, so I'm just going to blurt it out. He was Charles' lover, Elizabeth, your husband was gay."

Elizabeth's whole body reeled backward from hearing the astonishing words. Thinking there wasn't much information left about Charles that could surprise her; the startling news flash damn near knocked the wind right out of her. Quickly sitting down in a nearby chair she gasped to catch a breath of air. It was horrible to watch the reaction caused by such a wretched outburst, but Nicole couldn't spare the time for her to get over it and treaded on.

"It was quite apparent that he had been jilted by your husband. I think his goal was to get even with Charles so he had certain confidential information that he eagerly shared with us. This might be very difficult for you to handle, Elizabeth, but I must tell you," hesitating slightly to let Elizabeth get her bearings and she was definitely going to need them, she continued. "He told us that your father never gave your daughter up for adoption after he took her away from you."

Watching the color drain from Elizabeth's face was enough to make her acutely aware of what a strain this was putting on the poor woman. Time was of the essence and it was something that couldn't be helped, she knew she had to continue.

When she thought enough time had lapsed allowing her to recoup a bit, she asked, "Are you O.K.? Can I continue?"

All Elizabeth could do was nod her head in a gesture indicating the answer was yes.

"Previous to your pregnancy your father obviously had a mistress and her name is Charlotte Evans. I would guess that they actually had a place already established in a town called Wayland. After you had the baby, he purchased the house there so the two of them could raise the child as their own. I don't believe she has any knowledge that you or Justin even exist. There has been a private detective following every move your father has made and he led him right to the house where they live. For fifteen years they have been raising your child as their own, just a stones throw away from you. Charles must have figured out that we were on to him because the accident happened while he was trying to run us off the road. If he knew anything, he probably called your father before he came looking for us. If he did make that phone call, we figured that they would try and get your child out of town before we could find her. Just to be on the safe side, we have her under surveillance as we speak. Justin and Garret are on their way to your father's house right now to confront him. Davis, the private detective, is watching the house in Wayland so Charlotte can't pack up and run off with your daughter."

Elizabeth started to shake, but she didn't know whether to laugh or to cry. It sounded so foreign to hear the words 'her daughter' spoken directly to her. Having put the fact that she was a mother out of her mind a long time ago, it had a wonderful ring to it. In forty-eight hours her life had been totally turned upside down. In one day, she lost a husband she could never learn to love and after he turns up in the morgue, she finds out that he is gay. It suddenly dawned on her why he never pushed her to consummate their marriage; not that she would have allowed it, gay or not. Why...he must have thought he won the lottery when her father suggested a marriage to his broken down daughter. It was a perfect cover to hide his unusual way of life.

The father she had grown to hate had taken a mistress; and then deceived her by stealing her daughter. How could he have been so cruel to his own flesh and blood? It was beginning to feel as though her life had been some sort of nightmare that she was just waking up from. Justin had wanted to marry her all along, but she had disappeared and he couldn't locate her whereabouts to ask her. How much more was she expected to take? The news that her daughter had been in Wayland all this time should have pushed her over the edge. Instead, there was a strange warmth flowing through her. All this misery would soon be over and there was so much to look forward to. Now was not the time to fall apart, she would have to be strong and face whatever it was the future was going to hand her. There must be some reward for all of the trauma she had faced for so many years.

Nicole watched Elizabeth closely trying to read her body language but she couldn't tell what was going on in her mind. Was she going to be O.K.? Could she handle the information that she had been burdened so quickly with? The persisting silence began to worry Nicole.

"We're going to get her back, Elizabeth, I promise." Speaking rapidly with hope of bringing the woman out of the trance, she continued, "I'm going to take you to her right now."

Elizabeth still kept silent and had become increasingly pale. The fact that she was really going to meet her daughter for the second time in her life, actually face to face, was just a little more than she could handle.

"Elizabeth, are you O.K.? Answer me, please; you're beginning to scare me!"

Nicole thought that she might be going into shock; she hated the way she was forced to reveal the details. Finding out about her daughter should have been a pleasant experience, but telling her that way made it just another tragic piece of information she would have to bear. Nicole rushed to the back of the house where she found the kitchen and rummaged in the drawers for a cloth. Dousing it with cold water, she returned to Elizabeth and began to bath her face.

When she started to come around, Nicole asked again, "Are you O.K. now, Elizabeth?"

"Yes, I think so," she said, slowly. "My daughter has been in Wayland? It's so hard to believe, all this time she was just an hour away, and my own father was raising her? That bastard. I will never forgive him for this. May he rot in Hell." she seethed. "And Justin, he knows too?"

"Yes, we're going to go meet them as soon as you are able to travel. Do you feel strong enough?" she asked, knowing that she had shaken her up pretty badly.

Immobilized for a moment more, she continued to sort through the information in her mind.

"Yes," she said. "In fact, I'm very anxious to finally meet my daughter. Let's go."

Getting up nimbly from the chair she grabbed her purse and then stopped dead in her tracks to look directly at Nicole.

"Do they call her Rae Anne?"

Nicole wasn't surprised at her question. Elizabeth seemed to be a sharp cookie.

"Yes, they call her Rae Anne."

"Then Charles knew too, didn't he?" she said, with a hint of shock in her voice.

"Yes, Charles knew too. I think that's the information that killed him."

"Good," she said softly, with no mercy in her tone of voice.

Garret and J.C. pulled up the long, winding drive to Buck's house. When they got out of the car they headed to the massive front door. J.C. rang the bell and they stood there for a moment before the butler finally answered the door.

"May I help you?" the older gentleman asked.

"Yes, tell Buck that Justin Collins is here to see him. Tell him it's urgent."

"Wait here," the butler replied as he shuffled off to inform his employer. It wasn't long before he came shuffling back.

"Mr. Bordeo will see you now," he stated as he motioned them toward the library.

"Whatever you have to say, say it fast Collins. You're not welcome in my home," he barked at him from behind the massive desk.

"That suits me fine, Buck. I just stopped by to tell you I'm on my way to pick up my daughter, Rae Anne," he answered in a rather smug tone.

Buck leered at him as he reached for the phone and started punching numbers on the pad.

"Hope you're not trying to call your worthless son-in-law."

Buck glanced up with a surprised look on his face as he stopped pressing numbers for a moment in order to hear what else it was that J.C. had to say.

"You can find him in the morgue. Crashed into a tree and broke his fool neck while trying to run my friend here off the road. Surprised you haven't been notified about it yet!"

A look of horror crossed Buck's face. Pushing the button to disconnect the line, he waited for a dial tone and frantically started jamming his fingers on the numbered pad again. Perspiration visibly covered his bloated face as he missed the correct keys and had to re-dial Charlotte's phone number. His breathing became more labored as the seconds ticked by with no answer, making it feel like hours while the two men just stood there and stared.

J.C. felt quite comfortable while he patiently watched as the big man began to crumble before his eyes. It pleased him that he knew there was no possibility of reaching the party he was dialing. There wasn't going to be anybody to run to the aide of the monster sitting before him.

"Hope you're not trying to call Charlotte. She packed her gear and headed out a while ago. Left Rae Anne all alone at the house in Wayland."

That remark was the one that reached home. If they knew where the house was, he couldn't be bluffing about Charlotte running off and leaving his granddaughter behind. Buck pulled his massive body out of the chair, his face turning beat red as rage began to engulf him.

"You son-of-a-bitch!" he bellowed in a tone full of venom.

He wasn't standing long before a riveting pain shot through him. Taking a sharp breath, he grabbed at his chest and fell heavily into a heap onto the floor. J.C. walked over and stood over top of him, looking down at the pitiful sight.

Feeling as though he shouldn't be totally heartless, he growled, "Garret, call the butler."

Garret ran out of the room to find the old butler. J.C. sure wasn't helping the old man, but the butler could. The evident pain that Buck was wallowing in still wasn't enough to stop him from continuing the tirade.

"Nicole has gone to get Elizabeth. I would guess that she knows everything by now; how you and your mistress stole our baby, how you married her off to a homosexual, how you raised our baby right around the corner from where she lived. Am I leaving anything out, old man? We're taking Rae Anne away from here. You'll never set eyes on her again."

Buck's eyes were bulging as he tried to speak. His tongue had swelled and saliva slid down the corner of his mouth, but no words would come.

J.C. wasn't through, "You made me suffer for sixteen years, old man. I'm going to make you suffer for the rest of your life."

With that, he turned and walked out of the room. The butler scurried in to tend to Buck. His eyes were rolled back in his head while his limbs quivered helplessly at his side. The powerful old man sure was a sorry looking sight.

TWENTY

Elizabeth didn't want to wait another minute for the chance to meet her daughter. If she didn't go right then, she was afraid she might wake up from a dream only to realize she was still stuck in the nightmare she was living in far too long. It was time to put the misery away and move on. As they walked out to the car, Nicole's mind was on the verge of drowning. There were so many questions swimming around in her head. Knowing what a pitiful series of events Elizabeth had endured in the past twenty-four hours was all that kept Nicole silent. Swiftly maneuvering the car onto the street, she stole a quick glance at Elizabeth. The steady, but remote gaze was a tell-tale sign that her mind was off to some far away place. There were so many vital answers Nicole desperately needed for the story, but she just didn't have the heart to pull her from the secret place. Silence filled the air for a short time before Elizabeth finally spoke.

"Have you seen her yet?" she asked in a voice that was soft, but her eyes glistened with anxiety.

"No, I haven't, Elizabeth," replied Nicole. In an effort to flush away the disappointed look that shadowed Elizabeth's features, Nicole quickly added, "Davis has seen her, though. He said that she was the spitting image of her father."

The statement brought a slight nod from Elizabeth as she tried to conceal a broad smile that snuck across her pale lips.

"Do you want to know something that absolutely amazes me, Nicole?" she paused for a moment, drew a deep breath, and then continued. "It's truly amazing to me how a few choice words spoken in anger can alter your life forever. Such small words spoken with such a shattering impact! I have thought, over and over, if only I had kept my mouth shut that night. My father's actions infuriated me into stupidity. I should have just slipped out of the house that night and gone to meet Justin. If I could have told him what was going on, he would have taken care of everything. We could have eloped or something. I definitely would have been disowned from my family, but it would have been worth it. If the truth be known, being disowned had to be better than what my father has put me through. Just to have those sixteen years back to spend with Justin and our daughter. Those exact thoughts have haunted me for those same sixteen years," heaving a deep sigh, she finished the confession.

"Elizabeth, I have been so curious and I know it's none of my business, but why didn't your mother intervene? Surely she could have done something to stop your father? Why did she let her only child be sent away? How could she possibly let her only grandchild be given up for adoption? Surely, she couldn't have known where she did end up, or did she?"

Southern woman tended to handle their men a little differently than other women. Nicole intentionally had skirted around the word 'mistress', not knowing what the exact situation was with her mother.

"Mother, step in, or intervene as you called it? That thought is really quite humorous Nicole," she snickered sarcastically as her eyes suddenly held a haunting look. "I destroyed my relationship with my mother when I was a teenager, and she never was a woman to show forgiveness. Somehow, I ended up in the middle of an argument that was being pursued by my parents. I had wanted desperately to go to a school dance. The final decision as to whether I would be allowed to attend the dance or not belonged solely to my father. So, like any other teenager that might be looking out for their own best interest, I foolishly sided with my father. That sent my mother into a state of madness. If I had known then that my selfishness would have cost my mother's affection forever, my choice would definitely been different. In a fit of rage, she screamed at my father that his blood ran thicker through my veins than hers did. From that day forth he was to take full responsibility for my actions; from that very day I was totally excluded from her existence. The only time I was allowed to see her or speak with her was if we shared an occasional dinner together. She treated me no less than a visitor in her home, but no more either. The sad thing is that I have never been able to recall what they had been arguing about in the first place. At the time, I excused her behavior as a little eccentric, even a little crazy sometimes. It wasn't until years later, when I had realized what a monster my father really was, did I even try to understand my mother's actions. Silence and solitude were her only means of survival. By the time I really understood her demeanor, she had already become a virtual recluse. There was no way for me to reach her, and Lord knows, I tried. That bastard ruined my mother's life, just as he has tried to ruin mine. Mother may not even know she's a grandmother, or even that he sent me away to the convent. It was rumored that he told everyone I had been sent to Europe to attend school. Even if she had been interested in where I was, which I highly doubt, he could have told her the same lie. Whether or not she was aware of the fact that her husband kept a mistress is also a mystery to me, I know I wasn't ware of it. I couldn't even tell you if she had attended the wedding. They had me pumped so full of drugs, I could hardly walk down the aisle. So I definitely couldn't tell you who attended the ceremony, if that's what you want to call that three-ringed-circus," finishing, she swiped at a lone tear that had slid down her cheek.

"Why did they drug you on your wedding day? That was a bit peculiar, don't you think?"

Nicole knew why, but she wanted to hear it from Elizabeth. She found it still very hard to believe. A genuine chuckle escaped from Elizabeth's throat.

"Back in those days, I still had some spunk left in me. Father must have figured that if he didn't drug me, I would have kicked and screamed all the way down the aisle. That certainly would have been a correct assumption on his part too. I never would have married Charles willingly; I had never even laid eyes on the man. When I did meet him a couple of hours before the ceremony, I took an instant dislike to him. I suppose that could have been because of the circumstance he helped to put me in, but my opinion of him never wavered! The whole awful situation was planned so I couldn't go racing after Justin when I got home. I think Charles assumed that just because I chose not talk around the house meant that I couldn't hear either. He would carry on conversations about me and in front of me as if I didn't exist. The real truth was he only married me to get a partnership in my father's firm. Anyhow, the day after the wedding when the effects from the drugs had worn off, I just wanted to curl up and die. All my dreams had gone up in smoke. I realized then that the home my mother shared with my father was really just a very fancy version of a prison. My father was the warden and she had received an unjust sentence. The one he doled out to me wasn't one of the fairest, either. My father had been right about one thing though. I couldn't go running after Justin with Charles attached to my hip. I decided right then that there was nothing left for me, I would just continue to exist in a very dull life until the day I died. Maybe when this is all over with, I'll go to my mother and try and make some sort of peace with her. I'll try to get her to leave that hellhole and I'll let her know that she's a grandmother. Maybe that will put some spark back into her life. She can meet Rae Anne....,"

Elizabeth stopped short in the middle of her sentence; a horrible look crossed her face.

"What is it, Elizabeth? What's the matter?" Nicole began to panic as she watched the color drain from her passengers face, and she quickly asked, "Are you going to be ill? Do you want me to pull over?"

As a distorted look came across her face Nicole really began to worry. What if this was a delayed breakdown of some kind. Why had she been talking right along, acting as if she were in a jovial mood and then suddenly stop talking and look like death warmed over? Feeling totally helpless, all she could do was watch the obvious pain Elizabeth was tormented with.

"What if she doesn't accept me? Rae Anne? What if she hates me for giving her up for adoption? Oh, Nicole, I couldn't bear the thought."

Wringing her hands in distress, the tears were streaming like a waterfall down her cheeks.

"Oh, my God, I can't be this close to finally getting her back and then have her not want me!"

"Oh, Elizabeth! Please, put that thought out of your mind. You're a warm and compassionate woman. Why on earth wouldn't your daughter want you? Please stop those crazy thoughts! Once we get there, you can evaluate the situation and go from there, but don't put any more obstacles in your way right now. Come on now, snap out of it. We're almost there."

Elizabeth continued to sob, the deep, echoing wails kept coming. It sounded as though there was a wounded animal caught under the tire of the car. There were only a few miles left that separated the reunion of a mother and her long, lost daughter. It wasn't going to be good for Rae Anne to meet a hysterical woman claiming to be her mother. Nicole was running out of ideas so she pulled the car over to the side of the road.

"Come on now, Elizabeth, compose yourself! You don't want your daughter to see you for the first time with big welts on your face from crying, do you? Justin will be there too. You don't want him to see you like that either."

The mention of Justin's name seemed to snap her back to life. Pulling down the sun visor, she flipped the little cover open to inspect her face in the mirror. Grabbing her purse from the floor, she removed her make-up case and did a quick touchup. It was a strange feeling to actually care about her appearance again. After she straightened her hair and applied a bit of blush she turned to look at Nicole.

"How do you think Justin will react?" she asked, quietly.

"I don't know, but I can tell you truthfully that he's been very anxious to find both you and Rae Anne. Right now he's probably having the same thoughts that you are. I'm sure everything will turn out for the best," Nicole replied, praying that she was giving the right answers.

As she pulled back onto the road she witnessed Elizabeth visibly squaring her shoulders, as if she were gathering her courage. She seemed to be lost in her own thoughts, so Nicole's mind wandered over the situation that was about to unfold. Giving it some thought, it was pretty fascinating, the things going on around them. There were two people about to be reunited after a sixteen year separation. Their young love had been ripped away from them by a man cruel enough to steal their youth right along with their infant child. It was almost like they were prisoners of war and each of them had to serve a hideous sentence imposed by the same man. One prisoner had to live her life knowing that somewhere out there was her precious little girl, the only link left to the one man she had ever loved. Losing that little girl meant she couldn't bear to face him again. And then, to be drugged and led down the matrimonial aisle to be wed to a man she didn't even love. To be wed to a man of her father's choosing for fifteen long years and to never know one ounce of bliss was a crime in itself. How did Elizabeth do it? How did she come this far with her sanity still in tact? Then, to find out her husband was gay on the day of his sudden death. In addition, learning that the infant that was torn from her on the day of her birth was being raised by her father and his mistress! She glanced over at Elizabeth. There were no tell-tale signs that she was going to lose it again. In fact, for everything she had been through in just one day,

Elizabeth looked too composed. Nicole was amazed by her integrity, her grit. In a very few moments this woman was going to join her long, lost, love and together, they would be reunited with a daughter she hadn't seen since birth, fifteen years ago. A daughter J.C. hadn't even known existed. How on earth was Elizabeth holding it together?

Nicole thought about J.C. Was he holding it together? He, too, had paid a big price at the hands of Buck Bordoe. Losing Elizabeth had nearly torn him apart. If it hadn't been for Garret, J.C. might not have made it. How was it possible for one man to do so much damage? It seemed so unfair. J.C. had been overwhelmed at the thought of having a daughter. She remembered the wounded look that shadowed his face when Jason revealed the news. Remembering what a temper J.C. had displayed at that moment made Nicole fear for what he would do to Buck when they arrived at his home. It would be a whole lot better to keep his temper in check; he didn't need to get thrown in prison at this point in his life. Both J.C. and Elizabeth certainly deserved some happiness after all these years. Although Buck deserved to pay for what he had done, she hoped Garret would keep J.C. in line. Who did she think she was kidding with that thought? Garret's temper couldn't be controlled when it came to any situation concerning J.C. She hoped and prayed that they would both be there when they arrived at Charlotte's house.

TWENTY-ONE

"You were pretty hard on the old man, don't you think, J.C.?" Garret asked while they were walking toward the car.

An occasion to be formally introduced to the man had never occurred, but Garret took an instant dislike to Buck the minute they stepped into the library. To leave him writhing on the floor soaked in his own body fluids still seemed kind of cruel, even for a man of his malicious stature. Hardly believing that anyone would defend a monster like that, J.C. shot a look of disgust directly at Garret.

"That old man got everything he deserved. Even if he was fortunate enough to die right there, it would still be too good for him. I hope the bastard rots in Hell!"

J. C. had reached the door on the driver's side and placed one hand on the door handle and rested his other arm across the roof of the car. Glaring across the span of the roof at his friend, he continued to speak.

"Garret, do you realize what that man took from me? Damn it all, he stole my own flesh and blood!" he yelled as he slammed his fist down on the roof in a fit of rage. "It was bad enough that he hid Elizabeth away from me, but to steal my child, that's unforgivable. No man should have that right. I have spent the last sixteen years wondering how life would have been if I could have spent them with Elizabeth. It was so wrong that I had to find out from a total stranger that we had actually made a baby together. That baby was an extenuation of me, living and breathing, and all this shit was happening practically under Elizabeth's nose for fifteen years! Yeah, sure, I'm finally going to get the chance to meet my daughter. But what about those fifteen years I missed, Garret? What about that? I can't turn back the hands of time. I'll never get to see her take her first step or be there when she gets her first tooth, that's already happened a long time ago. I'll never get to hear the first words she spoke. Was it Buck that she called 'Daddy' all these years, instead of me? That was all taken away from me, he took it away from Elizabeth, too and he had no right to do that, Garret!"

Anger was pouring out of J.C. as he spoke. The more he talked the more he realized how much of Rae Anne's past was gone and he was never going to be a part of it. It wasn't fair that he would never feel the joy of holding the newborn infant in his arms, or count the tiny fingers and toes just to make sure they were all there and accounted for. Or that he missed the toddler years when her motor skills were being developed. If there had been a time when she suddenly awoke frightened by a nightmare, it hadn't been his arms that had comforted and cradled her until she fell back asleep. Even worse than that, she would never see him as a hero when he held her steady so she could peddle a bike for the first time. Oh, how he hated Buck Bordoe.

"You're right J.C., he didn't have that right. I guess I never thought of it in those terms. Still, I wonder if the old man croaked. He didn't look very good while he was lying there on the floor."

As Garret reached for the car door, he could still picture Buck grabbing his chest as he tumbled to the floor like a sack of feed.

"I told you, death would be too good for him! Besides, he's got no place to go. God doesn't want him and the Devil won't take his sorry ass."

Pulling his arm from the hood, he yanked the door open and slid into the driver's seat. Positioning the car in the direction of Wayland, he slammed a foot down on the accelerator and laid a long patch of rubber at the end of the driveway, just for good measure.

J.C. wondered how Elizabeth would take the news of her father's condition. Hell, he wasn't even sure what that condition was. Even so, he felt badly for Elizabeth, but certainly not for Buck. If he was the cause of whatever it was that happened to Buck in the library, he'd do it again in a heart beat.

"I wonder how Elizabeth took the news about Rae Anne. That had to be one hell of a shock for her, too," Garret said once they got out onto the road and the car stopped fishtailing from the stunt J.C. had pulled when they left the driveway. Garret was worried that she might not hold up after everything that had been heaped in her lap.

THE COVER STORY

"To tell you the truth Garret, I'm a little worried about that myself. At least I got the outrageous news in small doses; it's been piled on her at a steady pace. It had to be a hell of a shock when she found out that her husband was gay just after he killed himself in a car accident. Add insult to injury when she finds out that her old man didn't really put our child up for adoption, instead he chose to keep her and raise her with the help of a mistress. Not to mention that she's only been an hour away from her all this time. That's a lot for anyone to handle. I have no idea what her mental state has been." Looking in Garret's direction he asked, "How did she look to you when you saw her?"

There was genuine concern in J.C.'s tone. Despite everything that had happened, Elizabeth had spent more than sixteen years occupying a good portion of his heart. He couldn't erase that fact now.

A mental picture of Elizabeth popped into Garret's head. The image he saw looked tired and somewhat frail. When she was crying by the river bank, she looked so defeated, like she had truly fought a long, hard, battle and had severely lost. Garret didn't want to burden his friend with his opinion; he had enough to deal with without another negative response.

"Let's just say, I hope she's stronger than she looks, J.C."

Garret didn't feel as though he had to expand on his reply. Leaving the remark open like that, J.C. could interpret it anyway that he wanted to. As they approached the outskirts of Wayland, silence began to descend on the interior of the vehicle.

J.C. was trying to anticipate what his reaction would be when he saw Elizabeth again for the first time in so long. If he were to give an opinion of how he really felt, right at the moment, his answer would be 'scared'. That's how he really felt and he hated like hell to admit it, even if it was just to himself. There were major business decisions to be made every day, some that could make or break the company. Managing to stay on top by calculating which risks to take and when the right time was to take them was how he made the company such a success. These decisions didn't have anything to do with the company, this was his life and he felt completely out of his comfort zone. That's what scared him, lack of control. After trying to take control of his heart for sixteen years and failing, he knew it was hopeless now. What if he saw her and fell in love with her all over again? How would he react if she didn't show the same response? What if he saw her and he just felt contempt for her? Blamed her for the loss of his daughter for so long? Nicole's voice boomed in his subconscious mind 'she's as much a victim as you are', and she was right. He didn't have the whole story yet, but he did know that Rae Anne was taken from her at birth. That had to be worse than not knowing she had even been born. He was going crazy waiting to get to her now, and he'd only known of her existence for a few days. On the other hand, Elizabeth had known she was out there someplace for fifteen years but didn't know where she was or who was taking care of her. She had to live with that every day of her life.

Because they were almost to Charlotte's house J.C. decided, right then, that his first concern was going to be for Rae Anne. She was only fifteen years old and the only mother she had ever known had just driven off and left her alone crying her eyes out. If J.C. did nothing else, he was going to spend the rest of his life trying to make up for those lost years. As far as Elizabeth was concerned, he had to let the chips fall where they may. Did he believe in second chances? There had never been a real reason to think about it. Fantasized about it? Yeah, maybe he had, but he never thought she'd ever be available to him. He had loved her endlessly at one time. Maybe that in itself would be enough to get them through this ordeal. Keeping an open mind seemed to be the fairest way to handle the unknown, but the rest would be up to her.

Garret was on a different train of attention altogether. Thoughts of Nicole occupied every inch of his mind. What would happen now? Would she go back to California with them and spend those few vacation days she had spoken about? If so, he'd take some time off and spend every moment he could with her. Settling down and raising a family of his own had really been on his mind lately. Who better to settle down with than Nicole? Somehow he was going to figure out how to make her fall in love with him; the way Garret had fallen hopelessly in love with her. It didn't matter anymore if J.C. was interested in her. From now on it was every man for himself, he would win her away somehow and it really didn't matter how long it took. All he wanted was to be with Nicole. What if she doesn't want to stay, what if she decides to leave right from Dalton? The thought made Garret's stomach lunge. They hadn't been able to spend enough time together. How could he possibly make her see how he felt about her if she left so soon?

THE COVER STORY

Garret had managed to work himself into pure misery by the time they reached Charlotte's house. How was he going to get lost in those beautiful, green eyes if she didn't stay? How was he going to know how wonderful it would be to kiss those sweet lips? Or how soft her skin would feel beneath his touch? If he didn't find some way to make her stay surely he would go nuts. Why couldn't she write her story from California! It would be the same story no matter where she wrote it from.

"Garret, hey…Garret we're here," J.C. spoke in a loud voice trying to get his attention.

When he noticed Garret was in some sort of fog he asked, "Are you O.K.? You look kind of pale. I'm the one that's supposed to be nervous! What the hell's going on in your head?"

J.C. chuckled as Garret tried to pull himself together.

"Nothing, just forget it," Garret grumbled as he undid his seatbelt.

Nicole and Elizabeth were just pulling up to the house as the two men got out of the car; their timing couldn't have been more perfect. J.C. watched with nervous anticipation as Elizabeth emerged from the Buick. Still mesmerized by her beauty and grace, he felt as though the years were melting away like layers of ice standing in the direct sunlight. Everything seemed to be happening in slow motion. What an affect she was having on him as she stepped away from the car. Drawing hard for a breath of air, his heartbeat felt like it was racing out of control. A knot about the size of a baseball settled in his throat and his eyes began to well up with tears. Oh, how he had missed her. Not now, for Christ's sakes, he thought, this is not the time. Blinking as hard as he could to push away the tears, he cleared his throat and rolled his shoulders back and forth to gain some control of his emotions. When he felt stable, he put one foot in front of the other, and started toward Elizabeth. Please don't let me trip and make a fool of myself, he thought, as he looked up toward the sky. If there really is a God, right then was when he needed him the most.

When Elizabeth stepped out of the car, her attention was immediately drawn in the direction of where J.C.'s stood. When she made eye contact, her body suddenly froze. Oh, how wonderful he looked, time had certainly been more than generous to him. Unfamiliar ripples of excitement fluttered through her body, leaving her flushed with a warm sensation. She hadn't had feelings like that since she was....when was that? Ah, yes, she remembered, since she had been with Justin last. Just the sight of him seemed to wash those sixteen years right away, if only it were that easy to go back. When she was able to move, she started toward him wondering what would happen when they finally met in the middle. There was only about one more step to go before she would find out.

J.C. gathered her in his arms and hugged her as tight as he could without hurting her.

When he was sure the sound of his voice would be steady he said, "Oh, Elizabeth, how I've missed you."

Slightly leaning her away from his body, just far enough to get a good look at her face, he gathered her up close again for another hug. Tears stung the corners of Elizabeth's eyes. For the first time that day they were good tears. She felt so complete for the first time in sixteen years.

"I can't believe it's really you, Justin," she sighed. "I never thought I'd see you again."

This time she backed away to get a better look.

"It is really me, Elizabeth and I promise you, you'll never get away from me again! But, right now, we've got something bigger to take care of. It's time for our daughter to meet her parents! I can't believe I am a father, Elizabeth, thank you."

He kissed the top of her head as they turned to go up the walk where Rae Anne was nervously waiting.

TWENTY-TWO

The suspense had started to rise the minute the two cars pulled up to the curb. No one had any idea what the outcome of the reunion was going to be so they stood there, silently waiting. It looked as though someone had hit the pause button right in the middle of a good movie. Nicole didn't realize it, but she had been standing there holding her breath. It felt like she had been waiting in the wings breathlessly watching as a great love scene was taking place on the center stage. Sometimes a helpless romantic, she secretly swiped away a tear that had escaped before she could catch it. If there had been any doubt about how those two felt about each other, it was gone now.

J.C. slid his arm around Elizabeth's waist as they made their way up the walk to finally meet their daughter. Davis had been sitting patiently on the steps beside her, but he stood and stepped aside as the pair approached. Rae Anne sat quietly watching with peaked curiosity as the show of affection had taken place before her, still wondering who all those people were. The man that called himself Davis said that some special people were coming to get her. Were these the special people? And if they were, what made them so special to her? She was still feeling terrified and now she was totally baffled.

When J.C. got closer to Rae Anne, he saw the shock registering on her face. Without a doubt, she did look exactly like her father. It was no wonder they had kept her hidden. Even though her eyes were a little damp and swollen from crying, it had absolutely no effect on the beauty she had been blessed with. The look of confusion began to cloud the pretty face; J.C. could see that in her eyes so he gently stepped closer. Unable to control herself, she just couldn't stop staring into his face. It was so uncanny, she had the same shape and color of his eyes, the same slender nose, and even her lips followed the same pattern of curves as his. It was as though Rae Anne were looking into a mirror. A very strange feeling settled over her.

"Rae Anne," J.C. bent down so he could have direct eye contact with her while he spoke. Continuing in a soft voice, he said, "I know you've had a very rough day. And I know how confusing all of this must seem to you right now. I don't know if you've been told anything about me, but I'm Justin Collins, your father."

A warm glow emitted from his eyes. This young girl sitting before him really was his daughter; there wasn't the slightest doubt about that. Nothing could have prepared him for this moment, the heart that had been empty for so long finally felt so full. It still seemed like a miracle that he really was a father.

"Mother…I mean, Charlotte," she stammered, "told me that my father was dead and I was never to mention him again. Today she told me that she wasn't really my mother. She also told me that Uncle Buck wasn't my uncle, that he was really my grandfather. I'm so confused that I'm not really even sure that I'm Rae Anne!"

It was no wonder the poor girl was bewildered. After she spurted all that out, the tears started to stream down her face again. It was impossible to stop them even though she had been trying so hard to be brave. Seeing a larger version of herself standing right in front of her and claiming to be the father that was suppose to be dead, just took away all the composure that she had left.

J.C. wrapped his arms around her in an effort to comfort her. As the sobbing continued, he could feel her shoulders heaving and her whole body trembling. How would they ever make her understand what had happened to her? It was hard enough to comprehend all this confusion himself, and he was an adult.

"Rae Anne, I am so sorry you have had to go through this. I promise you, when this whole mess is over with, you will never have to go through anything like this again. Your mother and I will protect you from anymore harm, I promise."

The instant he mentioned the name 'mother'; she quickly ran the back of her hands across her cheeks trying to wipe away the tears and pushed herself away from J.C. as she stood up. Whipping her head around in search of Charlotte, her eyes feverishly scoured the area for any sign that she was there. That was the last person Rae Anne wanted to see right now. When J.C. saw her eyes darting around the vicinity, he instantly figured out who she was looking for.

"Charlotte told you the truth, Rae Anne; she's not your mother," as he said those words, Elizabeth stepped forward. "This is your real mother, her name is Elizabeth."

Elizabeth folded her arms around the bewildered child as she whispered in her ear, "I lost you once, my baby girl, and no one will ever take you away from me again. That's a promise!"

As she cradled her close to her chest Rae Anne tried to snuff out the rest of her tears. She still didn't have a clue about what was going on, but it did feel good to be folded protectively in Elizabeth's arms. Rae Anne couldn't remember a single time when Charlotte had given her any kind of love or affection. As he watched the bonding begin between the mother and daughter, J.C. sat back down on the steps with a sigh of relief.

"Why don't we sit here for a while and maybe we can sort through some of this confusion together. We'll see if we can shed some light on this situation, O.K.?"

Patting the empty spot next to him, he motioned for her to join him. Rae Anne nodded her head slowly and then sat down beside him. Elizabeth joined them, sitting on the other side of Rae Anne. Davis stood in the doorway of the house trying to get Nicole and Garret's attention so they would follow him inside.

"I'd like to explain to you in the best way that I can, how it is that you ended up here. This is all kind of new to me so I don't know how good I'm going to be at this, so try and bear with me, O.K.?"

Rae Anne was very anxious for someone to explain why it was that Charlotte just sped away in the car and left her behind. And especially why she told her that horrible story about Uncle Buck. She wanted to know who these people really were and why the man that said he was her father looked just like her. 'Yes', she indicated by shaking her head; she'd be more than willing to bear with him if he could explain all of these things to her.

"You're Uncle Buck really is your grandfather, Rae Anne. It would be my guess that you care an awful lot for him and I'm sorry to be the one to tell you this, but he's really not a very nice man. Umm…can you hold on for just a moment?"

Again Rae Anne shook her in a gesture meaning 'Yes'.

"Elizabeth, can I see you over here for a minute?" he asked, with a strange look in his eyes.

He got up and walked about twenty feet away from Rae Anne and Elizabeth followed.

"Do you think we should tell her about what happened to you? Do you think she knows about sex? Is she old enough to understand that we made love before we were married and that you got pregnant?" He just kept asking questions, never giving Elizabeth a chance to answer before he asked the next one, "I mean, we don't have to explain it in graphic detail. I just want her to know the truth. I don't want to start off with any secrets. I really hate secrets. Do you think she's ready for that kind of information?"

J.C. was so nervous; he just kept rambling on and on. Unconsciously his fingers kept sifting through his hair as he paced back and forth. How do you describe this stuff gently, he just didn't want to screw anything up. This wasn't at all like having a conversation with Garret; he didn't realize this was going to be so difficult. Would times like this have been easier if he had been included in Rae Anne's life all along? Elizabeth smiled deeply as her heart went out to him, he was trying so hard. She may have even laughed at his bewilderment if the situation hadn't been so serious. It was definitely time for her to come to the rescue.

"Why don't you let me handle this part? Maybe it would be easier."

Elizabeth laid her hand on his arm, as if to say, 'it's O.K., we can get through this together'.

J.C. let out a sigh of relief and said, "I think that's probably a good idea. Thank you Elizabeth," his voice carried a sheepish tone, but there was a look of gratitude gleaming in his eyes. Together, they walked back over to the steps where Rae Anne sat patiently waiting.

"Rae Anne, when we were younger, the times were much stricter than they are now. Justin, your father, and I had fallen in love and we had planned to be married. But, before we actually did get married, things got carried away and in the heat of the moment we ended up sleeping together. As a result of that experience, I became pregnant," her eyes grew warm and soft at that point. "With you. You were such a beautiful baby when you were born."

THE COVER STORY

Elizabeth grew quiet as she took a moment to study Rae Anne's facial structure. With features that resembled Justin's when she had first met him, it amazed her at what a beautiful daughter they had created.

"Anyhow, your grandfather, the man you know as Uncle Buck, didn't care for Justin. When he found out we had spent an evening together, he forbid me to see him again. That caused a terrible fight, and in my defense, I told him I had to marry Justin because I was pregnant with his child." Hesitating for a moment, she said with a smile, "that's what you did back in those days." And then her tone grew serious again, "As a result of my outburst, he sent me away before I could let Justin know that I was pregnant. Your grandfather was, and still is, a powerful man with plenty of money to do whatever he wanted, to whomever he wanted. I was sent to a convent until the end of my pregnancy. You were so tiny when you were born, and you really were *so* beautiful."

Looking into Rae Anne's face reminded Elizabeth of the first time, the only time, she had seen that perfect little face. The night she found Rae Anne in the nursery and brought her back to her room played over in her mind. The sound of a baby softly crying had awoken her. After she had returned to the room with the blanketed bundle, she placed her gently on her stomach so she could count her tiny fingers and toes. It was amazing what a powerful bond had formed for Elizabeth in those few moments of joy she shared with her infant child. When she awoke the next morning and her baby was gone, it felt like a part of her very being had been ripped from her body, never to be replaced. When it had become apparent that she would never know the joy of holding her child again, Elizabeth thought that she would surely die. That memory brought a flicker of pain that reflected in her eyes. Elizabeth quickly cleared her throat so she could continue speaking. Even after she cleared her throat the sound of her voice came in just a whisper.

"I fell asleep with you lying on my stomach and when I woke up, you were gone. Your grandfather took you away from me the morning after you were born. There was a married couple that wanted to adopt you, that's what he told me anyhow. He had said it would be better for our family's sake if no one found out that I had been pregnant. Rae Anne, I didn't know that he had lied to me; I never knew that he kept you so he could raise you on his own. I am so sorry. I never knew how near to me you were all of this time."

Elizabeth had tears welling in her eyes. It was getting harder for her to speak so J.C. thought that he had better take over before she broke down.

"Rae Anne, is this too much for you to handle? Do you want to stop for awhile?"

It was hard to tell how much she could process at fifteen years old. How much information of that nature could you unload on a young child? He certainly didn't want to overwhelm her. The poor kid had already been through enough.

Rae Anne was watching Elizabeth's face intently as she related the history of her birth. When she spoke of Rae Anne as a baby there was a soft glow flickering in her eyes that made her feel warm and loved. The breathtaking compassion that Elizabeth had revealed touched her immensely. Rae Anne wanted her to be her real mother; she wanted to be a part of her life. In fact, she had prayed for someone exactly like Elizabeth to rescue her from Charlotte; but yet, she was still confused.

"I knew I didn't belong to her," she spoke, softly. "But, how did you finally find me? And where did Charlotte go? I know you said that Uncle Buck, um…grandfather, wasn't a very nice man, but I know he really loved me. Where is he now? Will I ever see him again?"

If they could just answer her questions, she knew some of the feelings of uncertainty would go away. Rae Anne felt like she had been dropped into the middle of some fairy-tale; but she was too old to believe in fairy-tales.

"That is where things get a little complicated."

J.C. didn't know how to tell her exactly how they had found her.

"Buck had arranged the marriage of Charles Donovan to Elizabeth when she returned home from the convent, right after you were born."

"I know him," Rae Anne interrupted, "He used to come here and visit when Uncle, umm…. Grandfather, would be here"

Rae Anne had deeply resented him for being there, too. When Charles showed up, the two men would lock themselves away in her uncle's private room for hours. That room was always kept locked, even from Charlotte and she had no idea what was in there that could occupy their time for so long. But she did know that when he was there, he stole the time that she should have had to spend with her uncle. It was going to take a long time before she got used to the fact that Buck was really her grandfather and not her uncle.

Rae Anne couldn't picture Elizabeth married to a sleazy man like Charles. That information certainly came as a surprise.

J.C. exchanged glances with Elizabeth. What would make Charles travel to Wayland when their law offices were located in Dalton? If Buck had allowed him to come to the house, then he must have known about Rae Anne the whole time. J.C. looked back at Rae Anne and continued on.

"It was through a friend of his that we found out about you. As for Charlotte suddenly leaving, what they did was wrong. To hide you here and to raise you without our knowing it was wrong. I'm sure Charlotte knew that we would come for you and decided to clear out of here before she got into trouble. As for your grandfather, I know this is hard for you to believe, Rae Anne, but he's not a nice man and I don't think you will be seeing him for a long time." J.C. felt like a monster for telling her that, but it was the truth.

"What's going to happen to me?" she asked in a small voice.

The tears threatened to fall again even though Rae Anne was holding her eyes as wide open as she could so they wouldn't spill down her cheeks.

"Oh, baby," Elizabeth sighed as she wrapped her arms around her once more. "We're going to take care of you. We're going to take you home and nothing bad is ever going to happen to you again. I promise."

Rae Anne left her head buried in Elizabeth's shoulder and asked in a muted voice, "Where is home?"

J.C. looked at Elizabeth questioning her with his eyes. Where was home going to be? He didn't want to stay here, but he didn't want to lose Elizabeth again or his daughter.

"We've got plenty of time to figure that out! But right now, why don't you go get whatever belongings you want to bring with you and we'll go back to Dalton and spend the night at the Inn."

J.C. was ready to get away from that house. There had been enough excitement for one day.

"O.K.," Rae Anne replied, she was still sniffling a little bit as she wiped her eyes.

It was hard to leave the comfort of Elizabeth's arms, but the sooner she went into the house and got her things, the sooner she could get away from it and the memory of her life with Charlotte. Giving her parent's one last look, she turned and headed for the door. When she was out of hearing range, J.C. turned toward Elizabeth.

"Where is home going to be, Elizabeth? Would you consider moving to California with me? I don't really want to stay in Dalton, there are too many ghosts in that town," he said as he was silently praying that she would be willing to go to LA.

"I already have some stuff packed at the house. I was going to move anyway. If that's where home is to you, then California sounds wonderful! I think I would prefer to stay at the Inn tonight with you and Rae Anne, if you don't mind. I don't want to go back to that house. I think I'll just hire the movers to take care of the rest of my things."

J.C. stepped forward and lifted her chin gently with his fingers and planted a very soft kiss on her lips.

"Thank you Elizabeth. I don't want to lose you or Rae Anne again."

About that time, Rae Anne stepped slowly out of the doorway empty handed.

"I'd really rather not take anything if you don't mind. There is nothing here for me but unpleasant memories."

"That's fine Sweetie, I know exactly how you feel. We'll stop and get some toiletries and some pajamas for you to sleep in tonight and we'll get you some new things tomorrow. Come on, Kido, we'll meet you in the car Justin."

Elizabeth placed her arm over Rae Anne's shoulders and they walked together to the car.

"O.K., I'm going to run in the house real quick and see what Garret and Nicole are up to. I imagine Davis has got them scouring the place. I'll just be a moment."

'Justin', he hadn't been called that in sixteen years. That's something I'm going have to get used to! Not that I mind, J.C. thought, as he entered the house.

TWENTY-THREE

When J.C. entered the house, it looked like the place had been ransacked. All the cupboard doors in the kitchen were wide open and all the drawers were pulled out with their contents dumped into a pile on the floor. The cushions from the furniture were scattered all over the floor. Magazines and newspapers were tossed everywhere.

"Where are you guys?" J.C. shouted from the living room.

"In here," yelled Davis. "Is Rae Anne away from the house now?"

"Yeah, she's waiting in the car for me," he answered, as he walked down the hall to meet them.

Davis was positioned in front of a door with some sort of a pick in his hand, ready to put it in the lock.

"What's going on?" J.C. asked, curiously.

"We have checked every room in the house for any scrap of information that Charlotte may have left behind. We haven't touched Rae Anne's room yet; we were waiting until she was safely with you before we go through it. There's probably nothing in there anyway," he said as he crouched down to get a closer look at the lock. "This door won't open and we can't seem to find a key that fits the lock, so I'm just going to pick it. We were waiting to hear from you, we didn't want to do it in front of Rae Anne." Davis was working on the lock as he talked.

"Rae Anne said Charles would come over here to meet with Buck. What do you suppose that was all about? This is a long way from their offices in Dalton. I highly doubt it was a social visit, who invites their son-in-law over to have dinner with the mistress?"

J.C. watched as Davis nimbly picked at the lock. After hearing a distinct clicking noise, Davis turned the knob and gave the door a push. The heavy, old, wooden door creaked open with no further resistance. It was a much larger room than Rae Anne's, but sparsely furnished. An oversized desk sat in the middle of the floor with nothing but a phone and a lamp to occupy the vast space, causing the room to look quite intimidating. A big, leather chair was parked behind it; the seat was worn from the constant use of a large derriere. The pattern was branded in the leather. On either side of the window behind the desk were two, four drawer file cabinets. A small stand beside the desk held a copy/fax machine. If there had been an overhead light swinging from the ceiling, it could have looked damn near like an interrogation room. As soon as they saw the door was unlocked, Nicole and Garret appeared right behind J.C. and Davis.

"Don't touch anything without putting gloves on first!" Davis responded as he bent over a small leather case that could have passed as a doctor's bag and pulled out enough rubber gloves for everyone in the room. "I don't know what we're going to find in here so don't get any fingerprints on anything until I'm sure it's safe."

As soon as he pulled the gloves over his hands, he walked over to the file cabinets.

"Well, what do you know? What do you suppose are in these file cabinets?" Davis wasn't asking anyone in particular as he tried the first handle. "Locked. Check the desk for keys."

Nicole happened to be standing in front of the desk so she tried to pull out the drawer in the center, but had no luck, it wouldn't budge. It was apparent that it was locked, so she tried one of the other drawers located along the side and still had no luck.

"The drawers in this desk won't open unless the center drawer is unlocked. Where's your pick Davis?"

Davis reached in his pocket and drew out the pick and then walked over to the center drawer and popped the lock. Pulling the drawer open, he managed to find a ring of keys lying in a tray in the corner.

"Got em!" he said as he shook them around in the air to show the others what he had found.

Nicole went back to the drawer and started rifling through the papers. There was a small box stuffed way in the back, so she pulled it out and laid it on top of the desk to inspect the contents. Picking through the items in the box, she found Buck's passport, along with Charles' too. There was a passbook for a savings account that had Buck's name typed on the front from the Cayman Island International Bank. There were tons of deposits listed but the total registered well over a cool million. Going back to the drawer to see what other treasures might be hidden there; she moved a stack of papers and revealed the handle of a gun. Moving the papers aside so the gun would be in plain sight, she worked carefully because she didn't want to touch it. Just as she was about to check the other drawers, Davis let out a slow whistle.

"What is it? What did you find?" she asked as she crossed over to the file cabinet. "Holy shit!" she exclaimed as she saw what Davis had in his hand.

There, in living color, was Senator Leroy Thompson, standing as naked as a jay bird and holding a woman in his arms. That woman was definitely not his wife. Underneath that picture was a whole folder of him in just about the same type of pose, but with different women. On the jacket where the file name would normally be written, Nicole noticed a coded number in its place.

Davis quickly pulled an additional file. Again, there was a picture of another prominent figure, the ever popular evangelist, Tommy Tucker. The photos in his file would certainly douse the flames of fire he managed to instill on the congregation as he roared quotes of Hell and Damnation from the podium. It would be interesting to hear how he would explain the image of him dressed in a leather costume designed with the intent to leave his private parts exposed. The woman in the picture, also dressed in leather, stood behind him with a whip posed as if she were going to unleash the strap across his back. They must have used the same designer because none of her private parts were covered either. Again, Nicole noticed a coded number at the top of the file.

As Davis pulled file after file, unlike the other three who couldn't seem to get their fill, Nicole couldn't stand to look at another perverted picture. Only after they finished with a file and closed the jackets did she record the coded numbers. There had to be something to connect the files with the coded numbers, some sort book that might explain what the numbers meant. While they were still going through the files, she went to the desk and opened one of the drawers located along the side. After rifling through its contents and not finding what she was looking for, she moved on to the next one. Finally in the bottom drawer there were two black ledgers. The first book didn't have anything that even remotely resembled the coded numbers so she opened the second one. It was hard to contain the excitement when she saw the numbers listed in the book. LT500-30CD was the code on the senators file so she quickly thumbed through the pages until she found it. After studying the writing in the ledger, it took her a few minutes to figure out what the entries meant. It was a record of payment from Leroy Thompson, payment of $500, payable every 30 days, filed by Charles Donovan III. She quickly found TT1000-30CD. Tommy Tucker, payment of $1000, payable every 30 days, filed by Charles Donovan III.

As she read down the page, it dawned on her that they were blackmailing these men. No wonder the door was locked. There was a lot of dangerous material stored in the cabinets in the room. Looking down at the other ledger, Nicole wondered what that one was for.

"Davis, open the other one," she said as she carried the other book over to the locked cabinet.

When he got it opened, she found the drawers contained similar files, but there were no accompanying pictures. Grabbing the first folder she could get her hands on, she flipped it open to a cover sheet with the name of Douglas Parker typed at the top of the page. A series of strange numbers, as in—MB500-2ps, MW, YRS1000-YW—were in column after column; numbers coded in that fashion filled the whole page. Knowing she was really on to something, Nicole yanked the other book off the desk and searched for Douglas Parker's entry. MB—Miami-Buffalo game, $500 bet, two point spread, Miami to win—Parker lost the bet. Yankee-Red Sox's game, $1000 bet, Yankees to win—Parker won the bet. A wealth of information was recorded in the book. An entry dated 6-23-99 explained that Parker didn't pay up on a boxing bet, and he actually got his arm broken as a result of non-payment.

"This is unbelievable," she said as she read on. "They were running a gambling ring here. This ledger has all the information on who made the bet, the amount they put down, the point spreads, who was favored to win, and who ended up with the money. It's even recorded whether or not the payment was made, and if it wasn't, the date was recorded on which body part was broken. This is unbelievable! My God, these people were running an extortion ring and a gambling ring. Charles must have been in charge of the dirty work. Not one person's name appears on any of those files, except his!"

THE COVER STORY

Nicole just kept flipping through the pages in amazement. In the back of the book, there were dollar amounts with dates next to them. Nicole grabbed the passbook and checked the dates that each deposit was made. Every deposit matched every entry in both of the books, dollar amount and dates. It was a good thing Charles had already killed himself; there was enough evidence in the room to put him away for life. Buck wasn't going to be so lucky. Rae Anne wasn't the only reason they didn't want her snooping around. There was some very incriminating information on some very powerful people stored in the cabinets. How in the world did they get away with it for so long, she wondered?

"Oh, you gotta see this one! It's the sheriff of Wayland!"

Davis was laughing as he handed the file to Nicole. Inside was a picture of Sheriff Wade Drescoll wearing a mask over his eyes that resembled the one from the 'Lone Ranger'. The picture was disgusting, his head was bent back and his hands were holding onto a woman's shoulders as she knelt in front of him. It was very plain to see that she was definitely doing a very dirty deed.

"Jesus, Davis, I don't want to see that kind of shit!" she yelled at him as she swatted him with the file.

"Sorry," he replied, looking at Nicole a little sheepishly.

"J.C., aren't Elizabeth and Rae Anne waiting in the car for you?" Nicole asked when she noticed he was still in the room.

"Holy shit, you're right!"

The time had slipped away while he was busy going through the files with Davis. Having no idea how long he had been in the room, he quickly glanced at his watch. It had been almost an hour since he stepped into the house. What a great way to start a new relationship with Elizabeth, he thought.

"You guys are going to have to call the sheriff."

Just picturing the sheriff showing up at the house in his Lone Ranger mask nearly sent Davis into a fit of hysterics. Holding back as long as he could, it finally got the best of him and he burst into laughter.

"No, I'm serious. It's an election year and the DA will be pretty interested in this stuff. It's not going to hurt Charles, he's already dead. The old man could be too, for all we know. If this information gets into the wrong hands, I'm sure a lot of heads are going roll. I'm surprised there hasn't been some of that going around already. I'm only guessing that there hasn't been because we didn't read it in Charles' well kept notes!"

"What happened to Buck?" Nicole asked as she looked from J.C. to Garret, getting no answer. "Nobody told me anything about Buck!"

"Garret can fill you in later. Just get what information you need for your story, then call the cops. You better comb this place good, Nicole, and move the information you collect before they get here. I know damn well you won't be allowed to come back if you forget anything. I wouldn't let on that we went through all of these files either. That could mean trouble down the line if some of those people know we had privy to their private lives. I still can't believe the old man had balls enough to go after some of those shysters. Davis, after you've handled the police, you can take the car back to the airport and get a flight home. I think our work here is done. I really appreciate everything you have accomplished here. And thanks for staying with Rae Anne; you did a great job looking after her. I'll settle up with you when I get back to LA. Garret and Nicole, I'll see you back at the Inn. Elizabeth is going to stay there with me and Rae Anne tonight; she doesn't want to go back to the house. I've got to explain this to Elizabeth somehow. I'll be so glad when this is over. See you back at the Inn."

Slapping Davis on the shoulder with one arm and grabbing his hand to shake with the other, he said his goodbye's and raced out the door. He had already left his family in the car long enough. That was a line he never thought he'd be using—his family!

Nicole didn't waste any time. Grabbing the pass book, she copied the outside and the contents of the inside and she copied both Buck's and Charles' passports. Next came the black books and all the information stored in them. Only a few of the pictures were copied from the files; the ones that weren't so perverse. Not knowing what she would need for the story, she wanted to make sure there was plenty of material to work with. The gambling files were a different story. Each page was meticulously copied, both sides. There were some very large bets made by some very influential people. It made Nicole wonder if there was an underlying purpose for the gambling ring; such as hiding illegal donations. It also crossed her mind that bets made of such substantial amounts by the particular people that made them could also mean that they knew a game might have been rigged, or they may have done some rigging themselves. There could even be some syndicated mobster stuff going on here. What she did know was that there was some intense information, definitely worth its weight in gold, leaving this room that was going to provide her with one hell of a story.

"Some of that information you're taking could be dangerous to you, you know." Davis said, as he watched her.

"I don't plan on putting myself in any danger, Davis. I'll probably never get the opportunity to look at this stuff again. So, I'm going to take enough to keep everything fresh in my mind. Unless! Where's the sheriff's file?"

As she headed toward the cabinet, a dynamite plan was forming in her mind. Pulling the file out, she turned around with a devious smile.

"Why, what are you going to do with it?" asked Davis, wondering what she was up to.

The mischievous grin that appeared on her face didn't get by him.

"Nothing, just a little insurance policy!" she replied as she placed it on the desk until there was an extra minute to take care of it.

It took awhile to finish copying everything she thought would be necessary for research. When it was done, they quickly straightened the room putting everything back exactly where they had found it. All that was left was to straighten the other rooms they had torn apart earlier. Nicole picked up the cushions in the living room and tossed the magazines and newspapers in the trash. It wasn't likely that anyone would be around to read them anyway. While Garret and Davis stuffed the shit that was on the floor back into the drawers and finished the kitchen, Nicole went out to the garage to find some boxes to put her treasure in. As luck would have it she found enough to load all her copies in and took them out to the car. After all the material was safely stored in the trunk, Davis phoned the sheriff. Not long after the call, Sheriff Wade Drescoll's patrol car came screaming in the driveway. It sort of surprised the trio that he would make such a scene with the lights and the sirens blaring when he had to know what information might be lurking at Buck's house.

"What's going on here, boys?"

Sheriff Drescoll made a big production of hiking the belt up on his pants when he got out of the car. A big wad of chew made his cheek look as though he had a baseball shoved in his mouth. He leered at Nicole like she was some kind of showgirl on an X-rated movie.

"We've found some material that we think you'd be interested in, Sheriff." Nicole was the first to speak up.

He looked right at her and then looked at Davis. "I believe I said, what's going on here, *boys*?"

Davis and Garret both looked in Nicole's direction to see how she was going to receive the intentional brush-off. It wasn't hard to tell that she was seething inside, but she didn't say a word. Davis cleared his throat before he spoke, just so the chuckle that had lodged in there didn't escape.

"Well, Sheriff, it appears that we stumbled on some rather strange files in the house. We came here to pack the young ladies belongings because she's moving back to California with her folks. We were checking the last room to see if her birth certificate and social security papers were filed in one of the cabinets in there when we came across these other files. We're not exactly positive, but from what we found, it looks like Bartholamuel Bordoe and Charles Donovan III were running an extortion ring and a gambling ring from this house. All the proof is in a room in the back. We'll take you in and show you if you like."

"The files you found, they're all in there?" Sheriff Drescoll was getting pretty excited and he wasn't very good at hiding it. "Were there pictures in those files?"

"Funny you should mention pictures, but yes, there are pictures in there also. Quite descriptive pictures, I might add." Davis couldn't hide the smirk that came across his face.

"I'm going to call for some detectives to get down here. Then I want you to show me them files." Sheriff Wade grabbed his radio as he spoke, "Yeah, send a couple of detectives to 112 Eldorado Drive, ASAP. Possible extortion ring and gambling ring detected. Over." Replacing the radio, he straightened back up and said, "O.K., come on, show me where them files are."

He started toward the door with Davis, Nicole and Garret were right behind them.

"Who's the little lady?" he asked Davis as they walked.

"The little lady is a reporter, Sheriff. And I happen to be doing a story on those two men. We found this information, and I want to have access to it if I need it!"

Nicole's voice had raised a few notches as she spoke to him. The comment he made about 'the little lady' was the last straw. The man was obviously dumber than a box of rocks and he had really irritated the hell out of her and she wanted him to know it.

"Yeah, well, maybe you found it, little lady. But as soon as me and my boys get in there, it will belong to us! Now why don't you go relax somewhere and let us take care of our business?"

He tossed her a two-second grin and turned to enter the house. Davis led him back to the room where the files were located and Nicole and Garret were right on their heels.

"Which ones got the files with the pictures?" Sheriff Drescoll asked Davis.

"The one on the right," Davis replied as he pointed at the correct cabinet.

Davis stood just inside the door while the good sheriff nearly fell as he ran across the room trying to get to it. It didn't take him long to yank opened the first drawer and start plowing through the personal files. His arms were buried to the elbows just as the two detectives entered the room.

"Are you looking for anything in particular, Sheriff?" Nicole asked coyly from the doorway.

Sheriff Drescoll shot her a disgusted look and turned back to the hunt. It seemed as though he was on a mission from the speed he was executing as he pawed through the files in the second drawer.

"Do you think I could speak with you a moment, Sheriff?" Nicole asked him in her very best 'professional' tone.

"I thought I told you to find somewhere else to go, little lady. You're in the way here. We really don't need you anymore. Now git," he was frantically mauling through the third drawer as he spoke.

Nicole strolled over to the file cabinet he was searching through and lazily propped her elbow on the top and leaned her head against her hand. In an extremely low voice so only the sheriff could hear she said, "You sure do look different without your 'Lone Ranger' mask, Sheriff!"

Frozen in his tracks, he stopped rifling through the files and stared at her for a moment. In a raging voice he said, "What did you say?"

Nicole smiled sweetly at him but chose not to speak for a moment. It brought her such a wave of pleasure just to watch as Sheriff Drescoll's face turned a lovely shade of purple. With a glare as cold as ice, he stood there with his hands on his hips waiting for an answer.

"I said may I speak with you in the other room, Sheriff."

With a broad smile on her face, she turned toward the door and headed to Charlotte's room. There was no doubt in her mind that the good sheriff would be right behind her.

"What the hell was that all about?" he snapped at her when he came barreling into Charlotte's room.

"Well, I was trying to get your attention and you kept ignoring me. I'm not a woman who tolerates being ignored, Sheriff. I wanted to speak with you in private."

Nicole looked at him with such innocent eyes.

"This had better be good," he growled at her. With a quick change in his tone and in a much lower voice, he asked, "How did you know about the mask?"

The sheriff didn't dare go too far with her until he found out what Nicole was up to. Nicole walked over to Charlotte's bed and stuck her hand between the mattresses. When she pulled it back out; she had a folder in her hand.

Pulling out the picture with the Sheriff dressed in his mask, she asked, "You mean this mask?" Then she held the picture in front of his face for him to see. Sheriff Drescoll ran across the room and quickly shut the door.

"What are you doing with that file? That's obstruction of justice," he snarled through clamped teeth.

"Oh...and this wasn't what you were so intent on finding when you were tearing those drawers apart?" she replied, with a throaty laugh.

The blood drained from Sheriff Drescoll's face as he walked over and dropped heavily, down on the bed.

In a tone sounding full of defeat he spoke, "When you people called tonight, I was hoping this whole thing would finally be over. What do you want? How much is it going to cost me now?"

Nicole laughed again as she walked over to the sheriff and dropped the file in his lap. When he looked up at her, his mouth dropped open, but no words came out.

"I don't want anything, Sheriff. I just thought it might be a little embarrassing for you to conduct an investigation with your picture hanging on the wall as part of the evidence! That's all. On the other hand, however, it would be nice if you would treat me with a little respect! Oh, and of course, it would be nice to know that I will have your full cooperation if I were to need anymore information for my story."

Knowing that she had him by the short hair, she looked down at the sheriff waiting for a reply.

When Sheriff Drescoll finally found his voice, he asked, "Are all the um….photographs in here?"

"Well, of course, Sheriff! What kind of girl do you take me for?" she asked him, acting as though he had insulted her integrity.

Putting him in a 'damned if you do' or 'damned if you don't' situation, he just sat there in silence.

"So, Sheriff, do we have a deal? If I need information, are you going to be willing to help me out?" she asked as she stared intently at him, waiting for an answer.

Sheriff Drescoll stood up and yanked his wallet from his back pocket. Pulling one of his business cards out, he handed it to Nicole.

"That's still blackmail, little lady."

"Don't call me 'little lady' again! My name is Nicole. Call it blackmail if you like, but any way that you look at it, Sheriff, I still saved your ass, and I mean that literally, too."

Nicole walked out of the room picturing Sheriff Wade's bare ass hanging on the bulletin board at the station. When she reached Garret she was still chuckling

"Garret, if we're done let's get out of here. I've had enough of this place," she said as she headed for the front door. She was leaning against the car when Garret and Davis joined her.

"What was going on with you and the sheriff?" Garret asked her curiously.

Chuckled again, she replied, "Oh, just a little gettin' even!"

"I think we're all done here," Davis sighed, looking exhausted. "I showed the detectives where the gun was located. I think we pretty much answered all their questions. If you guys don't need me any more I'm going to head for the airport. It was nice meeting you, Nicole. Good luck with your story."

Before he turned toward the car he was driving, he extended his hand to her. Bypassing the extended hand, Nicole gave Davis a hug goodbye.

"It was nice meeting you, too. And thanks for all your help, Davis."

"I'm not hugging you!" Garret joked with him as he extended his hand.

Laughing at his ill attempt at humor, Davis shook his hand and told him he'd catch up with him in LA. As he headed toward the car, he turned and waved goodbye.

"Well, I guess we might as well head to the Inn. By the way, Garret, what happened with Buck?"

"Come on," he said, as he guided her to the car by her elbow. "I'll tell you on the way to Dalton. After you tell me what happened with the sheriff!"

TWENTY-FOUR

Watching Garret as he tried to squeeze his large frame through the car door was like watching an elephant trying to squeeze into a phone booth. As he placed one leg inside the car, he had to use one hand to clutch the roof for support. Then, he twisted his torso around until he finally felt the seat underneath his rear-end. After uttering a sigh of frustration, he dragged his remaining leg inside and closed the door. As Nicole watched the whole process, she hadn't noticed what a struggle it was for him to fit into the mid-sized car. Maybe the driver's seat was built differently; he had gotten behind the wheel with no problem. Placing her hand in front of her face, she hoped to conceal the grin that had slid across her lips. Even though she tried to stifle the sound, the echo of her laughter filled the inside of the car.

"Did you find that quite amusing?" he growled at her. But the sweet sound of her laughter was contagious, and he found himself laughing right along with her.

When they finally got on the road, Garret asked again, "So...what was going on with the sheriff? He looked like a whipped pup when he came back into the room."

Considering what a large ego Sheriff Drescoll had been sporting, the image of him looking like a whipped pup made Nicole burst into laughter again.

"Did you see his face when I whispered to him, Garret?"

"Yes, what the hell did you say to him? I've never seen a man turn that color before!" Whatever she whispered had obviously been for the sheriff's ears only because he didn't hear a word of it.

"Well, I had tried to get him to come to Charlotte's room, where I had hidden the file. When I asked if I could see him for a moment, he totally ignored me. So finally, I went over and whispered that he looked different without his mask. I knew that would get his attention."

As she spoke, her eyes sparkled with mischief.

Garret looked over at her, his eye brows raised in surprise and said, "Wow Nicole, that was pretty subtle!" and then he burst into laughter too. "Why did you take his file?"

"I told him I took it to save him from the embarrassment of his co-workers seeing the pictures that were in it. He actually thought that I took it to blackmail him myself; but the real reason I took it was for a little bit of insurance. I thought that if I saved the sheriff's file from the public eye, he would be grateful enough to let me review the information whenever I needed to," she answered as she looked sheepishly over at Garret. "I guess that was a little shallow, but I never dreamed that we would be dealing with some backwoods, country woodchuck. I thought those days were over! When he asked what I expected in return for the file, I told him all I wanted was a little respect, and to have access to files when I needed it."

"And...what did he say?"

Garret was intrigued with the way she had handled the sheriff. It was plain to see how angry she had been when he brushed her off before they had even made into the house. The look she had given him and Davis clearly warned them to stay out of it. He had no idea at that point that she had already made plans of her own. Nicole just continued to impress him with her strategic capabilities and her inner strength. Those were two more reasons that he added to the long list of why he needed to make her stay.

"Well," she said, laughter still lacing her voice, "he told me that it was still considered blackmail. But he hauled his billfold out and handed me a business card. I told him that no matter which way he looked at it, I still saved his ass. Garret, could you picture Sheriff Drescoll's photo hanging on the board at the station with nothing on but his 'Lone Ranger' mask?"

Nicole grabbed a hold of her stomach as she erupted into another fit of giggles.

When she finally got control of herself, Garret asked, "What do you think will happen now, Nicole?"

"They will certainly have to conduct a full scale investigation. I'm sure there will be a lot of people taking a fall for the racketeering ring. Buck's clients are going to be real upset that Charles kept such accurate files. There were a lot of big names in the gambling aspect of it, too. The amount of money that was placed on some of those bets was pretty substantial. If you want my opinion, I think there was something more going on then just gambling bets. When they do a thorough investigation, I bet they find out somebody was hiding illegal funds. There will probably be an investigation in the athletic department as well to see if there was any tampering with the players, you know, point fixing or players throwing a game intentionally. As for the blackmail files, I wonder how many of those will disappear? If Charles wasn't already dead, I don't think he would have been walking around much longer anyway. And as for Buck, if he's in no condition…" Nicole remembered, as she spoke his name, that Garret hadn't told her about him yet. "Speaking of Buck, what did happen over there?" Nicole turned sideways on the seat, giving Garret her full attention.

"Hmm," sighed Garret, as a mental picture of Buck lying on the floor flashed through his mind. "That was a sorry sight to see."

"J.C. didn't get violent when you got over there, did he? He didn't actually hit him or anything, did he?"

Nicole had worried all along that his temper would get the best of him.

"Oh, no, it wasn't anything like that. It probably would have been easier on Buck if he had hit him. Instead, he tormented him for a while, before he actually told him what happened to Charles. When he realized how hard that news hit the old man, he couldn't wait to tell him that Charlotte had split, leaving Rae Anne behind. That was when the old man grabbed his chest, like he was having a heart attack. When he hit the floor like a ton of brick's, he didn't look too good. I ran to get the butler, but I could still hear J.C. screaming at him that he was never going to see Rae Anne again. I really don't know if he had a heart attack or a stroke."

As he continued to speak, he glanced over at Nicole. His tone had grown softer, and she could detect a trace of pity in the sound of his voice.

"He may not have even made it to the hospital; I don't know. But I do know that J.C. wasn't leaving there until he finished having his say. I thought maybe J.C. was being a little hard on him and I made the mistake of telling him so. It didn't take long to straighten me out!" he exclaimed as an impish grin poked across his face.

"Wow," whispered Nicole. "There's another thing Elizabeth is going to have to deal with."

"J.C. hated that man; and he didn't make any bones about showing him how he felt. After voicing his opinion to me, I don't blame him either. Buck sure did mess up his life."

Garret was growing tired of talking about Buck. That subject played too hard on his emotions. Although he couldn't help but feel sorry for the man, what he did to J.C. and Elizabeth, even to Rae Anne, was unspeakable.

Changing the subject to something more pleasant, he asked, "Do you think J.C. and Elizabeth have made any plans for the future, yet?"

He glanced over at Nicole, wondering what her thoughts were.

"I wouldn't be too surprised if Elizabeth moved to LA with J.C. When I arrived at her house to pick her up, she had quite a few of her belongings packed already. That was before she knew anything about Rae Anne, so she must have already decided to relocate. I don't imagine either of them is going to be willing to spend anymore time away from their daughter, unless it's absolutely necessary. Judging from the emotional scene that was displayed at Charlotte's house, I don't think they are going to be willing to spend anymore time away from each other, either. Call me a romantic, but I think they were destined to be together. Did you see how they actually glowed when they finally got to see each other face to face?"

Nicole's eyes were glistening and the tone of her voice had mellowed.

"It won't take them long to sort through those lost years and put them all behind. They never dreamed they would have the rest of their lives to spend together! Oh, how I love happy endings!"

Smiling sweetly at the thought of how happy their future would be now that they were back together, she turned her head and gazed out the window. Clearing his throat, Garret seized the opportunity he had been waiting for.

"What about you, Nicole? What happens next for you?"

"Oh," she said with a sad, little undertone creeping into her voice, "I'll go back to New York and write my story; it will keep me busy for a while. I'll have to contact the DA's office in Wayland and go over all the information with them." As she glanced over at Garret, she smiled and said, "I think it's going to be an unbelievably great story. I wonder if Jason Deveroe had any clue that the information he gave us would cause the total destruction of such a prominent family and their business. I guess he must have, he was so close to Charles. It was probably the only way he could get even with him for dumping him.

Right at the moment Garret didn't really care about Jason, or the story she was going to write. All he cared about was finding a way to try to get her to stay.

"What about the little vacation you said you'd like to take in California once you got the information you needed? Why don't you come back with us and spend a few days?"

Not wanting to lose the chance to really get to know her, he was beginning to feel a little desperate. There was nothing left for them to do in Texas so he either had to get her to go home with him, or he may never see her again.

"Oh, I couldn't possibly do that now, Garret! The information we uncovered today will become national news. The sooner I get the story written, the better it will be for the magazine," she finished saying as she looked over at him.

As he returned her gaze, there was a strange look in his eyes that she hadn't noticed before. Was that longing she saw as she gazed at the reflection of herself through his eyes? No, it couldn't be, she thought. But why not, she chastised herself. Knowing that she had felt a certain kind of attraction toward him, was it simply impossible for him to be attracted to her? Put it out of your head, Nicole, she thought to herself, you don't have time for this! From somewhere, deep within, a little voice surfaced.

"And when will you ever take that time?" the little voice said, "What's the matter, Nicole? Are you afraid?"

Little shivers ran down her spine as she took a deep breath. Get a grip, Nicole, she thought to herself.

Trying one last time, Garret said, "Why couldn't you write your story in LA?"

Suddenly feeling very vulnerable, Garret grew silent for a moment to prevent his voice from cracking like a nervous teenager. This was all very new to him and he didn't have the foggiest idea how to handle these emotions.

"I'd really like to get to know you better, Nicole."

He wanted to add that he'd grown very fond of her, and that he thought she was beautiful, and intelligent, but he didn't trust himself to say anything more. The last thing he needed was to sound like a love-sick fool.

Nicole could hear the strain in Garret's voice. The last thing she wanted to do was hurt him; but she knew she couldn't write the story in LA; all of her resources were in New York. And besides, Sam would have a fit if she didn't go home soon. Furthermore, what kind of relationship could they have when she lived in New York and he lived in California?

Rather than to go into a lot of detail that would probably cause him more grief, she just said, "I'm sorry, Garret, I can't."

Garret was grateful that they were only about a half a mile from Dalton. It was too hard on him to spend any more time alone with Nicole knowing that tomorrow she would disappear from his life forever. Disappointment began to smother him and his heart felt heavy with the loss of the one woman he knew he wanted to spend the rest of his life with. Just as they pulled into the parking lot of the Inn, J.C. was coming out of the side door. Wandering over to the car to greet them, he took one look at Garret and wondered what had happened to him. Nicole wasn't looking too cheerful herself.

"Hey, is everything O.K.?" he asked, looking first at Garret, then at Nicole. "Did something happen in Wayland that I missed?"

Nicole was the first to find her voice. "No, J.C., I think we're just winding down from all the excitement," she said in a sad tone.

Yeah, right, he thought, after he analyzed the undertones of the situation. Leaving that alone for a moment, he asked Garret, "Did Davis get on his way?"

"Yeah, after we went over everything with the detectives and they were sure that we had answered all their questions, they told us we could leave. Davis looked beat." Garret was leaning on the hood of the car as he asked, "Where are Elizabeth and Rae Anne?"

"Elizabeth had some phone calls to make. I told her what happened to Buck while we were at the house. When I left to come outside she was on the phone with the hospital trying to find out what his status was. Thank God she feels the same way about him as I do, so she doesn't hate me for what happened. She was also going to call Charles' family and tell them to take care of the funeral arrangements. I guess she's not even going to attend the funeral, not that I blame her. I think Rae Anne was pretty much worn out. We stopped on the way here to get her some clothes and a toothbrush and she could barely keep her eyes open then. It's been a long, hard day for her so I would guess that she's upstairs, fast asleep. You can bet wherever she decided to lie down, it's not too far away from Elizabeth. It's almost like she's afraid if she lets her out of her sight, Elizabeth will disappear. We've decided that we're going to head out in the morning. Elizabeth has agreed to move to LA with Rae Anne and me."

Garret and Nicole grinned at each other and then looked back at J.C.

"What?" J.C. asked, looking like a kid who had his hand caught in the cookie jar; but he also appeared to be a very happy man.

"I think I'm going to head back to New York in the morning, too. I'm pretty anxious to get going on this story," she said, feeling pretty tired herself and she still had to make flight reservations and pack. "I want to thank you, J.C., for all the help that you've given me, you too, Garret. Do I have your permission to use all the information I've put together so far, J.C.?" Nicole added.

"Everything, but that one item we discussed, remember?"

Knowing that J.C. was referring to his mother's letter, Nicole shook her head to say 'yes' she had remembered the discussion and silently swore that the information would go with her to the grave.

"Oh, and by the way, I had Tami make a reservation for you. You're flight leaves at 9:30 in the morning. I took the liberty of calling her because I figured you would be anxious to get home. If you would rather take a later flight, we can just call and reschedule."

"No, that's wonderful. Thank you, J.C. What time will you be heading out in the morning?"

Nicole was hoping to see them at breakfast so she could get Elizabeth's permission to write about her segment of the story. It would be nice to see Rae Anne again before they left.

"We're going to leave around 8:30, about the same time you will need to get started," as if J.C. had read her mind, he added, "So we'll see you at breakfast."

"Marvelous. Well then, I'm going upstairs to unwind a bit and then pack. It really has been wonderful meeting all of you." She turned and looked at Garret before she said, "When this story is done, maybe I'll get to LA to see you again."

Walking over to J.C. she kissed him lightly on the cheek. At first he gave her a quick hug, and then he kissed her on the cheek. As soon as J.C. released her, she walked over to where Garret was standing. As she leaned toward him about to kiss his cheek, he quickly turned his head. Her feathery, soft kiss landed directly upon his waiting lips. Stunned at the unexpected touch of his lips on hers, Nicole pulled back quickly, and looked into his face. Garret smiled sheepishly at her as she mutely backed away. She uttered an unsteady 'goodnight', but when she reached the steps, it felt as if she were floating on air. J.C. sat there chuckling at the two of them.

"What was that all about, Big Guy?" he asked, before he realized that Garret's eyes were welling up with tears. It took him completely by surprise as he had never seen his friend affected by a woman like this before. Trying to get control over his voice for the second time that day, Garret finally told J.C. what was going on.

"I feel like an absolute jerk! I have fallen hopelessly in love for the very first time, and I don't have a prayer in Hell of keeping the girl! I have racked my brain trying to figure out some way that I could to get her to stay. I even managed to get up enough courage to tell her I wanted to get to know her better. There was so much more I wanted to say but my brain was turning to mush and I chickened out. This is way too hard, this love thing. I even went so far as to ask her to write her story in California."

Garret was struggling to keep his tears at bay. What would his friend think if he started crying like an overgrown baby?

"And?" J.C. asked, waiting for the rest of the story.

"She said she couldn't. That was it, she didn't give me any reason why she couldn't, she just said that she couldn't. I'm not even sure that she has any feelings toward me at all," Garret replied in a defeated tone that coincided with looking physically and emotionally drained.

"Well, if you want my opinion, the way she glided up those steps after you kissed her, I think she felt something!" J.C. replied, as he thought he saw a little spark return to Garret's eyes.

"What am I going to do? I don't know how to make her stay. How am I going to know if she cares about me if I don't get the chance to ever see her again?" Garret let out a sigh as he ran his hand through his wavy, dark hair. "Man, I suck at this stuff! There ought to be a manual for this kind of thing! There ought to be some kind of rule book."

Knowing that Garret wouldn't find the humor in the situation, J.C. tried diligently to conceal his laughter. It was his friend's turn to find some happiness; he had stood behind J.C., so faithfully, for so many years. Now it was time for him to move on and find a life that completed him. Not that J.C. was willing to sever their friendship, or for them to go their separate ways. That wasn't it at all. He just wanted him to find some happiness of his own. At that moment in time, J.C. was still overflowing from euphoria and all he wanted was to share that feeling with Garret.

After giving Garret's dilemma some thought J.C. finally replied, "Well…Garret the way I see it, if Mohammed won't come to the mountain, then bring the mountain to Mohammed!"

Garret looked at him in complete bewilderment, and then asked, "What the hell are you talking about?"

J.C. slid his arm around Garret's shoulders and whispered in his ear. There wasn't a soul in hearing range, but that didn't seem to matter. When he finished whispering and finally stepped away from his ear, Garret was standing there nodding his head.

"Do you really think that would work?" he asked, in amazement.

J.C. smiled and said, "What have you got to lose, besides the girl?"

"You're right," he said and then stood still for a moment while he thought. "You're absolutely right. I'm going to pack and then I'm going to be as good as gone. I'll grab a cab so Nicole can have the rental car to take to the airport," he said as he looked at J.C. for a moment and then crunched him in his arms, giving him a real bear hug. "Thanks, J.C. I'm so happy for you and Elizabeth and Rae Anne. And I'm truly glad you finally found her!"

"So am I, Garret," J.C. told his friend, as they started up the steps to the Inn. "And I'm glad this mess is finally over."

Looking down at the two men from her window, Nicole wondered what they had been discussing. While she watched them talk, she studied Garret's handsome profile. She hadn't been able to take her mind off from him since he plucked that kiss from her lips. Though his size could be intimidating to some, even from the first day they met, it hadn't been to her. He was a kind and gentle man, and she had felt comfortable and safe in his presence. The more she thought about Garret's characteristics, the more she realized what a wonderful person he really was. He was funny and caring and strong, and yet, he was never afraid to show his emotions. All the qualities she had been looking for in a man were right there, right in front of her eyes. What was wrong with her head? The 'someone' she had been searching for was right in front of her. Was she going to take the chance of leaving without even letting him know that she was interested in him? And that kiss! That kiss had generated more emotion in Nicole than she had felt in a long time. And it was such a little kiss! As she glanced out the window to get another peek at Garret, she noticed they were gone. Finally moving away from the window, she turned her thoughts to the tasks she had left to do before she went to bed.

It was time to make a mental list of things she had to do in the morning. Calling Sam was first on that list and then she had to talk to Elizabeth. While she and Garret were riding to the airport together they could make some solid plans for her to come back to California, after she had finished writing the story. The real plan was to let him know she was definitely interested in him. If he thought that she had just shrugged him off it would make her feel horrible. Yes, she had been scared, but she was just going to have to get over it! It would be the furthest thing from Garret's mind to hurt her intentionally and in her heart, she knew that.

Thinking she had everything under control, she decided to get her packing done that night. That way she'd have more time to spend with J.C., Elizabeth and Rae Anne in the morning. There wasn't any reason to worry about the time she'd have to spend with Garret knowing it would take at least an hour to get to the airport, and they would be alone. Yes, she thought, I do love happy endings! As she climbed into bed, she knew there wasn't going to be any problem falling asleep.

TWENTY-FIVE

Instead of waking up in a great mood after having solved all the mysteries that were plaguing the town of Dalton and its residents, Nicole couldn't understand why she awoke feeling so blue. The morning sunshine was streaming through her window promising to offer another wonderful day, but that didn't seem to have an effect on her. Even the thought of going home didn't lighten her mood. Leaving the wonderful people she had met while working on the story was going to be hard. In just a few short days it had seemed like she had experienced a whole lifetime with them. Since she was already packed and ready to go, all that was left was to call Sam before she went downstairs to breakfast. After carrying her luggage to the door for the porter, she dialed the number for the office and waited.

"Good morning, Rose speaking. How may I help you?" Rose's cheerful response came across the line.

Even Rose's chipper voice didn't raise her spirits, which was very unusual.

"Good morning, Rose. This is Nicole. Is Sam in?"

"Nicole, it's so good to hear from you! How are you? When are you coming home?" she sounded so excited to hear from her.

"Today, I'm catching a morning flight, but I probably won't be into the office until tomorrow."

Although she tried, Nicole couldn't seem to put any life into her tone. What was probably going to be the story of the year was sitting in boxes in the trunk of the car downstairs and the excitement of it all just didn't seem to be fazing her.

"It'll be great to have you back. We've really missed you, Nicole. I'll put you through to Sam."

Rose immediately detected that something was wrong by the tone of her voice. It sounded like the investigation had been going really well when she had called in earlier in the week. It could have turned out to be a big hoax; in the news business anything was possible. For Nicole's sake, she hoped that the story hadn't turned out to be a bomb.

"Morning Red, how's the story coming?" Sam cheerfully asked as he came on the line.

"I think we got our cover, Sam," was her stony reply.

Even though she tried to make the statement sound as exciting as the news really was, the enthusiasm just wouldn't come.

"We found the mysterious baby, Rae Anne, and believe it or not, she's the daughter that J. Collins Savage never knew he had."

It had been two days since she had last spoken to Sam so there was a lot of material to brief him on. Quickly continuing over some of the details about meeting with Elizabeth and about Charles' death, she finally got to the information pertaining to Buck. Sam let out a low whistle when she told him about the files that were used to blackmail his client's and the ones used for the gambling ring and how the bank book they found tied all of the information together. Both of the illegal practices netted his little operation well over a millions dollars in deposits.

"You're intuition was right again, kid! Sounds like you got yourself quite a story to write! When are you heading east?" With all the exciting news she had related to him, Sam was disturbed by the heaviness in her tone, so he asked, "Is everything all right with you, Red? You don't sound like your usual self."

"I'm fine, Sam. Just tired, I guess. My plane leaves in about an hour and a half, but I won't be in the office until tomorrow morning though. I'll go over all the rest of the details with you then."

Relieved to finally finish with the business of calling, she had an idea of how pathetic she must have sounded to Sam, but she just couldn't help it.

"O.K., Red. Well, congratulations, I'm glad things went well for you. Guess we'll see you tomorrow," Sam replied as he disconnected.

There was definitely something wrong with her but he just couldn't put his finger on what it could be. For somebody that was about to land what was sure to be the next cover story, there was a whole lot of excitement missing in that phone call. A cover story had been her goal since she started at the magazine. Now the possibility was within her reach, she sounded more like she was depressed instead of elated; he just didn't understand where that was coming from. It bothered him to know there was nothing he could do about it, he would have to wait and find out what was eating at her tomorrow.

Nicole grabbed her bag and checked around the room making sure there wasn't anything left behind. When she was satisfied with the survey, she headed down the stairs to the dining room for breakfast. At least she'd be able to spend a little time with J.C., Elizabeth and Rae Anne before her and Garret left for the airport.

When she entered the dining room, she spotted J.C. and Rae Anne already seated at a table, but it didn't appear as though Garret or Elizabeth had joined them. As she wandered over to the table and sat down, the waiter brought her over a fresh, steaming cup of coffee.

"Good morning! You two look pretty chipper this morning, where's Elizabeth?" she asked, as she glanced around for Garret.

"Good morning, Nicole. It's a great morning and we're pretty anxious to get back to California. Elizabeth will be here soon, she said she had something to take care of before we left," J.C. answered as he took a sip of his coffee.

It wasn't like Garret to be late, but she didn't want to come right out and ask where he was so she just kept looking over J.C.'s shoulder waiting for him to appear. Watching curiously as her eyes darted around the room, it was obvious who she was looking for, but he couldn't figure out why she just didn't ask where he was. There was such an anxious look on her face that finally, he decided he would just tell her that he wasn't going to show up.

"He isn't coming Red. Garret took off early this morning, but he left the car for you to take back to the airport."

It was obvious she was missing his presence when he saw the look of disappointment cloud her face. It was equally apparent from that look that Garret did have quite an effect on her. It crossed his mind for a split second to let her in on the secret they had shared last night, but then he decided not to spoil anything and kept it to himself instead.

"Oh," she replied shortly, as she fought back the panicky feeling that suddenly swelled in her throat.

Never dreaming in a million years that Garret would have already left, she had taken it for granted he would be there for breakfast and they would naturally ride to the airport together. Now she didn't know what she was going to do. It felt like someone kicked her in the stomach and knocked the wind right out of her. How was she going to let him know that she was attracted to him? Slowly she sipped at her coffee, trying to calm herself before she spoke.

"What time are you leaving?" she asked, hoping that J.C. wouldn't hear the quivering in her voice.

"As soon as Elizabeth gets back," he replied, as he leaned his chair up on two legs and crossed his hands behind his head.

Before she could leave town, there was one thing left that Elizabeth had to do. As her steps echoed down the corridor of the hospital it occurred to her how ironic her father's life would end. Stopping at the nurse's station to locate his room number, it didn't come as a big surprise that her mother didn't seem to be anywhere around. Of course she couldn't blame her.

The room was a typical hospital room but when she stepped into the doorway there was nothing that could have prepared her for the sight of him. It was shocking how he looked like nothing more than a broken down old man. There wasn't anything left to indicate that he had once been the thunderous, controlling Bartholomeuel Bordoe. An image of the shadow of a man he used to be, just laying there helplessly in the bed, burned into her mind.

As she slowly approached the bed his eyes began to glisten. The extent of the stroke he experienced caused the loss of speech so when he tried to communicate with her, the only noise he could make sounded like an animal grunting. Saliva continuously dribbled down the side of his mouth. Although there wasn't much control left in his arm, he still attempted to reach his hand out to her pleading with his eyes for her to take a hold of it.

"No, Daddy," she said softly, as she ignored the hand that was reaching for her in desperation. "I don't want to touch you. I just wanted to come by and see what you've done to yourself."

A garbled noise left his throat, but she had no idea what he was trying to say, nor did she care. It was useless to hold his hand out any longer, it was clear that she wasn't going to take it so the extended arm dropped heavily back onto the bed. The haunting look in his eyes never left her face.

"I can't feel sorry for you." Elizabeth's voice was calm and steady as she stared evenly into Buck's eyes. Knowing that she wouldn't feel complete until she spoke her mind, she continued, "You lied when you took my daughter away from me. I tried to live with the fact that some stranger was raising my child because you said it would hurt the family name if I kept her, but you were the one that watched her grow from a baby into a fine, young woman. You were the one that was there to enjoy the experience of her first tooth, her first step, her first smile. Where was I, Daddy, while you were stealing my role? I was cast aside, married off to a cruel, heartless excuse for a husband. That was the man that you chose for me, your only daughter, your only child, Daddy. You took everything away from me, Justin, Rae Anne, my happiness, everything."

Staring at him relentlessly, she watched as the pain crept over his distorted face. A lone tear escaped the corner of his eye and rolled slowly down his cheek. The display of remorse was way too little, way too late and it didn't make an impression on her. There was still words left unsaid, she wasn't leaving the room until she was finished.

"Now, you've left yourself with no choice, you're going to lay there and die, a broken down, lonely, old man with no one left to care for you, just the way you've made it. You drove Mamma away and you have driven me away, but I'm taking Rae Anne with me! And you know what, Daddy? You deserve everything that's happened to you."

Taking a deep breath after her final words were spoken, Elizabeth turned on her heel and walked out the door. Loud, garbled noises followed her out of the room, but she kept walking and never looked back. When she stepped through the hospital doors, the warm sunshine touched her face and thawed her heart. Her nightmare was finally over.

When she returned to the Inn, Nicole was sitting with J.C. and Rae Anne in the dining area. There was something different about her demeanor as she stood at the table, she was radiant and it showed.

"Are we ready to go?" she asked, looking at her new family.

Everything that had needed to be done was now completed and Elizabeth was anxious to begin her new life! Gathering their belongings, they all headed out to the parking lot.

"Before you go, Elizabeth, I have to ask for your permission to write the segments of the story that concern you. Is there anything you don't want me to cover?" asked Nicole, giving Elizabeth the same courtesy as she had given J.C.

After giving it some thought, Elizabeth answered, "Yes, you have my permission to write whatever you like. Maybe when the story comes out, it will help Rae Anne to fully understand what actually happened. Thank you, Nicole, for everything. If it hadn't been for you, I wouldn't be free at this very moment. I wouldn't be with my daughter, or with J.C. I owe all that to you." Elizabeth stepped forward and embraced Nicole. "If ever you get the chance, would you please come to LA and spend some time with us? I would like that so much."

Nicole got a little choked up over Elizabeth's eloquent words, proving yet again what a true aristocrat the lady was. Waiting for her voice to clear, she finally replied.

"I would love to come and visit, thank you for the offer. And Rae Anne," she said as she took the young girl by the shoulder's and studied her features. "You are a very beautiful girl. I hope you enjoy your new home and that everything turns out the way you hoped it would." Nicole pulled the girl to her and gave her a hug.

"Thank you, Nicole, for all you've done for me, too. I think I'm going to be very happy!"

Rae Anne put her arm around her mother as soon as she stepped away from Nicole. It looked as though the pair had already gotten a good start at bonding. Last, but not least, she gave J.C. a huge hug.

"Thanks, Red. Please do come and see us. You've done some great work and I hope your story turns out spectacularly. You take care of yourself, O.K.? If you ever need anything, just call. I promise I won't pawn you off on anyone else next time." J.C. gave her a bear hug and whispered 'thank you for everything' in her ear, before he got into the car.

THE COVER STORY

Nicole was left standing by the rental car as they pulled away feeling desperately and totally alone. Where the hell was Garret? Why wasn't he here ready to drive to the airport with her? All her plans had been spoiled when he didn't show up at breakfast. What made matters even worse was that he never even told her goodbye. As she loaded her suitcase into the trunk the tears start to fall. Why was it that she was feeling so miserable? What more could she possibly want? She was going home to write the story of a lifetime and yet, there she was, standing in the middle of the parking lot crying like a baby. Walking around to the side of the car, she felt around in her pockets for the keys. When she got behind the wheel of the car, she cranked the radio so loud it was impossible to think about anything but the music.

The trip to the airport was made in a fog. In fact, she was there before she realized she had even left Dalton. There was no waiting to board the plane, so she gave her ticket to the stewardess and found her seat. The laptop she had brought along was stuffed in the empty seat beside her. Originally she had planned to work on the story while the plane was in the air. Instead, she laid her head back and closed her eyes and waited for the take off. It had to be the most miserable day of her life.

Going over the details of the trip in her mind, she recalled the day she had spent in J.C.'s office. All the memories that she had guarded so closely and had pushed so deeply into her subconscious mind had surfaced that day. It was the first time in her adult life that she had dealt with every one of them. Like a flood bank ready to break loose, the tears started rolling down Nicole's cheeks. As she gazed absently out the window, she didn't even try to stop them. She cried for the little girl, hiding outside of her parent's door overhearing the hurtful words that were spoken. She cried for the teenager who stood, frozen in her tracks at the sight of her boyfriend and her best friend naked in the haymow together. She cried for the woman standing in the parking lot feeling lost and alone, wondering what she had missed because she had been afraid. What if Garret had been the one for her, like J.C. was the one for Elizabeth and vise-versa? Why couldn't she have just given him a hint that she was attracted to him while they were on the way back to Dalton? If they were destined to be together, they could have figured out some way to close the miles between them. Was she doomed to be alone for the rest of her life? She had felt so comfortable and so complete around those people; the people that she considered to be dear friends. Yes, she loved the people at the paper, but she had never given them so much of herself as she had with Garret, and J.C. and Elizabeth, and they had given so much in return.

Oh, why didn't Garret show up this morning she cried to herself. Right from the start she had felt so comfortable with him. Maybe that's why she hadn't noticed the strong attraction to him. It wasn't until he had kissed her that she realized it. Oh, the kiss! One tiny, soft, casual kiss, the tiny kiss that was big enough to send her right over the edge. Not knowing where the tears were coming from, Nicole cried even more.

Before the plane landed in New York, she went to the tiny restroom and tried to repair the damage that had been done by crying almost the whole way home. The salty tears that were shed caused her eyes to become red and swollen. It felt soothing to splash the cool water on her face. Running a comb through her hair helped her appearance a little, but unfortunately, that was the best that she could do. No one from the office knew what flight she was coming in on, so she didn't have to worry about anybody seeing her. If she had to, she could spend the whole evening putting cold compresses on her face to get the swelling down before tomorrow. What she was going to do about the depressed state she was in, she had no idea. The seatbelt sign was lit as she made her way back to the seat. A hand softly touched her on the shoulder as she was buckling up.

"Are you all right, Miss?" asked a concerned stewardess.

Nicole looked up at the kind face and said, "Yes, I'm fine, thank you."

Laying her head back on the seat, she closed her eyes until the plane was clearly on the ground. There was no reason to rush so she waited until everyone else had unloaded before she gathered up her belongings. It seemed as though everyone was hugging or kissing or crying with someone as she walked out of the terminal and it agitated her even more. People were just happy to be reunited with their loved ones which caused another pang of loneliness to spread through her. It was easier to walk with her head down so she didn't happen to notice the man with the big hat walking toward her.

"Howdy, Miss Bentley. Names Garret, Garret McCormick," Garret said as he stopped in front of her, waiting for her to lift her head.

Nicole thought she was becoming delusional; she was starting to hear things that weren't really spoken. If she didn't know better, she could have sworn she heard Garret's voice. When she popped her head up; there he was, standing right there in front of her.

"How did you…." she stammered as she looked around the airport. "How did you get here?" she finally got the question out.

"I came in on an earlier flight. I wasn't taking the chance that you wouldn't let me come."

He looked deep into her swollen, green eyes; wondering if the tears she had been crying were for him.

"Oh, Garret," she cried, as she dropped the laptop she had been carrying down to the floor and wrapped her arms around him. "I don't care how you got here! I'm just so glad that you came! I wanted to talk to you this morning, I had all these plans and you didn't show up. I thought I'd never see you again!" she cried as she buried her head in his chest.

"Well, here I am, and I'm not going anywhere for awhile."

He tipped her head back and this time he gave her a real kiss. When he released her, she felt light headed and all fuzzy inside, she couldn't stop herself from smiling. Garret bent down and retrieved the laptop. Placing her arm in his, they headed for the baggage claim.

"Hope this thing passed the dropping test," he said, as he raised the bag that held her laptop.

"Who cares," she laughed, as she raised her head and gave him a glorious smile. "It can be replaced. I'm just so glad you're here, Garret. Why didn't J.C. tell me you were going to be here?"

"What? And ruin the surprise! Come on, let's get your bag and get out of here. You know something? I've never been to New York City," as he spoke, he pulled her closer to him.

"Well, come on Cowboy, I'll give you the tour!"

Yep, she said to herself, I do like happy endings!

Ces liens qui nous séparent